SUMMER WEDDING ON ARRAN

A Scottish summer romance to fall in love with

ELLIE HENDERSON

Choc Lit
A JOFFE BOOKS COMPANY

Choc Lit
A Joffe Books company
www.choc-lit.com

This edition first published in Great Britain in 2023

Cover art by Jarmila Takač

ISBN: 978-1-78189-567-2

ACKNOWLEDGEMENTS

I would like to thank the Choc Lit and Joffe Books team for their support and encouragement. I feel very lucky to have you as my publisher. I would like to extend a special thanks to Lyn Vernham and Lu Taylor for their belief in me as a writer.

Thank you to my incredible editor, Sarah Pursey, whose amazing eye for details helped to strengthen and shape this book. Thank you for getting my writing! And for your sense of humour and encouragement. I have learned so much from working with you. Thanks also to Jasper Joffe, Emma Grundy Haigh, Jasmine Callaghan, Abbie Dodson-Shanks and Alice Latchford for help and support.

Thank you to the wonderful Choc Lit family for their ongoing support. It means a lot to me.

Thank you to the very talented book cover designer - Jarmila Takač - for the gorgeous cover!

Thank you to the Tasting Panel who said 'yes' to the manuscript and made publication possible: Aileen M, Alma H, Brigette H, Fran S, Hilary B, Janet A, Jenny K, Jenny M, Kate A, Laura S, Margaret M, Marie W, Michele R and Sallie D.

Thank you to Frankie Greenwood and Frances Wells for support and encouragement and reading early drafts of the book; and to all my other friends who offer a listening ear and advice! Thanks also to Dougie, Claudia and Grace for happily visiting Arran with me many, many times! I couldn't do any of this without your love and support.

PROLOGUE

'I think Mum would have been pleased by the turnout,' said Amy as she and her sisters, Kirsty and Emma, filed out of the church and followed their dad into the bright sunshine.

It was a glorious spring morning and the sky was a beautiful azure blue with just a few fluffs of white cloud. Clumps of bright daffodils bloomed against the red sandstone building, bringing flashes of yellow to the very sombre day. Daffodils and bluebells were their mum's favourite flowers and the girls had managed to fill the church with them. They had all been grateful that she'd managed to cling on to life long enough to see the start of spring and the flowers begin to bloom. She had passed away two weeks ago, after battling ovarian cancer, with her three daughters and husband at her side.

'She would have loved having everyone gathered together like this,' said Kirsty, nodding her head.

'Yes,' said Emma. 'All her favourite people in one place, wearing something blue or yellow as she wanted, the sun shining and gazillions of daffodils and bluebells. And the water looking at its best.' She gestured at the bay in front of them, the sea glassy and bright.

They were on the isle of Arran off the west coast of Scotland. The stunning coastline curved its way around the island and while their village of Brodick, on the east coast, had a sandy cove, the island had its fair share of pebble beaches and outcrops too. Arran was known as Scotland in miniature and rightly so for all that it offered. The Highland boundary fault ran through it, dividing the mountainous highland landscape on one side from lush green lowland countryside on the other.

The guests had started to drift out of the car park, no doubt heading back to the wake. The girls gathered around their dad, who had paused to dab his eyes with a handkerchief embroidered with his initials.

He looked lost. 'It just all feels so surreal,' he said, staring at the ground.

That morning, while getting ready, he had unscrewed the lid from his wife's jar of face cream and sniffed it. He'd told his daughters that he could picture her standing there beside him, massaging it into her cheeks as she used to do each morning.

Kirsty squeezed his hand. 'It's okay, Dad,' she said, managing to keep her voice steady. But her eyes welled up.

He smiled at them all, evidently thankful to have them with him. Amy linked her arm through his and Kirsty joined her husband, Steve, and their twins, Tom and Becky, who were waiting at the gate with Emma's partner, Max.

'Come on, girls,' said Max. 'We should get back to the house. People will be waiting.'

* * *

The wake was being held at Meadowbank Cottage, the family home the girls had all been raised in. It was now run as a B&B by Kirsty and Steve who had moved there with the twins fifteen years ago from their tiny London flat when their dad and mum had decided to downsize.

Family friend Edie was already at the house and was in charge of making sure everyone pitched in to hand out platters of sandwiches and mini quiches the girls had prepared earlier. Living on an island had several frustrations: there was no Amazon Prime delivery, or Marks and Spencer treats on hand, but there were so many other advantages and Kirsty wouldn't swap it for anywhere else.

Kirsty smiled gratefully at Edie who was refilling the kettle at the kitchen sink as they all entered. 'Thanks so much for helping. But you go and sit down now and have a cup of tea.'

Edie reached over to hug Kirsty. 'I'm just so sorry, my love. Your mum will be very missed.'

Amy puffed her cheeks out and exhaled. 'I keep expecting her to come through that door.'

Edie smiled kindly at her. 'I know, dear. It all feels very strange. When do you head back to Vancouver?'

Amy had been living in Canada for the past four years. She frowned and chewed her lip. 'I don't know . . .'

'You need to get on with your own life,' Dad said, patting her hand as he made his way to a seat at the kitchen table. 'The last thing your mum would want is for you to mope around. It's the same for Emma, she has her own life in Edinburgh to go back to.'

'He's right,' said Kirsty. 'Mum was just glad that you made it back in time to see her.'

Amy choked back a sob and moved into Dad's arms for a hug. Emma followed suit, as did Kirsty and they all held each other.

Kirsty mouthed her thanks to Edie who gave a sad smile and retreated into the lounge, taking a fresh pot of tea with her.

Their mum's death had rocked them to their very cores and all their hearts were broken. None of them knew how on earth they could move forward without her in their lives, but each of the girls knew that they owed it to her memory to do their best.

CHAPTER ONE

Two Years Later

Kirsty was reaching down to take a tray of shortbread from the oven when she heard the crunch of tyres on the gravel driveway outside. Frowning, she glanced at the clock and wondered who it might be. The next guests weren't due to arrive until after 2 p.m. and Steve was on the other side of the island on a walking tour to the King's Caves.

She carefully placed the hot tray on a wire rack and looked out of the window, briefly admiring the creamy pink clematis tumbling over the fence and the view ahead. Her heart soared every time she looked at the sparkling bay stretched out before her.

It was Steve's car. That was strange, she thought, something must be wrong.

She made her way out the kitchen and through the bright hallway. Opening the back door, she stepped outside and met her husband as he jumped out the car. 'Hey, what's wrong? I wasn't expecting you back yet. Where are the guests?' she asked, confused.

He walked towards her and kissed her on the lips. Then caught her hand and pulled her towards the bench under the sycamore tree at the side of the house. 'Come on, let's have a wee seat together while we can.'

A light breeze ruffled through the branches, causing some green blossom to flutter down and land on Steve's head. Kirsty tenderly brushed it away. 'Are you going to tell me why you're home? And more importantly what you've done with the guests? I thought you were supposed to be walking for most of the day?'

Steve stretched his long legs out in front of him. They were brown and the hairs on them had turned golden due to his rule that he would wear shorts for as much of the year as possible; he started in March and would keep it going until the end of October. One year he even lasted into mid-November. It was a far cry from their London days when they were permanently stressed and so busy with work that they barely knew what day of the week it was. He put his hands behind his head and chuckled.

'Well, we made it about a quarter of the way down the path,' he said. 'Then Trudy and Chuck decided they didn't fancy it.'

'How come?'

'They said it was much further away than they thought.'

Kirsty shook her head. 'But I thought that was why they were here? On Arran? To walk and explore the island properly? I though they chose our B&B because of your guided walks?'

'Meh,' said Steve, shrugging. 'I think they maybe quite liked the idea of it, but the reality was a bit different.'

'What a shame. They seemed so excited about it when we talked about it this morning. I can't believe they didn't go for it especially with your fabulous spider chat!'

'I know,' said Steve, grinning. 'The spider story normally does the trick.'

The circular trail was one of the island's most famous and was said to be where Robert the Bruce sheltered after a defeat in his attempt to claim the Scottish throne. While in a cave, the story went, he encountered a spider which he watched trying but repeatedly failing to make a web. The spider's perseverance, ultimately securing a web to the cave wall, was said to inspire Bruce to try again to take the throne and eventually his efforts led to his own success. Whether the story about Robert the Bruce was true or not didn't seem to matter. Tourists tended to be fascinated by the cave, and its ancient carvings of animals, tucked into the sandstone cliffs.

The walk took you through beautiful forestry and down a steep descent onto a shingle beach shoreline with views across to the Kilbrannan Sound on the Mull of Kintyre. It was a good walk, taking about two hours from the car park and round in a loop and back again. But most people managed it no problem and Trudy and Chuck had all the right gear for walking including boots and a stick which wasn't really required for today's terrain. But they insisted on taking it with them which seemed rather ironic now that they had bailed out.

'Did you tell them about Paul?' asked Kirsty. The tourists loved hearing about Paul and Linda McCartney's bolt hole across the water in the Mull of Kintyre. It was where he went to escape The Beatles' fame and where he started writing again. Over the years, and even as a child, Kirsty had seen people with telescopes standing on the shoreline, hoping to catch a glimpse of his farmhouse even though it was in deepest, rural countryside.

'Indeed. But that didn't sway them. They said they would look at the views online.'

Kirsty shook her head in disbelief. 'Unbelievable. Why bother coming here at all then if they can look at everything online?'

Steve burst out laughing. 'Each to their own.'

'Where are they now, Steve? What have you done with them?'

'They wanted me to drop them back in Brodick so they could go for lunch and chill.'

'Wow, oh well then.' Over the years, Kirsty had taken to most of their guests, but there were the odd ones, like

Trudy and Chuck, who irked her with their rude demands and expectations. Only this morning, Trudy had brought her wet towel into the kitchen and asked, in a rather demanding tone, for a fresh one.

Kirsty had wanted to tell her this wasn't the Hilton and could she say please. But thought it best to smile sweetly, especially as she knew the mystery inspector was doing the rounds of the hotels and guesthouses and could arrive at any moment. There was a cash prize of £25,000 up for grabs — and they had expansion plans.

'How I would love to tell them what to do with their walking stick poles,' she said with a sigh.

'How about I go and make you a cuppa and we can have five minutes peace before getting on with the day?'

'The shortbread,' she said suddenly. 'I've left the shortbread out and I need to go and box it up. I'll make the tea and bring it out.'

'Okay, if you insist,' he said, pulling out his phone and starting to scroll through his messages.

Kirsty filled the kettle and while waiting for it to boil, sprinkled caster sugar over the top of the trays. Then she carefully lifted the shortbread out with the greaseproof paper, laid it on a chopping board and reached for her sharpest knife and deftly began slicing it into squares. When they'd taken over the B&B, she'd decided that a little box of shortbread in each guest's room would be a nice touch and she'd been right. The reviews all mentioned the extra thought that Meadowbank's owners had gone to. She scowled as she thought of Trudy asking, without as much as a please, if she could have another box. Thinking of the reviews that they were so dependent on, Kirsty had smiled sweetly, again, and said yes of course.

'Here you go,' Kirsty said, handing over the mug to Steve.

'Thanks, love.'

She sighed. 'Isn't this nice? Peace at last.'

'I might take the paddle board out later on if that's okay?'

'Of course. The water looks perfect for it,' said Kirsty.

Steve was learning the sport and definitely spent more of his time in the water than on the board. Their seventeen-year-old daughter, Becky, who was brilliant at it, was mortified that her dad had taken it up and warned him not to be out there if she was. This spurred Steve on to make sure he did arrive when she was with her friends as he loved nothing more than embarrassing his children. Although to be fair, nothing embarrassed Tom, Becky's twin brother, who was as laid-back as his dad.

They sat in a comfortable silence for a few minutes until Kirsty's phone pinged. She pulled it from her pocket and read the text. She groaned.

'What's up?' Steve looked at her in concern.

'Just a message from Emma saying Dad called her earlier and sounded confused.' She shook her head. 'I think he's getting worse, Steve . . .'

'Remember, though, this isn't a good time of year for him.'

Kirsty nodded. That was true. They all tended to feel a bit wobblier in spring.

'Your sisters will be home soon for the wedding, and it will probably be good to get their thoughts then on how he is. Especially Amy as she hasn't seen him since the funeral.'

Amy was the youngest of the sisters and still lived in Vancouver. Kirsty couldn't wait to see her; she really missed her company.

Emma was the middle sister and an ambitious lawyer in Edinburgh who was always working. When she and her fiancé Max announced their engagement, she'd requested a very low-key wedding at home and so Kirsty immediately blocked out the diary to make sure the house was free of guests for Emma's big day. Somehow Kirsty had also ended up organizing the wedding. She felt it was her responsibility as the oldest and it was the sort of thing their mum would have thrived on doing. She felt a stab of sadness when she thought of how much she missed her mum who she used to see every day.

'You're right. I'm sure I'm worrying too much. One step at a time.'

He reached for Kirsty's hand and drew it to his mouth and kissed it.

'Hello there,' shouted a voice. 'We're back.'

It was Trudy and Chuck.

'Already?' Kirsty muttered.

'It's okay. I'll go and see to them,' said Steve.

Kirsty swallowed the rest of her tea, stood up and stretched her neck. Regardless of what Steve said, she *was* worried about her dad, among other things. She glanced back at Emma's text and frowned. She also needed to call Emma to talk about the wedding. There was always something to do. She looked at her watch. But in the meantime, she had better go down to her dad's house, a five-minute drive away, and check that he was okay.

CHAPTER TWO

As Amy neared the townhouse across the street from the park and tennis courts, she momentarily wondered how she had ended up living in the suburbs after being happy in downtown Vancouver for so many years. It was a lovely area and close to the beach and Ross's two-bedroom home was beautiful; it had an open living and dining area with a wood burning fireplace, cosy for wet and cold winters, and a spacious patio which was great for BBQs and stargazing late at night. Amy even had a walk-in closet in the vast upstairs bedroom which had views over the tree-lined street. However, her belongings scarcely filled a third of it. She'd never been one for having lots of stuff.

Amy unlocked the front door and dumped her yoga mat in the hallway and went into the modern kitchen with its custom millwork storage, stainless steel appliances and huge breakfast bar. Yet today it looked as though a small army of toddlers had rampaged through it. Which they almost had. Ross's six-year-old son, Caleb, was staying with them this week and there were trails of cereal and puddles of milk on the counter. Her heart sank as she felt her feet crunch over food on the floor. She had always been tidy and houseproud and she couldn't help but sigh as she began straightening things out. Wiping the surfaces down, she finally rinsed the cloth at the sink and wrung it out to dry. Then she bent down and opened the cupboard below, grabbing the dustpan and brush and quickly swept the floor.

What was she doing? It was a question she was starting to ask herself more regularly.

She fixed herself a mug of tea and then perched on a stool at the counter and opened out the magazine article that she had started reading earlier.

Help! Need a Change but Don't Know Where to Start . . .
Should you move house, change career or end your relationship? Follow our simple chart to find out . . .

Amy exhaled quietly as she traced her finger under the words '*Feel it's time for a new job?*' That was easy to answer. Definitely not. She loved her job as a yoga instructor and massage therapist. She leaned forward and looked again at the page. '*If you answered no, then that's great. Turn over, you don't need this feature.*' She frowned. What about the rest? Come on, she said to herself, pushing the magazine aside. She was determined to face up to the other questions the magazine had asked, and which had been rattling about inside her head for the past few weeks.

Do you need a change? Yes. *Do you have a clear idea of what you want to do?* No.

Are you a risk taker? She didn't know. Kind of yes, but also kind of no. She had taken a risk when she decided to stay in Vancouver six years ago when she came for a working trip. That had been a huge risk. Back then she had a well-paid, but very dull, job in accountancy in Glasgow. She worked hard but also had a busy social life, but she had started to feel a bit empty. She saw the same people at weekends, in the same bars and restaurants. It was all a bit 'samey'. The trip to the west coast of Canada had piqued her interest again in travel, especially as she had always told her sisters she would live there one day. So, she quit her job, packed up her things and flew back from Glasgow to Vancouver. Then she had taken the ferry from Horseshoe Bay over to Nanaimo on Vancouver Island and booked herself into a three-week yoga teacher training course in the village of Tofino. That had been a big risk and she smiled as she thought about how carefree she was back then and how happy those three weeks were.

Tofino was at the western edge of Vancouver Island overlooking the Pacific Ocean. As soon as she arrived, she knew she had made the right decision. It had a charming harbour and some cute shops and galleries. However, most people visited for its stunning wildlife and scenery, including the rainforest and hot springs. There were some beautiful beaches, where she practiced yoga, and also learned to surf. Because she was there in spring, she even saw the migration of the grey whales travelling between Alaska and Hawaii. It truly had been a magical time.

At the end of the course she had almost stayed there instead of returning to Vancouver. However, things started to fall into place as someone on the course mentioned his friend, Josh, had a room to rent in downtown Vancouver. It couldn't have worked out better. Josh was also a yoga instructor and he helped Amy get started and grow her business, as he had too many clients and was always looking for someone to refer students to. So yes, she was a risk taker. Or perhaps she *had been* a risk taker.

But now, six years later, she felt stuck in a rut.

For the past few months, she had been thinking about home, prompted by her sister's up and coming wedding. Then she had started to make pros and cons lists of the reasons she should extend her visit back to Scotland. She made sure her reasons for and against were always on scrap bits of paper which she had to hide in the recycling box. She had embraced meditation and in her balanced moments reminded herself to trust her intuition and that the universe would take care of her. She always told everyone else to trust that things would unfold the way they were supposed to. Why couldn't she take her own advice?

She kind of loved Ross and was fond of Caleb even though the feeling wasn't reciprocated, and she wondered if she would ever form a bond with him. She didn't realize how hard being a stepmum would be. She had tried so hard to connect with him, but he kept her at arm's length. Despite that, she felt a massive amount of guilt at the thought of walking away. She bit her lip as she stared at his paintings, stuck to the fridge.

Could she really leave and disrupt things for him again? She had been told so often that kids were resilient, and it was better to be honest with them. Another wave of guilt. Was she really going to compromise her own happiness for a life she didn't want to keep a six-year-old boy happy? A boy who clearly wasn't keen on her . . .

Perhaps the time away for Emma's wedding would be good. A change of scene would give her a break and offer her a fresh perspective. It would be great to see her sisters again and Dad, of course. They all kept in touch and spoke regularly, but it wasn't the same as being there. She was very aware how different their lives were.

Kirsty was the oldest and eight years her senior which meant they'd never been particularly close. She and Steve were married and settled with kids, which triggered another stab of guilt that she didn't actually know her niece and nephew very well. She and Emma on the other hand had always been close growing up, as there was only two years between them, but even they had drifted apart. Emma was so focused on her job and didn't give herself much time for fun. She wasn't sure of Max — again because she only met over Facetime calls and once at their mother's funeral. But he seemed kind and loved her sister who was obviously happy and ready to settle down. That was something Amy had always resisted until she met Ross.

She had always valued her freedom yet with Ross, well, she thought it was maybe about time she tried to give commitment a go. Especially given that she was approaching thirty-five. Ross had been one of her regulars at a yoga class near Stanley Park and later admitted that he started going to yoga as a coping strategy for his divorce rather than turning to alcohol. They were friends before anything happened and then it just kind of did. When he asked her to move in after a year of dating her instinct had made her hesitate, especially as she and Caleb hadn't exactly hit it off. She tried to rationalize the niggle that wormed away inside her, telling herself that it was new, and she was out of her comfort zone, and she would settle.

Amy always thought six months was a good amount of time to aim for before making any decisions. But they had been living together for four months now and she wasn't sure that things could improve hugely over the next eight weeks. She knew if she was to be true to herself then she needed to follow her gut. Her intuition was telling her what to do, she just had to listen. This wasn't the life she wanted . . .

She gasped out loud as she realized she had *finally* admitted it.

Her phone beeped. It was *another* text message from Ross asking what she was doing. She had already told him at breakfast that she had several massage appointments at the clinic across the street. He clearly hadn't listened. Sighing, she quickly sent him a reply and then slipped off the stool and ran upstairs, stripped off and had a quick shower before changing into her other work clothes — a pair of loose drawstring pants and T-shirt. She pulled her dark blonde hair away from her face and into a ponytail. She half wished she was the one having the massage. She looked around the ensuite and although it was all very familiar, it didn't feel like home. She could easily imagine herself packing up her few belongings into her rucksack and walking away without a backward glance.

She shook her head sadly at her reflection in the mirror. What kind of person did that make her? She sighed. She needed to tell him sooner rather than later that she was returning to Scotland. Alone.

CHAPTER THREE

Emma didn't like spicy food. It made her face flush, more than usual, and created an extreme thirst in her which made her swallow pints of water and then run to the loo. However, she knew how much Max loved it. Tonight, he'd invited along their friends, Ruth and Oliver, who were further along life's journey than they were. Ruth and Oliver had decided against marrying, as neither wanted to be bound by the social constraints that tying the knot represented. Instead, they wanted a baby to be their priority and Ruth was seven months pregnant after a trying round of IVF. In fact, it was very much touch and go whether they would make Emma and Max's wedding. However, perhaps a bit unkindly, Emma didn't mind as Ruth had made so many withering comments to her over the years about weddings and how she would never understand being tied down to one person for life. Their non-attendance might be best for everyone.

'I mean obviously we'll do our best to be there,' Ruth said, before putting a forkful of rice into her mouth.

'We just don't want to take the risk of being stuck on an island if she goes into labour,' said Oliver, realizing Ruth's mouth was full of food.

The way he said *island* irked her, as though it was a remote outpost in the middle of the Atlantic that took days to get to rather than a fifty-minute ferry ride from the mainland.

'They do have doctors and nurses there you know.' She stopped short of pointing out that she and her two sisters had been born at home; it would make Ruth anxious.

'We know that,' said Ruth. 'But we must do what is right for us now we're going to be a family.' She paused and shrugged. 'It's just such a shame about the dates.'

Emma eyed them both and momentarily wondered why they were still friends. She and Ruth had met at university in Edinburgh, aged eighteen, and shared flats over the years from tiny apartments tucked down cobbled lanes off the Royal Mile to grander tenements in Bruntsfield. Now, as she watched Ruth slowly pat her bump, she wondered what on earth had kept them together. All Ruth seemed to do was make constant digs at her. She had already explained that the wedding date was planned around everyone else's hectic schedules. Her sister had cleared her B&B bookings for a week so they could be at Meadowbank Cottage together. Amy was flying in from Vancouver and had worked her teaching schedule and massage therapy appointments around the date.

'It's just one of those things, I guess. I'm just sorry that it clashes with your due date,' Emma said now with as much diplomacy as she could muster.

'Indeed,' said Ruth flippantly. 'We know where we stand, don't we, Oliver?' Her attempt to make the words sound jokey failed.

Oliver took a sip from his beer glass. 'What was that, love?'

'Doesn't matter. Just saying that it's a shame the dates clash.'

Oliver rolled his eyes. 'Yip.'

In that moment, Emma felt a wave of dislike for them both which was so out of character for her. 'Well, you just need to do what's best for you.' She tried not to say it unkindly, but realized her tone was slightly barbed.

'Of course you must,' said Max smoothly, tilting his head in surprise at Emma. 'And we'll totally understand, won't we Emma?'

'Yes of course.' She wiped her mouth and dumped the napkin on the plate next to her.

What was wrong with her tonight? Why was she being so moody and mean? She couldn't seem to stop herself. In fact, she wanted to leave. *Now!*

The foursome continued making small talk for another ten minutes and then Ruth started to fuss about being tired. Emma could have hugged her — in complete contrast to the rest of the evening. It was the most sensible thing Ruth had said all night. They settled the bill and went their separate ways.

Max asked Emma if she was okay as they walked home, but she was so annoyed with herself that she brushed off his concern and just held his hand, not trusting herself to talk.

His mobile rang as they let themselves into their flat.

'Sorry, I need to take this,' Max said as he headed to the study to take the work call.

He'd been locked away in there for the past hour and Emma was about to head to bed when a message dropped from Kirsty.

Hey sis, are you up? Can I call?

Emma immediately phoned Kirsty, worried something was wrong.

'Hey. Is everything okay?'

'That was quick,' said Kirsty.

'You caught me at a good time. Is Dad okay?'

'Yes . . . he's fine. I popped down to see him earlier. Anyway, how are you? Being a bridezilla yet?'

Emma laughed. Her sisters teased that she was the most laid-back bride-to-be ever which was unusual as she was so meticulous about every other aspect of her life. Her brief to Kirsty had been: a simple wedding, in a beautiful setting, with plenty of food and wine and her small circle of friends and family around her. The family minister had agreed to take the ceremony wherever Emma wanted it.

'That's it?' Kirsty had said. 'That's all you're giving me to go on?'

Emma had laughed. 'Yes, you can go wild and do what you want.'

'But, I mean, don't you want a particular theme or colour? And what about flowers? And music? And food? What kind of wine do you want? Italian or Spanish? Do you want cava, prosecco or champagne served at the reception?'

She had laughed, feeling quite liberated at the thought of letting go of the organization. 'I don't mind.'

'Bridesmaids? Dresses? Tell me you'll manage to sort out your own dress?'

'You and Amy and Becky will be my right-hand women on the day and, yes, just leave the dresses for me to sort. I will of course let you know what I find, and you can give me your thoughts.'

'No meringues or flouncy gowns, please?' Kirsty had pleaded. She and Steve had married in the grounds of Brodick Castle on a hot summer's day almost twenty years before. Kirsty swore her photos still haunted her. And certainly they haunted her sisters too. Emma and Amy had been unable to hide from the photographer their looks of disgust at their yellow, satin full-bodied dresses. Being dressed up as giant Quality Street sweets had been traumatizing for their teenage selves.

'I will make sure it is stylish and sophisticated. No bright chocolate wrapper colours, worry not,' Emma had promised.

Emma was just thankful that Kirsty was happy to take on the rest of the planning and she knew her sister would also add a few wee touches to make the day extra special. Feeling a wave of love and gratitude wash over her, she really wanted to share with Kirsty what was on her mind. She could really do with some sisterly advice as she was so out of sorts and didn't like the way she was behaving with Max and their friends too. But it wasn't a conversation for the phone. She would have to wait until she got to Arran.

'So how are you? Has work been busy?' said Kirsty, her tone sympathetic.

'Yes crazy. Which is why I'm so glad we are having such a small and low-key wedding.'

'That's actually why I'm calling. I have a proposal.'

That had Emma's attention. 'What's that then?'

'Well, and hear me out, before you say anything . . .'

'Mmm, mmm.' Emma felt a flutter of anxiety start in the pit of her stomach.

'I know you would like it all to be held at Meadowbank . . . however Steve went to see the new distillery the other day which has opened right down by the beach. By the way, you'll never guess who is back and running it?'

'Who?' said Emma impatiently, willing Kirsty to get to the point.

'James.'

'James, as in James from school? As in *Amy*'s James?'

'The very one.'

'Does she know?'

'No, I don't think so. I thought I'd share the news when she gets home. Though I'd better tell her before the big day. Especially if she's bringing Ross.'

'If?'

'Well, I'm assuming she is. She hasn't said otherwise, has she?'

'No,' said Emma. 'Wonder what she'll say when she sees James?'

Kirsty chuckled. 'I know. Blast from the past, eh?'

'Yeah! Anyway, sorry, what were you saying about the distillery?'

'Yes, the distillery is beautiful, and the views are to die for. Right on the beach and across the water. I can send you a video and pictures.'

'Okay . . . why?'

'Well, I, we wondered how you and Max would feel about having your big day there?'

'Instead of Meadowbank? How come?'

She heard Kirsty take a breath. 'We can still do it here if you want to, Emma. It's your choice. I just thought it might be nice to have us all here together at home, without caterers and florists bustling around. And I'm a bit worried about space inside should the weather turn.'

Emma frowned. It wasn't like her sister not to embrace an event at home. 'Okay. How much is it costing?'

'That's the thing. Because they haven't done any weddings yet they'll let us have the venue free of charge as a trial run so they can see how it goes. We can still use the caterers and everyone else that would have been at the house. This just keeps it a bit more . . . tidy and simple.'

'Okay,' said Emma slowly. 'What do you think?'

'Well, the windows are floor to ceiling looking out across the bay so even if the weather turns, which I hope it won't as it's been so lovely of late, then the ceremony can be moved inside. If it's fine, then you can actually take your vows on the beach. How cool is that?'

Emma was intrigued. It did sound quite nice and as long as she got to spend some time at Meadowbank with her sisters and her dad that was all that mattered. 'If you send me the pictures, I'll take a look and talk to Max. We'd better decide soon as time is ticking on.'

She felt herself tense even as she said it. She needed to speak to Max. *But how and when*? There was never going to be a good time. Yet her worries were dominating her thoughts and distracting her from what should be one of the happiest days of her life.

'Are you sure you're okay, Emma?' Kirsty sounded concerned.

'Yes, honestly, I'm fine.'

'You just sound a bit tired.'

'Mmm, I probably need to go for a lie down. We were out for a curry with Oliver and Ruth.'

Kirsty laughed. 'I bet you need to go and recharge in a darkened cupboard?'

'Something like that,' mumbled Emma, still embarrassed at how irritated she was earlier.

'How's Max?'

'Oh, you know just the same as always. Busy with work but quite happy.'

'Okay, well have a chat with him and let me know.'

'Thanks,' said Emma. 'I really appreciate all you're doing for us.'

'That's what big sisters are for.' Her words hung there in the silence for a moment and there was so much more they could have said to one another.

Then Emma coughed, breaking the silence. 'Look I'd better go but will be in touch.'

'Okay dokey. Speak soon. Bye. Love you.'

Emma ended the call and curled on up on the sofa, letting tears silently fall down her face. She didn't cry — why was she crying? She needed to pull herself together. Emma had never ever given into emotion before, and she certainly wasn't about to start now. Her determination kicked in and she opened up her laptop, vowing to get on with things. Thank goodness Max was still on his call and couldn't see her like this. She had a chance to pull herself together and her inbox would quickly focus her attention. Then she saw a reminder in her calendar for later in the week. She needed to collect her dress from a boutique in the New Town.

Surely once she saw herself in that it would all start to feel more real? She'd begin to feel flutters of excitement to replace the anxiety that seemed to greet her when she woke up every morning. If only she could get to the bottom of what was causing her to feel like this.

CHAPTER FOUR

Kirsty sat at the kitchen table, flicking through the recipe book, wondering whether to make risotto for dinner or not. A piece of paper floated from between the pages. Kirsty opened it up, her eyes welling with tears when she realized it was a handwritten note from her mum with her flapjack recipe.

Mum had been the parent who taught her how to bake and Dad had shown her how to cook. Out of the three sisters, she was always the one who took most interest in what her parents were doing in the kitchen and would always watch as they chopped and whisked and stirred things. Mum shared all the recipes she'd been taught by her own mum and which had passed down through the generations: scones, pancakes, shortbread, rhubarb crumbles, coconut cakes, apple pies and rich, berry jams. Meanwhile her dad taught her how to make pots of soup, pasta sauces, casseroles and curries while cheerfully telling her tales from his past. He'd spent time in the Royal Navy as a young man and had plenty of anecdotes to share — some funny and some gripping — and had become very efficient at looking after himself. That was just as well as when he met Jean her signature dish was beans on toast. The girls never tired of hearing the stories about how he wooed their mother with his culinary skills.

Kirsty's official rule was to offer only breakfasts for guests and she kept her other dishes for family and friends. Although on the odd occasion guests had joined them around the large wooden kitchen table in their warm and welcoming kitchen. Its log fire made it especially cosy in the winter months when fewer restaurants were open and there were fewer tourists on the island anyway.

She thought about her dad and the pride he took in cooking for them all. Since Jean's death he hadn't bothered as much as he said there was little point in cooking meals for one. Kirsty tried her best to invite him to join them or would take Tupperware containers to his cottage. She had been dismayed though when she went to the fridge that morning and realized that several were still there untouched.

Always loyal and discreet about her dad and his grief, she'd resisted the urge to offload to anyone about her worries for him. Especially when he'd assured her that he was fine, and had simply forgotten they were there.

'Why don't you come and have dinner with us tonight?' she suggested. 'The kids would love to see you . . . and I'm trialling a new risotto that I can get you to taste.'

'Risotto?' he'd said in surprise. 'What's that?'

Kirsty fought back a wave of frustration. 'The rice dish, you know. The one that you taught me to make.'

Her dad didn't seem to register what she said.

'Dad, how about it then?'

He glanced out the window. 'Sure dear. That sounds fine.'

'I'll send Steve down to get you. In the meantime, let's have a cup of tea and a sandwich?' She reached over to fill the kettle and flicked it on, then quickly emptied the fridge of things that had gone well past their sell-by date. She was all against wasting food, but these items were way beyond using.

Fortunately, she had brought some fresh milk in and a couple of rolls from the bakery. Her father had a lump of cheese in the fridge which looked okay, so she set about cutting slices from it and popped them inside the rolls. She could really have done without the cheese today, especially as she needed to get into a dress for Emma's wedding. She placed a mug on the coffee table in front of her dad and handed him a plate. Then she sat down and took a bite from her own roll to encourage her dad to do the same.

'What have you been up to this morning then? Did you play golf?' Tuesday was always his morning to play a few holes with a group of friends.

He shook his head. 'No. I didn't.'

'That's not like you. Are you feeling all right?' she said, concerned. 'You don't seem yourself . . .'

A frown flitted across his face. 'I just miss your mum.'

Kirsty had returned home with a heavy heart and began preparing dinner, messaging Steve to ask him if he would collect her dad on his way back. She didn't know what to do. There seemed little point in worrying her sisters and she didn't want to offload to Steve, especially when he already did so much for her dad.

That evening, Dad sat at her table and seemed his usual self, chatting to the kids and Steve quite animatedly to the point that Kirsty wondered if she'd been imagining things. Perhaps he was just a bit lonely. She knew how overwhelming grief could be. Maybe there wasn't any need to panic quite yet. She was probably being too sensitive. However, she made a mental note to keep more of an eye on him.

'Have you got your father-of-the-bride speech written yet, Alex?' Steve asked Dad.

His eyes widened in panic. 'No. Not yet. Why? Do I have to?'

Steve looked helplessly at Kirsty.

'No, Dad, you don't have to,' she said. 'But I'm sure Emma would appreciate it. I can do it though, if that would make you feel less worried?'

'Yuck,' said Tom. 'I'm never getting married.'

'Nobody will want to marry you, so you don't have to worry,' Becky said curtly. 'Though Lucy at the pool seems to have the hots for you. I keep catching her staring at you when you're blowing your whistle.'

'Shut up,' he said, scowling at his sister.

'There's still time, though, right?' Kirsty's dad rested his fork on his plate, oblivious to the kids' bickering.

Kirsty looked across the table at him. 'Yes, Dad there's still time. You've got a couple weeks to go.'

'The wedding is in . . .' His voice trailed away.

Kirsty noticed Steve raising an eyebrow at her. 'It's in June,' she said, trying her hardest not to sound frustrated. 'A few weeks to go so there is plenty of time.'

He smiled, seemingly reassured, but Kirsty could tell he was worried. She leaned back in her chair and took a sip of water, thinking about her own wedding day and what a brilliant speech he had given then. She could remember every word of it as though it was last week. Her parents had been so proud that their oldest daughter was getting married, and she had floated about on cloud nine and enjoyed every minute of the attention.

When it came to the speeches, he stood up from his chair and toasted everyone with a glass of bubbly and then proceeded to talk about how much he loved his girls and how proud of each and every one of them he was. He spoke of how blessed they were when Kirsty arrived in their life and how he was thrilled that she had found such a wonderful husband in Steve. She remembered wiping away the tears of happiness that had pooled in her eyes as she listened to him, Mum smiling up at him in adoration. She hoped now that he would be able to say something that Emma could always cherish, and she vowed to make sure she helped him pen a few words.

'Right kids, you can do the washing-up,' said Steve, clapping his hands.

'What about pudding?' said Tom, eyeing up the chocolate cake that his sister had baked earlier.

'You can have some when you've helped me tidy up,' said Becky, scowling at her brother.

Kirsty looked at them briefly, scarcely able to believe that the twins were now approaching their eighteenth birthdays and would be leaving home after the summer holidays. Becky was going to Dundee to study dentistry and Tom had an apprenticeship lined up with the Forestry Commission in Perthshire. They'd always been completely different and quite independent of each other. However, she wondered how it would feel to be living in different places. They'd finished their final few exams earlier in May, and she hadn't seen much of them since. They were both busy working, desperate to earn money to fund their way off the island. Kirsty, Emma and Amy had all been exactly the same when they were younger. She didn't even want to think about the house without them in it. She decided to park that in a corner of her mind until after the wedding.

'This is nice,' said her dad to Steve, as he chewed a piece of cake.

'Becky made it. I can't take credit.'

'It's Gran's recipe,' said Becky.

'She was a good baker, wasn't she?'

'She was, Gramps.'

'I wish she could come to the wedding.'

Kirsty could feel a well of tears building up behind her eyes. 'She will be with us in spirit I'm sure, Dad.'

'We all miss her.' Becky reached over and squeezed his hand.

Kirsty smiled gratefully at her daughter and tried to ignore that constant feeling of dread that seemed to be permanently lurking in her stomach.

CHAPTER FIVE

Amy sat back in her seat after she'd said the words and watched Josh frown. 'But you seemed to have made a great life for yourself here. I had no idea that you had been feeling like this, darling.'

They always ate brunch together after classes on Fridays. However, they'd both cancelled the last couple of weeks. She had suggested to Ross, several times, that they could invite Josh and his partner, Andy, to the house for dinner or lunch especially as they had the outdoor space and the huge BBQ. However, Ross always seemed to have an excuse not to.

Amy frowned. 'It's been swirling about in my head for a while and, you know me, I like to think about stuff before I talk about it.'

Josh nodded. 'I know, I get that. I do.'

'I guess with my sister's wedding, it's making me think about home a lot. Dad isn't getting any younger and, well, maybe things have changed. I've loved my time here. I wouldn't have met you, Josh, if I hadn't come here. But with Ross . . . well, I feel . . .' Her voice trailed away as she tried to figure out what she was trying to say. 'I feel constrained. Suffocated. He always wants to know where I am. It's just making me want to bolt. That's the reality.'

'Whoa, okay,' he said, clasping his hands together and leaning in towards her. 'I wasn't expecting that.'

They were sitting in a booth in their favourite brunch spot in Yaletown. Amy smiled at the waitress as she delivered a huge plate of the most delicious and wholesome food she had seen for a while: fresh mashed avocado with tomato jam on sourdough bread.

'I have been so used to having my own freedom without having to answer questions about where I am or who I'm with. I'm only just beginning to realize how much I hate it when he needs to know my every move.' She took a sip from her almond milk latte then frowned as her phone buzzed. 'That's the fifth text message from him this morning.'

Josh shook his head. 'That is a *lot*. I totally get where you're coming from. I couldn't stand it if Andy was like that. He respects my freedom and I give him space too. If he was needy that would be it. I had no idea Ross was so clingy.'

'Neither did I until recently. I just thought he was attentive. Then I started to feel hemmed in . . . How's your smoothie?' Amy pointed at the glass of green sludge which contained spinach, avocado, pineapple and chia seeds.

'It balances out what is about to come,' he said, smiling. Just then the waitress placed down his plate piled high with Belgian waffles, berries and drizzled with maple syrup. 'Could I have some extra syrup please?' he asked. He waited until she had walked away. 'Never know why they skimp so much on it. This is *Canada*. We should be swimming in the stuff.' He looked over at Amy, his face etched with concern. 'You need to do what's right for you. Maybe the trip back home will do you good? It may give you some space to think and work out what it is you really want, my love?'

She rested her fork against her plate. 'That's the thing, Josh. I know what I want and what I don't want.'

'What are you saying?' He took a mouthful of waffle and closed his eyes as he savoured the taste. 'Heavenly. Sorry, darling, I am listening.' He focused his attention back completely on Amy.

She took a deep breath. 'I need to break up with Ross. Does that make me a terrible person?'

Josh reached across the table and squeezed her hand. 'It makes you human and brave and honest.'

Amy gazed at Josh, a wave of affection washing over her. He always knew what to say. No wonder they were such good friends. He was always so calm and kind in a crisis. 'Thank you. What would I do without you? Thanks for listening as always.'

'Hey,' he said, smiling. 'You would do the same for me. And have done. Think of all those late-night chats we had about Andy in the early days.'

She laughed as she thought back to the angst and worry he'd had over his relationship and whether he was doing the right thing when he met Andy. The two friends used to sit up late discussing every detail of their dates and conversations together, analysing every text and email and comment. Those were special times when life just seemed simpler.

He rolled his eyes at her.

'I know,' she said, 'But look at you now. Stronger than ever. I am so happy things worked out for you guys.'

Josh beamed. It was lovely seeing him so settled and in love. That was what she wanted for herself. A balanced and respectful relationship where they gave each other space to be themselves. She didn't want to settle for second best. She wanted to be honest and be true to herself and if that meant being on her own then she was more than happy with that.

He gave her a sympathetic look. 'When will you tell him?'

'Soon.' She blurted the word out before she could change her mind. 'It has to be soon. I mean, my flight's booked.'

'Well, you know you're very welcome to come and stay at ours if you need to.'

'Thanks,' she said gratefully.

'Have you told him that you're going?'

'To the wedding?' She shook her head. 'No. He doesn't even know my sister's getting married, nor that he's been invited as my plus one.'

Josh dropped his fork. 'Oh, crikey. What are you going to tell him?'

She pulled a face and thought for a moment. 'I am just going to have to be honest and speak to him. Sooner rather than later.'

'Are you sure you're going to be okay?' he asked again, flashing her a kind smile.

'Yes, I will be and thank you. Knowing you have my classes covered is great.'

'No problem at all and take as long as you need to. I'll cover them for however long you're away.'

Now probably wasn't the time to grab his offer. Although she had provisionally asked Josh to cover her for two weeks, she wanted to wait until she was home before she made any final decisions about what she was going to do.

'Are you nervous about going back?' he asked now.

'I am. More than I thought I would be. It's been a couple of years. Well, since Mum's funeral,' she said sadly. 'I've missed my sisters and my dad and, well, I guess he's not getting any younger either. But I'm excited, too. It feels like a bit of a calling. I'm desperate to smell the air and see the Scottish grass.'

Josh burst out laughing. 'I didn't realize that was a thing.'

'It's hard to explain. It's green and mossy and damp and smells of wet leaves and . . .'

'I get the picture . . . kind of,' he said. 'You miss wet, damp outdoorsy stuff.' He pulled a face. 'It sounds like it will be a bittersweet trip with your mum not there, but at least the wedding will be a really positive focus.'

She looked at him. 'Exactly. Now eat up before that plateful goes cold.'

'Cheers,' he said, knocking his smoothie against her mug.

Amy felt a wave of sadness ripple inside her. She would really miss him when she left. That was the thing, too, she really didn't know if she would be coming back at all.

CHAPTER SIX

When Emma was a teenager, she was desperate to escape home and explore. As a student, she spent summers backpacking in Europe and Asia. She finally settled in Edinburgh and had carved out a successful career as a lawyer and had never intended to settle down.

Then a few years ago she had met Max through work. He was also a lawyer and despite her intentions to remain single, she'd fallen for him instantly. But she didn't tell him that. To begin with they met with a mutual group of work colleagues in a wine bar for drinks after work on a Friday. Then as the weeks passed, they started spending more and more time together. Then one night Max invited her out for dinner on her own. He took her to a small, French bistro tucked away down a cobbled lane. It was cosy and intimate, and each table had a flickering candle. They both drank Kir Royales and took far too long to order because they were so absorbed in their conversation.

Eventually they had shared steamed Shetland mussels, to start, then roast confit of duck leg. It was the first time Emma had ever tried duck but it became evident Max was a foodie and passionate about eating good food. Afterwards they had shared a plate of cheese and full-bodied red wine.

It was only when she glanced up and saw the restaurant had emptied of all the other diners, that they realized the staff were keen to get home and it was definitely time to leave. When he walked her back to her apartment in Stockbridge, everything seemed to have a rose-tinted gloss to it. She had never quite noticed before how elegant the Georgian and Victorian terraced houses were. Max lived near the Meadows, and didn't know the area so well, and kept stopping to look in the delis and at the menus of gastropubs whose customers were also starting to spill out onto the pavement. It was only as they approached her flat, right by the Water of Leith, that he finally admitted that he wanted to kiss her.

'When did you decide that?' she'd asked him coyly.

'When you ate a mussel tonight,' he joked.

'And you saw the sauce dripping down my chin?'

'Yes, that did it for me. But I also wanted to kiss you when I saw you arguing with that numpty that I work with,' he said.

Emma laughed. She knew exactly who he was talking about. Max's colleague, Raymond, a man of a certain age who held outdated and sexist attitudes and had a habit of mansplaining whenever he spoke to, or at, a member of the opposite sex. Emma quickly derided his comments with her razor-sharp wit.

'I don't think anyone has told me they want to kiss me because of my put-downs and mussel-eating prowess,' she said with a giggle.

'I also wanted to kiss you the first time I saw you and then every time after that . . .'

They'd reached her front door and as he stepped towards her, he cupped her face in his hands and finally kissed her. It had been worth the wait.

That was almost three years ago and apart from being intelligent and handsome, he was kind and that was what she loved most about him. She switched off her terminal and then began to gather her things, swallowing back the lump in her throat for the umpteenth time that day when she thought about her husband-to-be.

They'd moved in together two years ago and bought an apartment in Leith Docks which was small but the view over the harbour made up for its compact size. The area was trendy and vibrant with bus routes to the city centre and there were plenty of pubs, clubs and restaurants within walking distance.

Emma tended to walk to her office in St Andrew Square, at the east end of George Street in town, if she could. Aside from anything else it was quicker as Leith Walk had been ripped apart for the new tram lines which seemed to be taking forever to sort out. For that reason, she always kept trainers in her bag, so she had no excuses and tonight was dry and mild so decided to walk home.

Max was a criminal lawyer, but she knew his heart was no longer in it. He had been exposed to a lot of vicarious trauma over the years and it had started to take its toll. The passion he once felt for law and for justice had started to wane and he had become disillusioned with what was once his dream job. Now he spoke of ambitions to open a restaurant.

His family lived in North Berwick, a pretty seaside town around thirty minutes from the capital. It was place they visited often as Max was close to his mother, a widow, and his younger sister who also lived in the town with her girlfriend. Emma realized she could actually imagine them living there one day and raising a family. She quickened her pace as the thought gave her a slight jolt.

By the time she arrived home, her heart was racing. Why on earth was she feeling so jittery? She had cut way back on caffeine and was trying to make sure she did her Wim Hof breathing exercises several times a week. She had even begun finishing her daily shower with a sixty-second blast of cold water in a bid to help her stay calm. She didn't feel particularly nervous or stressed about the wedding preparations. It was very small and informal so she couldn't blame that on the swirl of anxiety constantly sitting at the pit of her stomach. So what was it?

The couple had an agreement that whoever arrived home first would prepare dinner. She always preferred it when Max beat her to it because he was so good in the kitchen and, she thought wryly, every other room too. But when she let herself in, the flat was empty. She glanced at her watch which told her she'd beaten her step-count target for the day. And it was just after 8 p.m.

Reaching for her phone, purposefully shoved to the bottom of her bag, so she wouldn't be tempted to scroll through it as she walked home, she saw he'd sent a text.

Sorry love. Held up. Should be home at 9 x

Her heart sank. That meant it was down to her. She kicked her shoes off and decided to have a quick shower to wash away the grime of the day and her walk home.

Feeling refreshed, she pulled on her sweatpants and a T-shirt and wrapped her hair in a turban towel. She opened the fridge and peered in.

There was a punnet of squashed cherry tomatoes, a couple of onions and a block of mature cheddar. Then she checked the cupboard for pasta. That would do. She poured herself a glass of wine to sip while she chopped the onions and browned them in a pan with a drizzle of olive oil. While the onions softened — apparently you had to leave them for a while Max had told her —she walked over to the window and stared out at the view.

She could hardly believe there were just a few weeks to go until their wedding. It seemed surreal. She thought about work and what she needed to do before going on annual leave. Emma was a family lawyer and much of her work involved divorce settlements and childcare proceedings which could be tricky. Many of the divorces she handled had come about because of social media and jealous spouses who snooped on their partners online. Or indeed a spouse reconnecting with a past lover and being emotionally and physically unfaithful. It was a minefield.

Taking a swig of wine, she gazed at the horizon. She was glad she and Max were united on their view of social media. Emma limited her use as much as possible because of the negative impacts it could have. Max didn't use it due to his work. He didn't want to become a target for trolls or clients. Emma was glad about this as she had friends whose partners were obsessive with their scrolling. It didn't surprise her that social media was the cause of arguments in one in every five couples. *You're not perfect*, said the little voice in her head. Emma tried to shake it off and went to check on the onions. She added some garlic, tomatoes and herbs and popped the lid on to let the sauce simmer.

Just then her phone pinged with a notification on her sisters' WhatsApp chat.

Hey girls. Can't wait to see you both. How is the bride-to-be? It was Amy. She couldn't wait to see her little sister and meet the man who appeared to have captured her sister's heart. She adored Amy and rued their having drifted apart over the years. But she was so glad that she seemed to have finally settled down even though she was on the other side of the Atlantic. Emma started typing.

Good thanks. Just making dinner for my husband-to-be! Where have I gone wrong? Can't wait to see you either and meet Ross! Is he excited about a visit to the motherland and meeting us all?

Emma could see Amy had read the reply and was still online but hadn't replied. Maybe she was distracted with something else. She would leave it for now and perhaps Amy would reply later. Just then she heard Max's key in the door.

'Hey you,' he called.

Her heart fluttered and she smiled. 'I'm being a good wife,' she said over her shoulder.

He laughed as he hugged her from behind and pulled her close. 'Smells divine. You do too.'

Just then her phone pinged again, several times.

'You're popular,' he said.

'Just my sisters,' she said, glancing at the phone on the worktop. Reaching for it she saw that Kirsty had joined the conversation.

Here are the pictures of the distillery. Sorry forgot to send the other day! x

'Wow,' said Emma. 'Look at these images!' She immediately showed Max. 'Don't they look amazing?'

Max nodded, his eyes widening. 'I can't wait for our wedding, Emma and for our married life to begin.'

CHAPTER SEVEN

The kitchen at Meadowbank Cottage was a picture of chaos, although it was an organized mess and Kirsty had everything under control. Kirsty's mother, Jean, had always been a stickler for tidiness. It didn't matter that she'd been dead for two years, Kirsty could still sense her mum casting a critical eye over the kitchen. She had inherited her mum's need to always be wiping down surfaces and skirting boards. She even liked touching up the slightest scuff marks on the white walls with the tiny pot of paint she kept underneath the sink. Jean had been the same with her need to make sure her house always looked immaculate, and it had passed down to Kirsty who was currently scrubbing the kitchen sink and would soon have the rest of the place looking spotless.

When Jean was alive, she used to walk in the front door without pausing to knock or ring the doorbell. It took Kirsty's husband Steve a while to get his head around it especially when they first moved into the house. 'What if we'd been in the middle of something?' he had said suggestively. 'Or I'd been walking around starkers?'

'Then we would have very dodgy reviews on Trip Advisor, wouldn't we?' said Kirsty when Steve raised his eyebrow yet again. 'I still think of it as my family home.'

Of course, she never had stopped thinking of it as her family home and this morning Kirsty wiped away a tear as she thought how much she would just love to see her mum bustle through the front door again. She didn't know if she would ever get used to the thought that she would never see her again. She thought about one of the final memories she had of her before she fell sick.

'I've got you some marmalade. You know the stuff Edie makes? I was in the coffee shop on the bay, and they had some and so I thought I would get it before they sell out,' Jean had said all of this while opening the cupboard door and quickly rearranging its contents to fit in three jars of Edie's delicious Seville orange and cranberry marmalade.

'Thanks, Mum,' she said.

'How's business?'

'Ticking along nicely, thanks.'

'Are you making enough of it though? I really think there's potential to expand out there,' she said, pointing to the outhouses.

Kirsty looked bewildered. 'Why all the questions, Mum? Is everything all right with you?'

'Oh nothing. You know me. I like to worry. Just ignore me.'

That was true, she was a worrier, but Kirsty often wondered if her mum knew then that she wasn't well and was just making sure her brood were all okay.

A bird flew against the window which made Kirsty jump and brought her back into the present. She looked down at the gleaming sink with pride. She absolutely loved this house even though it seemed to need constant cleaning and attention. She just hoped all their painstaking hard work would pay off in the end. Sometimes it felt that working in hospitality was getting harder and harder to actually make a decent profit. They had all sorts of plans to expand but not enough of a budget.

The guesthouse was a substantial blonde sandstone villa with an elegant timber staircase which led to a wide hallway where there were six bedrooms, three of which were ensuite, and a family bathroom. The house had always been full of character and charm, which she and Steve had tried to retain. However, they'd also enjoyed adding a modern twist. Each of the three guest rooms had white linen and thick duvets and the plumpest pillows with cosy throws in different colours to match the room names: yellow, orange and green.

Outside the garden was a rainbow of colourful blooms and palm trees thanks to its warming position in the Gulf Stream. Her dad had always been a keen gardener which made the garden such a beautiful place today. Behind, was the glen which led on to a lovely meandering walk through trees and past rivers all the way to Lamlash.

Over the years they had got used to tourists in flip-flops and light T-shirts knocking on the door and asking if they could use the loo or if they could buy a coffee. That had eventually led them to buying a campervan which sold coffee in the busy months and which the kids were supposed to help out in during the school holidays. However, they had got better paid jobs as lifeguards in the nearby hotel so usually Kirsty and Steve were left to open up the van which meant it had been a bit neglected lately.

Kirsty smiled as she looked across to the dilapidated barn where the wedding was originally going to take place. It needed some attention, and she was relieved that the pressure was off to make it wedding ready. She didn't mind that Emma had appointed her as the wedding planner, but her skills didn't quite extend to the dilapidated barn. That was a job for Phil and the other Kirsty from the TV series *Location, Location, Location* and unfortunately she didn't have their number.

When she and her sisters were young, they had often found random kids playing on their things. Dad had set up a slide at the bottom of the garden and a tree swing which some mistook for a public play park. 'It's better people enjoy it than things not getting used', he would say cheerily.

It had been a while since she'd seen him smile. She hoped Emma's wedding would give him something to be happy about although she did wonder how he'd be with the speech. Kirsty reached for her to-do list and spreadsheet and sat down at the kitchen table, relieved that Emma and Max had loved the photos of the distillery and were delighted at the new choice of venue.

She scanned through the latest version which wasn't actually too daunting. Emma had never liked fuss and attention. The cake was being made in Lamlash at Cèic coffee shop and bakery. Its Kurdish owners were the most beautiful bakers and quite happy to make Emma's unusual request for a three-layered cake: rich fruit on the bottom, vanilla on the next layer and then carrot cake. In fact, to be fair, thought Kirsty, the cake was the most demanding request Emma had made.

Their dad was taking care of the bouquets and sourcing the flowers from Meadowbank's gardens. She would need to remind him of this later.

'Hi, love,' called Steve as he walked in the back door. She could hear him kicking off his boots. 'How's your morning been?'

'Fine,' she said with a shrug. 'Same old. Laundry, dishes, tidying up. And scrubbing the sink,' she said with a giggle. 'Life on the edge.'

'But at least the sun is shining.'

'Yes, that is true. We are living the dream. I just hope it stays like this for the wedding. Anyway, how was the walk?'

'Great.' He smiled. 'They were over the moon this time to see so much. I mean sheep, otters and a Highland cow in the same day.'

'Really?' she said, wondering if he was being sarcastic.

'Yes,' he said. 'It would seem they want to make the most of their last day with us.'

Kirsty laughed, knowing full well how much Steve wanted to impress Trudy and Chuck and it seemed like the wildlife had done the trick.

'Yes, and they said they would add it to their Trip Advisor review.'

'Great,' said Kirsty. 'Let's hope they leave it at that and don't complain about the towels.' Much as she didn't like online reviews, she knew they were a necessary part of the business and, touch wood, they had all been positive so far. She always made the effort to send a follow-up email to all guests thanking them for their visit and also asking them to leave a review if they didn't mind.

However, she always worried that their luck would one day run out. All it took was for one disgruntled customer to make a complaint and it could affect their bookings. She knew plenty of small business owners who took great exception to negative reviews and would go on and reply to each one. Kirsty sometimes cringed at the tone some of these took as they could be both quite defensive and aggressive, and she didn't think it made good business sense. She knew the customer was always right, in theory, but even if you disagreed then it wasn't ideal to start getting into a hostile exchange on a public platform.

She reached across to the cupboard to take out a couple of mugs and then turned back to see Steve filling the kettle. He was whistling an upbeat tune and she couldn't help smiling at his general cheeriness. He was so happy here.

Steve grew up in the Highlands and had struggled to adjust to life in London even though he told Kirsty, when they met, he saw it as a rite of passage and had to be done. But he was a country boy at heart, always had been, and he jumped at the chance to move to Arran when the kids were small. Now, he was in his element and loved showing off the wildlife and natural beauty to the tourists.

'I had an enquiry for the first week of July,' she told him as he dropped a couple of teabags in the mugs and filled them with boiling water.

He frowned. 'I thought we were fully booked?'

'Yes. But it just goes to show that if we had another couple of rooms, we would probably fill them.'

'I know, love, but it's just going to cost too much at the moment.'

The couple had ambitions to restore the barn at some point and turn it into a studio with an ensuite shower room. Steve was usually ever the optimist while Kirsty tended to worry about the cash side of things, and it worried her slightly he was now becoming more cautious like her. She was also concerned that the roof of the main house would need attention soon and prayed that the dry spell continued so she didn't need to think about putting buckets out to catch drips. Steve was great around the house and good at doing odd jobs, but he had a tendency to start jobs then get waylaid when other areas needing attention distracted him.

'You look tired, are you okay?' he said as they sat down at the scrubbed pine table.

'Yes, I'm fine. Just a busy head and lots going on . . .'

Steve reached across and squeezed her hand. 'I worry about you sometimes. You've had so much on your mind . . .' He looked at her pointedly as said gently, 'Especially these past few months.'

She looked away and pursed her lips. 'I'll be fine, Steve. Honestly, don't worry. I just want to get through the wedding. Then I'll talk to them. I don't like keeping secrets.'

Steve knew better than to argue, so he changed the subject. 'Do you know when Amy arrives?'

She shook her head. 'No. She's being a bit evasive. She did say it would be at least a week before the wedding. But I'll try and pin her down and work out what her plans are. It would be good to have her here sooner rather than later.'

'I'm sure she'll be here before you know it.'

Kirsty hoped so. Right now, she needed her sisters around her more than ever.

CHAPTER EIGHT

'I know there's something on your mind,' said Ross as he pulled into the driveway and turned off the ignition. They sat in silence for a moment.

'I'm fine,' said Amy, doing her best to convince him she was. She smiled but turned into more of a grimace.

Ross sighed and leaned back, resting his head against the seat.

Amy hated what she knew she was going to have to tell him. She studied the contours of his nose and mouth, finally looking at his eyes.

Ross sighed again. 'Just tell me what the matter is, Amy. You're behaving strangely. I can tell something's bothering you and I'd rather you told me what it is.'

'Uh . . . I'm just preoccupied with work.'

'But it's yoga and massage, Amy. How can that be stressful? You should be all Zen and relaxed . . .'

Wow, she thought. *Say what you think why don't you?* 'Erm . . . it's not quite as straightforward as that,' she said, trying not to sound too annoyed. 'I'm thinking about the admin that I'm falling behind on, the clients I've been supporting, class cover . . .'

He looked at her. 'Class cover? What do you mean by that?'

She could have kicked herself for letting that slip. What an idiot. There was no way that he would let it lie. 'Oh, you know, in case any holidays come up. I just need to know who I can call on to cover my sessions.'

He didn't seem too rattled, and her answer actually seemed to pacify him. In fact, weirdly, he was smiling at her. 'A holiday? You're right. What a brilliant idea. We could do with a break. I'd love to go away, and I know the little guy would too. Wouldn't that be amazing if the three of us went away somewhere together?'

Amy's heart sank. But she knew as Ross reached to open the door, things were all settled in his mind. That was the end of the conversation, and his mind was now in planning mode. This was what he always did. He pulled the key from the ignition, jumped out the car and whistled as he walked towards the front door. 'Leave it with me,' he said over his shoulder. 'I'll look into it and sort something out.'

Amy followed him into the house, her feet trailing behind her. She wanted to scream at him that she didn't want to go on holiday with them and that he never listened to her. He never did. It was all about him.

She lightly touched the natural curve of the wooden banister and looked around the hallway. She felt empty and detached. This wasn't her home, and it never would be. Despite the late afternoon sunshine streaming in through the windows, she felt really discombobulated and had a sudden urge to get as far away from this claustrophobic mess she had got herself into. She made a snap decision.

'Cup of coffee?' he asked.

She shook her head. She told him most days that she never drank coffee in the afternoon and yet still he regularly asked her the question even though they had been together almost eighteen months. It didn't make him bad but every little detail about him was now irritating her which said more about her and what she had to do. 'No thanks, not for me. I'm just going to go for a quick swim while I can.'

'Oh, okay,' he said, sounding disappointed. 'How long will you be?'

What does it bloody matter, she wanted to shout. 'Why, is there a rush?'

Glancing at his watch, he said, 'Remember we're collecting Caleb later.'

Amy tried hard to smile. She felt small splinters of her heart start to crumble as she realized, she was having to pretend. This was so against everything that was so dear to her — being genuine and honest and kind. She met his gaze. 'Okay, don't worry. I won't be too long.'

He turned away to walk into the kitchen. Amy sneaked another glance at him. She was fond of him, but as she watched him with compassionate detachment, she realized that was it. She gathered her swimming things then pulled the door closed behind her, wishing she could just keep walking.

It didn't take Amy long to make the walk down to Jericho Beach and she felt herself relax as she got nearer the shore. It was one of her favourite thinking spots and she liked to lean against one of the many logs and watch the world go by. It never failed to calm her. Today she wanted to be in the water to experience that feeling of being in a liminal space between the land and the sea and just float. As she slipped her clothes off, folding them neatly in a pile, she watched the wild black rabbits scampering around and playing. When did she forget to be playful and just enjoy the simple things?

This was one of the less-crowded beaches, which made it more appealing to her, and although it was a bit rocky, she knew which bits to avoid. She had learned her lesson previously and now always wore wet shoes to protect her feet from any sharp stones or shells.

The water was cool as she slowly walked through the gentle ripples and allowed her body to adjust to the temperature. A few kayakers and paddle boarders were out but she was the only one swimming today. Amy had taken an open water swimming safety course the previous year which helped her learn about the local tides. She knew the outgoing tide was always a bit more predictable as the water was flowing away from the beach. She gave a quick glance to the boats to check the current, but the surface was calm and still. In fact, the conditions were perfect.

Taking some deep breaths in and out, she then slowly braced herself as she lay on her back and floated, allowing her body to acclimatize to the drop in temperature. Even the process of lying on her back and watching the sky overhead had an immediate soothing effect. After a minute or so she turned onto her front and stuck her face in the water, gasping at how cold it felt. The water temperature was just over eight degrees which wasn't that different to the sea in Arran. In fact, according to her research, the water at home may have even been slightly warmer by about one degree.

She began swimming, her goggles allowing her to escape to another realm below the surface. She focused on bubbles and blurry shapes and within a few minutes she felt her anxiety subside and the tension she'd been holding begin to dissipate. Slicing her arms through the water, she kicked her legs and smiled. After a while she flipped on her back and floated again, staring at the empty sky above her.

She had always loved swimming in the sea when she was younger, but when Mum died, and she came back here after the funeral, she found cold water helped her deal with her grief. Perhaps it was the sensory overload of having to handle plunging change in temperature, but it distracted her from the visceral sadness and gave her something else to think about. She always felt calmer afterwards and it had definitely helped her mental health over the past few years. Being in the water was where she felt most like herself.

Even though she longed to stay there, floating on her back, her hands and feet began to feel a bit numb, and she knew she'd been in there long enough. Reluctantly, she rolled over onto her stomach and made her way to shore.

CHAPTER NINE

Emma was so glad she didn't have to think about caterers and flowers and that Kirsty was happy to handle that side of it. The main focus of the wedding was about her and Max becoming husband and wife. She wasn't a bride-to-be who spent hours poring over menus or tasting wine. As long as there was food and drink, she was happy.

Max, yes, was perhaps a bit fussier, being a foodie, but he had scanned the sample menus Kirsty had sent over and was happy with the BBQ dishes they'd suggested. This wasn't like him at all, and she knew he would have liked to have been more involved, but it was a sign of just how run ragged he was with work. They'd opted for canapés followed by sea bream with lemon thyme and paprika, prawns marinated in ginger, lime and coriander, steaks charred over applewood and sides of salad, new potato salad, crunchy coleslaw and cherry vine tomatoes with feta cheese.

They weren't so fussed about desserts, especially since they'd chosen a fancy wedding cake, but knew they'd better have a couple of options. She had left Kirsty and Steve to make the final decision on that, or namely Becky and Tom as they were the ones most likely to eat pudding. Even her dad had never had a particularly sweet tooth. Becky and Tom had taken their responsibility very seriously and insisted they would have to go to the distillery to sample a few of the options. Eventually, after some thorough research, they'd selected a strawberry and mint pavlova, a nectarine cheesecake and a salted caramel tart with crème fraiche.

She was glad they didn't have a wedding list either. They had been living together for two years now — they moved in together shortly after her mum's funeral — and really didn't need anything. It was going to be a small affair, just a party of around thirty, and she had said to guests that if they really felt they wanted to give a present would they mind donating to the Beatson Cancer Charity in memory of her mum. All the staff there had been amazing during her treatment, and it felt good to be able to give something back and also remember Jean in some way, so she was part of their celebration.

Time had flown by this past week as Emma and Max focused on settling outstanding work so they could focus fully on their wedding. Emma sat at her desk and gazed out the window as she thought about seeing her dad and sisters. She was planning on going home a few days before Max arrived with his mother and his sister and her partner. They had rented a holiday home near Meadowbank and Max would stay there the night before the wedding. His kilt, a family tartan of bright reds and blues, had been dry-cleaned and was hanging in a suit carrier in the spare room next to Emma's dress which she loved and couldn't wait to wear. It was simple and elegant with an off the shoulder neckline, Bardot sleeves and flattering ruching under the bust.

She was certain that the nerves and worry over the past few months were all down to stress and anxiety. Aside from anything else she was also feeling a bit helpless about not being nearer to help Kirsty with her dad. From what she said, and certainly from what Emma could tell when she spoke to him, he was starting to become confused. Hopefully when she saw him in person she'd be reassured. She was sure he was probably also feeling a bit anxious about the wedding, she reasoned, especially without Mum there to organize it in the efficient way they all knew she would have.

Taking a few deep breaths to try and ground herself, she placed her hands on her desk and closed her eyes. She pictured Max and only Max. Only then did she start to feel that lovely sense of anticipation that all brides should have.

She was busy answering emails when she realized, she had several missed calls and a voicemail on her mobile. She frowned when she saw it was from the GP. She listened to the message from her doctor asking her to call the surgery at her earliest convenience. She was about to do, so when an urgent call came in from a client and that snowballed into a legal emergency, regarding child custody. When she finally looked up from her laptop and saw the time, the surgery was closed for the weekend.

She shrugged and made a mental note to ring first thing Monday morning and then programmed it into her phone so she wouldn't forget. It would just be a follow-up from the blood tests she had run since the pregnancy scare. Emma had made an effort to eat more regularly and was trying to remember to take iron tablets; she was likely anaemic.

That weekend she was having a meal with some friends instead of an official hen do, the idea of which had filled her with horror. She had a facial and an appointment booked tomorrow to have her hair done and then a girls' night meal. She intended to enjoy every minute of it.

She grabbed her coat and bag and closed the office door behind her.

'Hey, Joy,' she said to the office PA, standing by the lift.

'Hi, Emma. I'm so glad it's Friday!'

'Me too,' she said.

'Are you getting excited?' she said in her enthusiastic voice which couldn't fail to engage you.

'Mmm . . .'

'*Ooh* nervous, are you?' she said, her eyes shining.

'I'm okay, I think probably as it's such a small affair.'

'I know, I can't believe you're managing to keep numbers so low. There's no way on earth we could have had such a small bash. Not with my lot.'

Emma smiled affectionately at her. Joy came from a large family and as the youngest, and only girl, her wedding was planned for about two years' time, and she shared every detail with Emma.

'How is Olive doing?'

'Ah, you know, growing up too quickly and has an opinion on everything.' She whipped her phone out of her pocket and scrolled through some images, thrusting it in front of Emma.

'She is so cute. I can't believe how quickly she's growing up.'

'I know. She's three going on thirty and she doesn't stop talking.'

Emma laughed. 'Wonder who she takes after then?'

Joy gasped in mock indignation. 'That's what everyone says. No idea why they think that.' She grinned. 'Anyway, I know you still have a week to go but you make sure to send some photos to me as soon as you can and have a lovely day. I know you hate fuss and will probably quietly slope away next week without saying bye . . .'

Emma was about to disagree but, actually, Joy was spot on.

'Here let me give you a cuddle now.' She leaned in and flung her arms around Emma who felt weirdly moved.

She was very fond of Joy and her enthusiasm for everything was so infectious. She ushered her into the lift as the doors opened. 'Thanks, Joy. I will definitely send you some photos. I just have to get through the hen night first.'

Joy squealed. 'Is that this weekend? Oh my. Are you having strippers and everything? I had strippers at mine and, I mean, I know it's totally inappropriate and I shouldn't even be admitting that to you but . . . Wow, it was fun!'

Emma's eyes widened in horror at the thought. 'Erm, no, just a quiet dinner with a few friends . . .' The lift opened, and they walked out onto George Street, busy with tourists and office workers ready to embrace the weekend.

'You take care and enjoy that wee munchkin of yours. She is a beauty. I'll see you Monday.'

Joy beamed. 'Aw, thanks, Emma. And I am sure that it won't be too long before we hear the patter of tiny feet for you as well.'

Smiling, Emma turned in the opposite direction and started to walk home.

CHAPTER TEN

The guests from the past couple of days were gathering their things, preparing to leave. Trudy and Chuck were now finally heading to Edinburgh and Kirsty was almost tempted to get out the bunting and farewell streamers. It felt as though they'd been there for weeks. But she would miss the other guests who she had grown fond of. Neil was a retired teacher from Hove and Alice was a repeat customer from Inverness who loved walking and always made it her mission to try and spot a golden eagle on one of the many hikes she embarked on during her stay.

Alice had found Meadowbank Cottage after an online search following the death of her husband five years ago. When she arrived that first time, she was clearly shy, and Kirsty did her best to put her at ease. After a few days she had opened up to Kirsty and told her about the plans she and her late husband had had to visit Arran. Sadly, they hadn't managed to before his sudden death and Alice promised herself that she would go. She had loved the island so much, and Meadowbank Cottage, that she'd started to visit at the same time of year every year since.

'Same time next year?' said Alice, smiling.

'I've already got you in the diary. Don't worry. It will be great to see you.'

Kirsty noticed Neil, the retired teacher, hovering in the background. She hadn't missed the cosy chats the pair had been having these past few days. They sat at the same table for breakfast and Neil had also offered to go walking with Alice yesterday. Kirsty had thought he looked pale and withdrawn on arrival but now he definitely had a skip in his step and his cheeks were a healthy pink.

'Do you know, Alice, I might just book for next year too. That is a great idea.'

Kirsty paused, her eyes flicking to check Alice's reaction. However, she needn't have worried as Alice clearly also thought it a great idea given the huge grin on her face.

'No problem at all,' Kirsty said. 'I'll pop you in now too and email you a confirmation. It would be lovely to have you back again.'

'I hope the wedding goes well, dearie, and that your sister has a fabulous time,' she said sincerely. 'Do let me know, won't you?'

'Of course I will.' Kirsty gave Alice a hug. 'I promise to send you some photos.'

Alice's eyes twinkled. 'I would love that. Please do!'

Just then, Steve arrived in the hallway, keen to get the guests to the ferry terminal in time. There was no way they were going to let Trudy and Chuck miss that boat. 'Come on,' he called to Alice. 'Let's get your luggage in the car.'

Trudy and Chuck were already outside sitting on one of the wooden benches positioned to catch the morning sunshine. A light breeze had started to pick up, but there was a lovely warmth in the air. 'This is such a calming view, isn't it? Thank you so much. We have loved it,' said Trudy.

Chuck nodded in agreement. 'It's one helluva place,' he said. 'We will definitely need to come back. And we'll tell all our friends in California about it too.'

Kirsty was slightly taken aback at his chatty enthusiasm. It had been the most he'd said throughout his stay at Meadowbank. 'It's been a pleasure and I hope you come back soon.' Kirsty crossed her fingers behind her back. She wasn't sure that she ever wanted to see them again.

Trudy nodded. 'It is a beautiful island. Full of magic. We are *so* sorry to leave. All being well we will be back.'

Kirsty wasn't quite sure what to make of their cryptic comments and she frowned, bemused.

'Well, there is plenty more magic to go and find,' said Steve, swinging the car keys and winking at his wife. 'Let's get you to that ferry. We can't have you missing out on the next leg of your journey.'

Kirsty waved as Steve drove the guests away in the people carrier. She stood for a moment enjoying the view. Trudy was spot on when she said it was calming. It certainly was and even just a few minutes looking at the sparkling waters were enough to soothe her busy mind when she was in her most emotional state whether annoyed, sad, angry or frustrated.

Normally, Kirsty would rush inside the minute guests left and strip the beds and get the sheets bundled into the washing machine then out on the line to dry. The worktop was also stacked with dirty breakfast dishes. However, she decided this morning she would sit on the bench in the sun and remind herself of a guest's perspective. Wasn't it important to remind herself why people came here? It was all too easy to take things for granted and to underappreciate what was right in front of you. She had a bit of time before the next guests arrived later that afternoon and so was going to make the most of it.

As she sat there, she became aware of the sounds around her. Birds were singing, the gentle breeze rippled through the tree and a lazy bee buzzed overhead. The air was salty, and she took in a few deep breaths, trying to settle her busy head. Closing her eyes, she smiled and she enjoyed the feel of the warm sun on her face. She could taste the salt on her lips and hear the swell of the waves. Moments like this made it all worthwhile. She had never regretted this move home, not at all. Yet sometimes the days felt mundane with never-ending chores such as laundry, scrubbing toilets and shopping for groceries yet again.

When she wasn't attending to the needs of guests, she felt as though she was running after Steve and the kids, always picking up wet towels from the bathroom floor. Steve was very hands-on, and she was grateful for all that he did. But Kirsty felt like she was starting to forget who she was, as though she had lost a part of herself these past few years. She could easily present a smile to people she met in the village or at the shops but there were times when keeping up appearances was exhausting. It felt like she was wearing a mask.

She thought of Steve and the way he still followed his passions with his trail running, hiking and now the paddle boarding. She still had to work out who she was and what she wanted. Before the kids were born, she loved writing and had tried to keep this up when they were little but then she became so involved in their lives and juggling that she was too exhausted to even try. She had volunteered at the local primary school as a reader helper when they were younger. Perhaps she could do some more volunteering? Helping and connecting with the community was supposed to be good for your mental health. Maybe she could think about that. The problem was right now she just wanted to curl up in a darkened room and go to sleep for a very time. She sighed. There was no chance of that anytime soon because everybody wanted a piece of her. She needed to make sure her sister had a magical wedding and then after that she would take time out for herself.

But worry gnawed inside her. Her problems were greater than that. No matter how much she tried to bury it, Kirsty knew that sooner or later she would have to deal with the huge secret she had uncovered only a few months ago. Because it wasn't going away, and she needed to tell her sisters about it. And soon.

CHAPTER ELEVEN

'Did you have a good swim?' asked Ross, as Amy let herself into the house and quietly closed the door behind her.

She was cold, a good mixture between still feeling the adrenaline rush from the water and the pressing need to go and warm up in the shower. She shivered slightly as she stood there considering her options. 'Yes, thanks. I'm just going to go and have a quick shower. It was cold.'

'Take your time. I just had a call from Caleb a while ago. Guess what? He's been invited to a sleepover with Danny, so there's no rush to go get him. It's just you and me for the rest of the evening.'

Amy forced a smile and ran upstairs before she blurted out what was on her mind, knowing she had to leave very soon. Peeling off her clothes, which now felt slightly damp, she flicked on the shower and stepped in, making sure the water was tepid rather than too hot. She couldn't quite believe that her life had got to this stage.

When she'd arrived in Vancouver all those years ago, she never expected to stay for so long. It had been a wonderful second home to her and she had made great friends. Yet once again she was reminded of that feeling of not knowing where home was any more. She felt rudderless and alone.

Perhaps Emma's forthcoming wedding and the fact her mum wouldn't be there were the factors. She vigorously rubbed the shampoo into her head and watched the soapy suds cascade down the plughole. She was going to speak to Ross. She'd tell him she couldn't be here any longer then she'd leave. It wasn't fair to stay, not now she knew that it wasn't love she felt for him. She knew this would be the last shower she would have here. It all felt so surreal.

She wrapped herself in a towel and quickly scooped her hair into a turban with a smaller towel. Reaching for her phone she sent a quick message to Josh.

I'm going to tell him. Please can I come and stay? x

He replied almost immediately. *Of course. Here for you and we are in all night xx*

Amy thought about her mum again. What would she say to Ross? She knew she could ask her sisters, but she didn't want to burden them with what was essentially her problem. As far as they were concerned, they'd meet Ross at the wedding. The fact she hadn't even told him about it said enough. She thought of her mum's motto that all the girls should always enjoy life and live it to its fullest. She wasn't in the least bit bothered when Amy moved to Canada. Quite the opposite. She was delighted and promised that they would go and visit her especially as it was a place she always wanted to visit. Sadly, she never made it thanks to cancer cutting her life so short.

Amy knew she was lucky to have supportive parents especially when so many of her friends complained that their parents' guilt-tripped them because they'd moved away for work or just because they wanted to live their own life. She closed her eyes, briefly picturing Mum's warm smile. *You know what to do, my lovely. The answers are all inside you. Just trust your instinct. What does your gut tell you?*

Amy opened her eyes, wiped away a tear and smiled sadly at her reflection in the mirror. It was time to be honest and treat Ross with the respect he deserved. Tidying away all her things from the bathroom, she gave it one last cursory glance before looking in the wardrobe and making sure she had packed all of her belongings.

'I've cooked some pasta,' he said proudly as she walked into the kitchen. He handed her a glass of wine. 'How was the water? Cold, or okay? Do you feel better for it?'

Amy couldn't help noticing that he was talking too quickly and asking her an awful lot of questions without giving her the chance to answer. Was he nervous or did he know she was about to say something? 'Um, it was fine thanks.' She glanced at the table and noticed the flickering candle. Oh no, what was he planning? He wasn't the type of guy to prepare candlelit dinners . . .

'Cheers,' he said, knocking his glass against hers.

She couldn't bring herself to take a sip.

'It's your favourite.' He frowned. 'The Italian one that you love.'

'Thanks,' she mumbled. It wasn't her favourite wine at all. It was his. Her favourite wine was French.

'Is something wrong?'

This was not good. He was jumpy and kept patting his pocket as though he was worried he had lost something. She put the glass down, noticing that he had changed into one of his better shirts.

'Amy, I just wanted to say . . .'

She had to do something, say something, and quickly before this all escalated. 'Can we eat?' she said, pointing at the Bolognese sauce simmering on the stove. 'I'm absolutely starving.' She lied. She was usually ravenous after her swims but tonight her stomach was churning.

'Okay, I suppose so. If you want to.' He put his hand on the small of her back and guided her towards the table. 'Sit down and I'll bring it over.'

Amy numbly lowered herself into a chair and watched as he drained the spaghetti then arranged it in bowls. He ladled the sauce on top.

'*Voilà*!' he said, and she cringed. It was one of the few things that he said that annoyed her, which made her feel even worse than she already did. Why couldn't she be more gracious? She was *such* an awful person for thinking badly of him. As he placed the bowl in front her, she tried to look engaged. This wasn't his fault, it was hers. Entirely hers.

'*Bon Appetit*.'

Amy forced herself to eat a few mouthfuls if only to provide a base for the wine which she was tempted to start gulping. *Breathe*, she told herself. *Ground yourself Amy and just breathe. And do the right thing*.

'So, as I was saying, I've got some good news . . .'

She held her breath for a moment then exhaled. 'Uh-huh?'

'I've managed to get some time off work and thought we could go away.' He beamed at her. 'Isn't that great?'

Blimey, he didn't hang around, did he? The holiday discussion, if that was what it even was, had only been a couple of hours ago. 'Um, well, the thing is . . .' she began, 'I'm actually going to be going home.'

'What do you mean?'

She saw the look of confusion flit across his face.

'I'm going home to Scotland.'

'Why?'

'To see my family and . . . well, my sister is getting married.'

'When?'

'Next month . . .' Her voice trailed off.

'I could come?' he suggested brightly.

She didn't reply.

'Hold on.' He scowled as the penny dropped. 'Why are you just telling me this now?'

'That's because it's quite a last-minute thing.'

He scratched his chin thoughtfully. 'Well, let me see what I can do. It might be tricky but I'll see if I can juggle things with work so I can come with you.'

'It's a small wedding,' said Amy.

'That sounds lovely. It will give me a chance to meet your family and get to know them all. I'm sure Caleb would love that too. Especially if he gets to see a real Highland cow.'

'No!' she shouted.

He was visibly taken aback. 'No?'

'What I mean,' she said slowly, urging herself to remain calm, 'is that I have to go alone.' There, she had finally said it.

He looked at her, surprised. 'Do you mean I'm not invited?'

Amy hesitated, almost tempted to use that as an excuse, but then her words started to tumble out. 'No, Ross. What I mean is that I'm going on my own. I'm going home alone, and I am going to my sister's wedding on my own. You're not coming, and you're not invited.'

'You mean that you don't want me there?'

She felt her cheeks redden and she fixed her eyes on his. 'This is something I need to do on my own. I haven't been back since Mum died and I need some time and space.'

'I get it,' he said, but he sounded hurt, as though he had no understanding at all of what she had just said. 'You want some time to process it. That's okay.' His voice was now clipped which confirmed to Amy that he didn't understand at all.

'Actually, Ross, I need some space from everything. From us, from here and from you.'

He put his fork down suddenly and looked away, avoiding her gaze. 'Is this about Lucinda?'

'Lucinda?' Amy was genuinely confused. Why would his ex-wife have anything to do with this?

He sighed. 'I wasn't going to say anything to you as there didn't seem much point in upsetting you. It was a complete mistake, a one-off . . .'

Amy reached for the glass and took a gulp of wine.

'It didn't mean anything. It really didn't. But you were away doing that yoga convention and she was lonely and . . . well, we do have history.'

Amy sighed, partly in relief. And it didn't escape her that he'd tried to blame her being away for work for why it happened. As though somehow it was her fault that he had been unfaithful. 'Look, Ross, there is no easy way to say this to you and I am genuinely sorry as I don't like hurting anyone. But I need to go home to Scotland. I don't want to be here anymore.'

'But it meant nothing! I'm sorry.' He shrugged. 'I probably shouldn't even have told you.'

'I am glad you told me. We need to be honest which is what I am trying to be with you. I want to go home. Alone.'

'Are you sure you actually know what you want, Amy?' he persisted. 'I mean you've seemed fairly happy to move in with me and live here for the past few months.'

'Yes,' she said, her voice steely. 'I am sure, and I am genuinely sorry, Ross. But this—' she pointed around the room — 'isn't what I want. I care for you and Caleb. But I'm not in love with you and my future isn't here. I'm sorry. I truly am.'

'Wait, what? You don't love me?' he said in a whisper.

'No,' she said confidently, realizing that she never had. 'And I don't think you love me either, Ross. Otherwise, you wouldn't have slept with your ex-wife.'

He looked at her in disbelief. 'You've been leading me on then? All this time?'

'No, Ross, I haven't been leading you on. I moved here because I wanted to. I wanted to be with you, and I wanted to give things a go. But things have changed. I've changed. And you aren't happy either given what you've just told me.' She pushed the plate of cold, congealing pasta away from her.

'But you're not listening to what I am saying! It was a one-off.'

'Even if it was and I wanted to stay, how could we move on from it? I mean she's always going to be part of your life.'

'What now then?'

Amy didn't like the slightly sneering tone in his voice, but she didn't suppose she could blame him. 'I fly home next week.'

He clenched his jaw tightly. 'Unbelievable. Were you going to string me along and get me to drop you at the airport? Then dump me at the departure gate?'

She shook her head sadly. He was angry with her, rightly so. Hopefully he wasn't too hurt. But this hadn't been right for either of them. She stood up, ready to clear the plates away.

'Leave them Amy. Please . . . just go. Get out. Get out of *my* house.'

She walked past him and paused, putting a hand on his shoulder. 'I am sorry. I didn't want to hurt you and I'm truly sorry that things haven't worked out.'

He pushed her hand off.

'Is there someone else? Is that what you mean? You've met someone else?'

'No, Ross. There's nobody else. That's not what this is about . . .' She paused. 'But maybe you and Lucinda could try and give things a go again? I'm sure Caleb would like that.' She walked out the room and went slowly upstairs. She called a taxi as she gathered her belongings.

When she came back downstairs, she looked into the kitchen. Ross was still sat at the table, staring at the wall. 'Just go,' he said flatly and emptied the remaining contents of the wine bottle into his glass. 'I never want to see you again.'

As the cab pulled away, she felt awful for the hurt she'd caused Ross, but fairly indifferent to the fact that he had cheated on her. She couldn't help but breathe a huge sigh of relief.

When Josh opened the door to his apartment, she fell into his arms. 'I am so glad to see you.'

'How did it go?' he asked.

'It was hard. I felt awful, even with what he told me.'

'Oh? Do tell?'

'Can we get you anything?' said Andy, coming through to greet and hug her too.

'Thanks, but no. Just being here is great and I can't tell you how much I appreciate you. Do you mind if I just crash guys? I'm absolutely exhausted.'

'Yes, of course,' said Josh, helping her with her bags and showing her into the spare room. He hugged her again. 'We're here for you. Just let me know if you need anything.'

'Thanks,' she said. 'I'll fill you in on all the details tomorrow.'

She watched as Josh closed the door, then sank into the pillows realizing just how emotionally and physically tired she was.

But for the first time in months, she slept well and when she woke up, she felt as though a huge weight had been lifted from her shoulders.

As she stretched her arms above her head, she felt a glimmer of something pooling inside her; a feeling that she hadn't felt for a very long time. Hope.

I knew you would do the right thing for you, darling girl. You trusted it would work out and it did.

'Thanks, Mum', she said out loud and smiled.

CHAPTER TWELVE

Emma remembered the exact moment she had the first inkling that something might be wrong. A couple of months earlier she had been in the bathroom putting some toothpaste in the cupboard when she saw all the sanitary pads and tampons. She frowned, briefly wondering why she was so well stocked as she tended to have to remind herself to get more. Then it struck her that she had missed a period . . . Or maybe it was two. She had been so absorbed with a high-profile case at work, working well into the small hours, the weeks had seemed to disappear.

Although she and Max weren't actively trying for a baby, they weren't not. She couldn't remember the last time they used contraception. Could she be pregnant? A wave of panic washed over her as to what this might mean. The timing wasn't great at all. There was too much happening what with work right now and, of course, the wedding.

Then the voice of reason whispered to her that none of that mattered. If she *was* pregnant, then they would make a plan and work around things. It wasn't the end of the world. She smiled as the reality dawned on her that this could indeed be the start of a new chapter for her and Max. It could be a dream come true. The wedding wasn't that far away, and she couldn't be that far along. Three months at the most and anyway, they weren't living in the 1950s. It would all be fine and add an extra layer of celebration to their big day.

But then she had taken the pregnancy test and the line had shown negative. She felt as though she had been punched in the gut. Thank God she hadn't said anything to Max about it and raised his hopes. She felt absolutely desolate and heart-broken which surprised her. She hadn't realized how much she wanted to be pregnant.

Since then, she had thrown herself back into work and tried not to think about it though she had to admit, she'd thought of nothing else. She then began to wonder why she hadn't become pregnant yet especially since she had been off the pill for a couple of years. She hadn't wanted to worry Max either, so had held back from telling him. Though she knew he would be kind and supportive as always, she didn't want to have to deal with his disappointment too.

The other signs which she'd dismissed over the past months — hot flushes and tiredness, then started to loom large in her mind and she had thought there was no harm in talking to the GP about it. She had fully expected her to tell her that this was all normal and with a stressful job and up and coming wedding it was probably all down to stress. Or anaemia of course. She remembered she had that as a teenager — and so did Amy!

Then she remembered that Kirsty's periods tailed off when she took up running to help her cope with stress and had taken things to the extreme so much so that her periods had stopped altogether. Maybe that was what happened with extreme periods of life stress? In fact, when she stopped to think about it, she realized that her cycle had started to become quite irregular after the death of her mum.

'I think we'll just run some blood tests to be sure,' the doctor had said.

Emma was surprised and hadn't expected her to say that. 'What for?'

'Just to check a few things like your iron levels and your thyroid especially if you're very tired. Would you say more than usual?'

Emma gave a dry laugh. 'Not especially,' she said. 'No more than usual or than anyone else.'

Now she sat in the waiting room glancing at the clock and wondering when the doctor would see her. She was clearly running late, and Emma was already anxious enough. Her phone kept pinging with work emails, and she was doing her best to keep up and reply to them all. She only had a few days left until she finished for the wedding. However, her focus was completely scattered. She just wanted to get this over with and get on with things. Why couldn't the doctor just have told her about the results over the phone? When she had called back on Monday, after she had missed last week's call, the receptionist insisted that the GP wanted to see her in person. It was now Wednesday and she had spent the past couple of days wondering if she had cancer and was dying? Why else would she want her to come into the surgery?

'Emma?' said the doctor, coming to the door of the waiting room. 'Come with me.' She smiled which made Emma relax. Surely that was a good sign? If she was dying then she wouldn't be smiling at her, would she?

The doctor pointed at the empty chair next to her desk and she took a seat and glanced at her screen. 'Sorry to keep you waiting. I know you're very busy.'

Emma shrugged. 'Don't worry. I understand.'

'Okay, Emma, I have had your blood results back and these initial results would indicate that the amount of progesterone in your system is very low.'

Emma didn't know what that meant. 'What does that mean?'

'As you know, the decline in fertility speeds up when you reach your mid-thirties . . .' She glanced at her notes. 'You said you and your partner have been having regular, unprotected sex for some time?'

Emma nodded.

'Emma, I would say these initial blood tests suggest that you're in the early stages of menopause.' She looked at Emma who was still listening and waiting for her to continue. 'Now there are other things we can explore. But with the additional symptoms you mentioned like the hot flushes and night sweats . . . everything would point to the menopause.'

She whipped her head up and looked at the doctor in disbelief. 'But I'm only thirty-seven,' she said.

'I know and let's not rule anything out at this stage. But I really think we need to investigate this further. I'm going to refer you for more tests, and we will try and get to the bottom of what's going on.'

'But I'm about to get married. How do I tell my fiancé this?'

'Let's take one step at a time,' she said, kindly. 'Let's just try and find out what's happening before you start to panic.' She paused. 'Early menopause can run in families. Is it something your mum had? Do you have sisters?'

'My mum is dead. My older sister has two children, and I don't know about my younger sister's monthly cycle.' She knew she was being rude and was embarrassed at her tone, especially when the doctor was trying her best to be kind.

'I am sorry to hear that,' she said, her tone sympathetic. 'Look, why don't you go home and let the news settle? Talk to your partner and in the meantime, I'll refer you for these further tests.'

Emma managed to thank the doctor before stumbling out of the surgery in a daze. Early menopause? Did that make her infertile? How on earth could she break this to Max when he had his heart set on having a family and they were due to get married in less than two weeks? How was she going to tell him that there was a chance she couldn't have kids?

CHAPTER THIRTEEN

Steve was peeling a banana and telling Kirsty, for the umpteenth time, that it was important for men to watch their blood pressure. He'd also added sweet potatoes to the shopping list as they were another excellent source of potassium, which was essential.

Kirsty didn't think there was anything wrong with his blood pressure. He always looked perfectly relaxed to her. She, on the other hand, could do with lowering her blood pressure with all that was going on.

Steve also liked to start the day with porridge in order to reduce high cholesterol. Now he was in the over-forty bracket, in fact make that the over-forty-five bracket, he was forever sharing such snippets of useful information.

She sighed. At least he was being mindful of his diet and didn't carry any extra weight. There were no signs of a middle-age paunch and he was as fit if not fitter than the day they had met all those years ago. The outdoors life suited him.

'I'm off to meet Nicola for a coffee this morning,' she said as she opened the dishwasher and started to unload it. Steve reached for the cutlery and began putting it away.

'You're quiet this morning, love. Is everything okay?' he said.

She frowned. 'Yes, just lots to think about. Wondering if the mystery guesthouse inspector will be here before the wedding or after and if we are actually in with a chance of winning. And wondering when Amy will arrive and how to find the time to get over to Glasgow to collect her.'

'Remind me . . . Emma's arriving next week and then a few days later Max will be here with his mum and sister?'

'Yip, that's correct,' she said, even though she'd told him all of this so many times already. 'They've hired Lilybank Cottage.' She mumbled something vague under her breath.

He looked at her for a moment then tucked a strand of hair behind her ear. 'Why don't you head off now? Let me finish this. You could walk down and meet Nicola rather than take the car. It will do you good rather than rushing there at the last minute.'

'Okay, thanks. I will do.'

An hour later she sat on the bench outside the bakery with two coffees, waiting for Nicola to arrive. Nicola was one of Kirsty's closest friends on the island and although they had always known each other to say 'hello', they became close when the twins started school. It was during their first few days here when Kirsty found herself walking out of the playground and trying to bite back the tears. Nicola, whose son was in the year above, had spotted her and insisted she take her for a coffee. Kirsty was so grateful Nicola had taken her under her wing that day. They had been firm friends since.

'Sorry I'm late,' said Nicola, as she arrived out of breath. 'You're a star — thank you.'

'Don't worry. It makes a change for me to be on time. I thought I'd bring them out as it's so nice.'

It was a glorious morning with not a cloud in the sky.

'You're looking pensive this morning,' said Nicola. 'Penny for them?'

Kirsty took a sip of the strong, hot coffee. 'Just feeling a bit tired. Perhaps a bit overwhelmed. A bit fed up . . . bet you're glad you asked!'

'Yes, I am because that doesn't sound good.'

Kirsty, to her horror, felt a tear slide down her cheek.

Nicola reached over and clutched her hand. 'If it's any consolation, it's no wonder. You never bloody stop, Kirsty! If you're not making beds or porridge, then you're worrying about the kids or Steve and your dad.'

Kirsty wiped away the tear.

'There's something else though isn't there?'

'I'm just a bit emotional,' she said. 'Worried about whether the wedding will all go to plan. But if I'm honest, Nic, I'm tired. I miss Mum. I *really* miss her. There are so many questions I want to ask her . . .'

'It's a difficult time for you especially with Emma's wedding and Amy coming home. You're bound to feel her loss more acutely at the moment.'

'I just don't want to go on about it to the girls.'

'I'm sure they'll be missing her, too. They just won't be feeling it as acutely as you because they don't live here.'

'That's true.'

Nicola reached into her bag and handed Kirsty a tissue. 'Are you sure that's all it is? Anything else on your mind?'

She sighed. She couldn't tell Nicola everything. It wasn't fair.

'Is all okay with Steve?'

'Yes, he is great . . . I'm very lucky, I know.'

Nicola chuckled. 'Yes, we would all like a Steve in our life.' Nicola was a single parent whose husband had upped and left after deciding that neither island life nor family life were for him.

'How's your dad?'

Kirsty exhaled then took another drink from her cup. 'Honestly? I don't know. It's hard to tell. He's been managing okay since Mum passed . . . but . . .'

'Have you noticed a change?' Nicola worked as a nurse at the local GP practice and her mum had lived with dementia, so she was a good friend to talk to this about.

'Not massively,' she said. 'Just a few small things.'

'What do you mean?'

'He's started acting differently.' She frowned. 'He'll say things completely out of character. I can't even think of an example so perhaps I'm imagining it.'

'Anything else?'

'He doesn't seem to grasp things in the way that he used to. And there are a couple of times we've been out, and he's become confused and a bit disorientated.' She paused. 'I keep thinking about the story you told me about your mum and the strawberry sauce . . .'

'When she wanted to know why we were having ketchup with our ice cream cones?'

'Yes,' said Kirsty. 'The other night I was going to get the sauce out the cupboard to have with our dessert and I stopped myself in case he thought it was ketchup. Isn't that stupid? There was no reason why he would have but I just didn't even want to give him the chance to say it.'

'Oh, Kirsty, it does sound like you're analysing everything that he's doing.'

She shrugged. 'It's hard not to as I feel so responsible for him. Yet other times it's all fairly normal and he's just Dad. You know my dad —he's always had a sense of humour — but I'm almost waiting for him to start saying things that are totally inappropriate and lose his filter completely.'

'Okay. Look it does sound like there have been some changes since we last spoke. It's maybe worth bringing him in to see the GP. It's best to catch anything early — if there is anything of course?'

'Yes, I'll suggest that again. I just need to tread carefully.' She raised an eyebrow. 'He doesn't like me making a fuss. You know how stubborn he is.'

She nodded in agreement. 'Yes, and he is doing incredibly well to live on his own.'

'That's what I'm worried about.'

'Try not to worry too much and don't catastrophize quite yet, Kirsty. Remember you're under huge amounts of stress just now and worrying about your dad . . . well things feel bigger than they are. One step at a time. Most of all, remember that he's still your dad.'

'You're right. Thanks for listening. You're a good friend.'

Nicola patted her arm and stood up. 'I am such a good friend that I'm going to get you another coffee.'

Kirsty smiled gratefully as she watched Nicola walk across the road and slip inside the door of the bakery. She sat contemplating for a moment and watched the birds swooping into the water.

'If only life was that simple, eh?' she said to Nicola when she returned with the coffees.

'Well, there's nothing to say it can't be,' she said. 'Look I've bought buns too. Let's just make this *our* simple for the moment.'

'Aw thanks. Enough about me and my woes, Nic. Tell me about you. What has been happening and how is Jamie?'

'Loving student life and being away from home,' she said.

Nicola's sole focus for a long time had been her son Jamie and Kirsty knew it was hard when he left to go to university on the mainland.

'I'm a bit gutted that he's not back for the summer but glad he's off exploring.' She smiled. 'At least he's given up asking his dad when he can take him to the next game at Ibrox. I'm just glad he's out making a life for himself.'

'You must really miss him?' Kirsty bit into the iced bun, savouring the sweet taste.

'Of course,' she said, the tears pooling in her eyes. 'But I need to get on with it. I always knew he would leave one day, and yeah, it's been hard. But because I know he's happy then I don't feel quite as bad as I thought I would. Plus, I get to go and spend weekends in Dundee which is a bit of a novelty.'

'I'm dreading the twins leaving,' admitted Kirsty. 'You're going to need to mentor me through it all when they go.'

'You'll be fine. Keeping busy is important and you are very good at that. And we can go for visits together and have wild weekends in Dundee.'

Kirsty smiled and rolled her eyes. 'We'll see about that.'

'Now promise me you'll call the surgery and make an appointment to bring your dad in?'

'I will. I promise. Thank you.'

'Any time. You're not alone. I know how independent you are and how stubborn — you clearly take after your dad — but I am here to help.'

Kirsty bit her lip and managed a small smile. If only she could tell Nicola everything. But she owed it to her sisters to tell them the truth first.

CHAPTER FOURTEEN

Amy yawned, realizing just how tired she was. The journey had been long and although she had only left Vancouver the night before, it felt as though she'd been on the go for days.

She had sobbed when Andy and Josh had embraced her and said their goodbyes at the airport. She still felt teary when she thought about leaving her dear friends.

When she'd landed at Heathrow, she collected her hold bags and checked in separately for her connecting journey to Glasgow. The flight had been delayed from Canada and she was anxious she would miss the connection. But somehow luck was on her side, and she just made it.

Now as the flight began its descent to Glasgow she gripped her seat, her eyes unexpectedly welling up as she saw the patchwork of green and yellow fields below. She was almost home.

She disembarked, feeling giddy with excitement. Everything was so familiar, yet she felt as though she was looking at it with a fresh perspective. There was something even homely about the airport that she couldn't quite put her finger on. Perhaps it was being surrounded by Scottish accents again. She had forgotten just how friendly people were.

When she'd retrieved her luggage, she followed signs for the shuttle bus to the city centre and waited behind some tourists to get on the modern double-decker. It had been a while since she'd been on one of these and she felt like a child who had seen snow for the first time. She wanted to tell people to hurry up and board. She was now desperate to get home. She hoped Kirsty wouldn't be annoyed that she hadn't shared her exact travel itinerary and would be happy to be surprised.

Twenty minutes later she was in Central Station buying a coffee and croissant to have on the train to Ardrossan. She smiled at the gaggle of school kids who looked like they were heading for the same train and quite possibly a day out to the beach at Ayr. Then she stopped to listen to the pianist who was playing a version of the theme song to *Game of Thrones*. The polished mahogany piano sat right in the middle of the concourse and was surrounded by a small picket fence and some fake grass. When the young guy finished his piece, people began to clap and then when there was a lull, an elderly lady sat down and launched into '*Für* Elise'. Amy smiled at her as she narrowed her brow in concentration. She was almost tempted to have a go herself but then when she looked up at the departures board, she realized her train would be going soon, so she picked up her bags and briskly made her way to the platform and onto the train.

The sun was shining which definitely improved passengers' spirits. Amy settled herself on a carriage near the front and became aware of a woman watching her. 'Hello, hen,' she said. 'You been somewhere nice?' She was gesturing at Amy's luggage.

Amy took a sip of her oat-milk latte. 'I've been in Canada but that's me on my way home now.'

'Oh, how lovely. I've got a cousin who lives in Canada. In Toronto.'

'Ah. It's a great city but I've been on the other side — in Vancouver.'

'That's on the west coast, isn't it?' she said.

Amy nodded. 'How about yourself? Where are you off to today?'

'Nowhere very exotic,' she joked. 'Just off to see my grandkids in Dalry.'

That was the last stop before Ardrossan Harbour, so Amy settled in for an interesting chat with the woman who shared her life story with her. The woman introduced herself as Lisa and seemed glad of the company. She was delighted when Amy told her she didn't look old enough to be a grandmother. Lisa used to work in the bar at the Theatre Royal in Glasgow and kept Amy entertained with her funny tales.

'You should write a book,' she said, wiping away tears of laughter.

'Aye, well maybe one day I will. Och, will you look at that. It's almost my stop. Thanks for listening to me, dearie,' she said.

'It's been an absolute pleasure.'

'You make sure you enjoy your sister's wedding.'

'I will.'

'Here — you never said what your dress is like?'

It suddenly dawned on Amy that she had no idea either. *Oops.* Was she supposed to have sorted her own bridesmaid dress? She felt mildly terrified at Emma's reaction when she told her she had forgotten one of her few main tasks. 'It's a . . . surprise,' she said, trying not to laugh hysterically at the panic she was now feeling.

'Well, I'll look out for you when I'm next over on Arran. Bye for now, love.'

'Goodbye and have a lovely time with your grandchildren.'

'Indeed, I will,' she said. 'I've got a bag full of illicit goods with me — chocolate and crisps. My daughter-in-law will do her nut.'

'That's what grannies are for. They're lucky to have you.' It was only as the train pulled away from the station that she realized that if she ever had kids then her mum wouldn't be there to be their gran. This homecoming was going to be so bittersweet.

CHAPTER FIFTEEN

After the doctor's appointment, Emma had staggered home in shock not quite sure what to do with herself. In a trance she had gone into the kitchen and pulled out flour, sugar, margarine and eggs and baked a cake. She could barely even remember mixing the ingredients together. But as she looked at the buttercream icing in the bowl, she frowned. It had turned grainy. She sighed, annoyed that she hadn't made it properly despite sifting the icing sugar. Maybe she should have softened the butter more?

Or maybe she should just have made date and walnut loaf instead? Her mum told her the secret of making it work was to toss the chopped dates in flour, so they didn't sink to the bottom of the tin. She scraped the icing into the food bin and frantically searched the cupboards for walnuts. Of course, there were none. Why would there be? She couldn't remember the last time she had baked a loaf, never mind a cake. She tipped that into the bin as well. Max would think she had lost the plot if he came home and found their flat had turned into an artisan baker's.

Baking used to be her go-to therapy and she always smiled when she was in the process of making cakes, but now it felt like a disaster. Anyway, what on earth was she doing at home on a busy workday when she should be in the office trying to clear her desk?

She sat down at the breakfast bar suddenly feeling light-headed. Then she grabbed her phone and started scrolling through a parenting site.

'Am I too old to be having my baby at forty?' someone had asked.

Emma glanced over the replies: *'No! Not at all! I had my first at thirty-nine and had baby number two at forty-three!'* The next response was, *'There are loads of women all over the world having babies after thirty-nine! Age is just a number!!'*

The amount of exclamation marks used in the discussions started to annoy her. It made all the comments seem a bit frivolous as if they were talking about something superficial.

'I had my baby at forty-one. I was really stressed about being old, but she keeps me young!' Then there was, *'Hilary Swank was pregnant at 48!'*

Feeling momentarily relieved, she closed the site down and slid her phone across the counter. Maybe she was jumping the gun and blowing things completely out of proportion. She wasn't definitely in the early menopause so she should hang fire until she had more details and more tests had been done.

Max was in Aberdeen on an urgent case, and she felt a pang of loneliness. How she longed to speak to him. Her mind went full circle at a hurtling pace. How could she just have a casual chat right now? How could she possibly tell her husband-to-be that she may be in the bloody early menopause? She grabbed her phone again and typed into the search bar '*Is menopause at 38 normal?*' There were over thirteen million results.

> *Menopause before the age of forty is called premature menopause. Approximately one per cent of women have early menopause. You're not alone . . .*

Except she was alone. She wished she could talk to her mum. She would know what to say and do. This was Emma's own fault. She should have been to see the doctor about this much earlier rather than burying herself in work. She'd had an inkling something was wrong for ages but had ignored it, telling herself that she was simply having cold feet about the wedding.

On some level, she must have known the doctor was going to tell her bad news. That was why she couldn't let herself get too excited about the wedding. She knew if she did, that would jinx it. Anyway, maybe once she told Max the truth there wouldn't be a wedding. She curled up on the sofa and reached for the picture of her and Mum in the snow-covered garden of Meadowbank Cottage.

That winter had been awful and there'd been a huge snow dump that cut the islanders off from the mainland. Emma had been home to visit for the weekend and ended up staying almost two weeks. She remembered that time with her mum with great fondness as it had been when they had a chance to bond over food.

Jean always said good food was fundamental in life. She took great satisfaction in home cooking using ingredients that Dad grew in the back garden. Although he tended to be the cook, Jean did love making soup with his vegetables. She made carrot soup, leek and potato soup, fruit crumbles using apples, berries and rhubarb. There were also supplies of kale, green beans and broccoli. Jean's thinking was that if they were cut off from the mainland due to the weather and ferries were unable to make deliveries then they should be able to be self-sufficient for a while.

There were always plenty of tins in the cupboard and vegetables in the freezer. She always made loads of jam and chutneys and baked their own bread, so they never went hungry. Even when they lost power that year and the island was blacked out, they managed with their camping stove and candles. Many of their neighbours were left completely without heat and lighting and cooking facilities.

Emma and her parents mucked in with the rest of the community and made sure they did what they could to help. With roads impassable, helicopters they had even ended up delivering blankets and flasks to islanders. Something she definitely hadn't told Ruth! But it was a reminder of the strong community they lived in.

She'd enjoyed life in Edinburgh but now was definitely getting restless; work was all so focused on money and budgets and hourly rates and sad stories. She and Max earned good salaries but rarely had the time to spend their earnings as work took over their lives. Now she wondered what it had all been for. Although she had never been in a desperate rush to have children, she realized she had taken it for granted that it would just happen. Now that she had been told it might not happen, she felt as though she'd been punched in the gut.

And she had to figure out how and when to tell Max.

She tried to convince herself that he would understand. This was Max after all. He knew whenever she was out of sorts, and something was bothering her.

Just then her phone began to ring. It was Max. She snatched it off the counter.

'Hello,' she said, feeling a flutter insider her stomach.

'Hello, beautiful. How are you?'

'I'm good,' she lied. 'I was just thinking about you. How are you?'

He hesitated. 'Well things are taking longer here than I thought.'

Emma knew what was coming. It was one of the perils of being married to a criminal lawyer. Especially one who had been working on a high profile murder case for months.

'There's been a delay and I'm having to stay on.'

'Oh,' she said. 'What does that mean exactly?'

'That I might not get back till Monday or Tuesday . . . we're still working on a few more witness statements.'

Emma sighed, wondering if this was the universe's way of helping her get her thoughts sorted out. 'Don't worry. I understand. It just means that I may be away before you get back.'

'I know and I'm sorry, but I can't walk away now. Not when we're so close to making a breakthrough.'

Max and his team were actively working on a cold case from fifteen years ago and were representing the mother of a young woman who was strangled in woods in Aberdeenshire.

'It's okay you don't need to explain. I know this is important and I just hope you get what you need especially for that poor woman.' She paused and tried to keep things light. 'As long as you don't miss the wedding! You will get away for the wedding, won't you?'

He took a sharp intake of breath. 'Don't even joke. There's no way I would miss it, Emma. I will swim there if I need to.'

She couldn't help but laugh at that comment, but at the back of her head she could hear the voice growing louder. *You need to tell him. You need to say something, it's only fair that he knows*. Her stomach lurched. The irony of being a family lawyer wasn't lost on her. She always told her clients about the importance of honesty in relationships.

'I love you, Max,' she said, desperate to let him know that which she hoped would see them through.

'Hey, are you okay?' He'd evidently detected a change in her tone.

She bit her lip. 'I'm fine. Just a bit emotional about the big day. And I miss you.'

'I am sorry. If I could be there right now, believe you me, I would.'

'I know and I don't mean to make you feel bad. Look if you're not due back till Monday or Tuesday then maybe I'll just head to Arran at the weekend. There's not much sense in me hanging around here when I could be back home, making myself useful.'

'Good thinking. And can I just remind you that you are the best thing that has ever happened to me and that I love you and can't wait to be your husband.'

She smiled, feeling reassured by his voice. For a moment she wondered if she should just blurt it out. But bringing it up on the phone didn't feel appropriate. It would have to wait until they were both together on the island.

CHAPTER SIXTEEN

Kirsty loved being up early. Steve had gone paddleboarding and she was quite happy sitting alone outside with her mug of coffee and listening to the birdsong and gazing at the view of the sea ahead. The salty tang in the morning air and the cool breeze tickled her cheeks. Even though it was early June, some of the trees still had late cherry blossom; clusters of pink flowers gently floated down to the ground like confetti. Beautiful. She closed her eyes and listened to the chirps and tweets of the birds.

'Hi, Mum,' said Tom, plonking himself down on the bench next to her.

Kirsty jumped. She had trained the twins to move as stealthily and quietly as they could when leaving for early shifts or returning late from work. She felt proud that they had the prowess of professional marksmen. 'Good morning, love. What's up?'

'Nothing. Just waiting for Becky to do her hair and then we're off.'

'You don't mind being on the same shift as her?'

'Nah. Not really. When do the aunts arrive?' He scratched his head and yawned.

'Good question.' She pursed her lips. 'Emma will be here on Monday. And Amy should be here by Wednesday, I think. At least I hope so.'

Amy was still being vague about her arrival, but she said she would make her own way back home. Emma was secretly relieved as factoring in a trip to Glasgow Airport was looking like it could prove tricky.

'It's going to be mad around here, isn't it?' he said, wrinkling his nose.

Kirsty's mind was racing ahead to the big day, never mind the lead up. 'It will be amazing, and we will be so happy to see Emma settled and happy. For as long as I can remember, her life has been all about work.'

'Well, she's got a nice life, hasn't she? Holidays abroad and a nice pad by the water?'

Kirsty nodded. 'Yes, but that's just stuff, isn't it? It doesn't necessarily bring you happiness . . .'

'Do you ever wish you and Dad had stayed in London?'

Kirsty put her mug down on the ground. 'Not at all. We were ready to leave and come back. It was all fun while we were young. But once you were born it all became a challenge.' She had told him this story several times before, but he seemed to want to hear it again. 'Our flat was tiny and at the top of an old building. Every time I wanted to take you out, I had to carry the buggy down and then go back upstairs and get you both and hope that it hadn't been stolen by the time I got you both back downstairs. It was exhausting . . . and you could have fitted that flat into a corner of the barn. It was tiny.'

He laughed. 'I don't know how you did it. I couldn't live in the city.'

She ruffled his hair. 'That's because you are your father's son. He didn't like it either but if he hadn't gone for that job at the hotel then he wouldn't have met me, and you wouldn't be here. In fact, we wouldn't be sitting here now having this conversation.'

Tom reflected for a moment before he spoke. 'So, you don't think I'm weird for not wanting to go to university in a city?'

'No, darling, of course I don't. What's brought all this on?'

'Just some of the guys are talking about what a great time they're going to have as students in Glasgow and . . . well, I feel a bit dull, I suppose.' He blushed.

She hugged him close to her and sniffed his head, desperate to inhale that baby scent from him that she was sure she could still smell. Tears glistened in her eyes. 'You listen to me, my darling. You are amazing and wonderful, and I am so proud that you are doing what is right for you rather than following the crowd. You can always go and visit them at weekends and then let them get on with their essays.'

He grunted. 'I know, I know I would hate the essays. It's just hard. What if I don't fit in as the apprentice?'

This was so unlike Tom, who normally took everything in his stride. 'You will fit in, Tom. I know you will, and do you know what? If it doesn't work out, then it's not the end of the world.'

'It's not the end of the world until it's the end of the world,' he said back quietly. It had become a family saying.

'That's right. You can come home, and we will help you to decide plan b. So don't worry.'

He sniffed. 'I'll just miss you . . . and Gramps . . .'

She clutched him closer and willed herself not to start crying. 'We will miss you, too, darling, but you can come home any time and we will come and visit. This is your time and your adventure, Tom.' She glanced over at the door and saw Becky checking her hair out in the reflection of the glass. 'Your sister is coming.'

He cleared his throat and sat up. 'Thanks, Mum. Don't tell her, please?'

She chuckled. 'I won't. I promise.' It didn't matter that they were almost eighteen, at times they were still like giant toddlers, and she couldn't believe that she would have to soon let them go.

'Hurry up, Tom,' called Becky.

'Unbelievable,' he said. 'She's the one who was taking ages and faffing about with her hair.' He stood up and walked over to the car. 'Thanks, Mum,' he called over his shoulder. 'Love you.'

Becky blew her mum a kiss, waved, then climbed in, started the engine and as soon as Tom closed the door, she sped away.

Kirsty stood up and stretched. It was time to head back inside and start breakfast. Reaching for the spurtle to make porridge, she glanced at the Trip Advisor page on her phone to check for new reviews. She tried not to be obsessive about it, but she did refresh it every few hours to find out what guests had said. The kids had been great this year and had set up on Instagram where they already had thousands of followers. Every time there was a good review, Kirsty shared it to the page. She didn't know whether to be annoyed or relieved when she saw there were no new posts. But she didn't have time to dwell on it because the guests, who were due to leave later that morning, appeared and were ready to be fed before boarding the early ferry.

An hour or so later, when she was pegging out washing, she heard the sound of Steve's car in the driveway behind her.

'Well, well, well,' he called out to her. 'You will never guess who I happened to find.'

'I've no idea,' she replied.

'Surprise!' called a voice.

Kirsty dropped the washing and spun round. 'Amy!' she said and ran to her little sister and the girls embraced.

CHAPTER SEVENTEEN

'Well, are you surprised?' said Amy pulling away from Kirsty and smiling at her.

'I most certainly am! Why didn't you tell us when you were coming? We could have come to get you at the airport?'

'Because I couldn't let you do that, and, apart from anything else, I wanted to surprise you.' Amy couldn't stop grinning. She was *so* happy to be back.

'Come on inside,' said Kirsty, smiling in delight.

Amy followed Kirsty into the cottage and as soon as she set foot over the threshold of the cottage, she felt about twelve years old again. Being home, and in her sister's company, tended to make her regress to being a child again.

'How was the journey?' said Kirsty, fussing around her.

Amy gave a tired smile. 'I am so glad to be home, but I am not going to lie. I am absolutely knackered. That was one lengthy journey. I know you are supposed to keep going to fight the jet lag but seriously, I really don't know if I can.'

'Let's get you a tea in the meantime. Or maybe a coffee?'

Amy sat down at the kitchen table and a memory of playing board games and doing homework floated through her mind. She traced her finger over the familiar grooves on the scrubbed pine surface.

'I'll put your bags upstairs in the green room,' said Steve.

Amy groaned and sunk her head in her hands. 'Sorry, sis, totally forgetting that an unannounced arrival isn't ideal when you are running a guesthouse. I can go stay somewhere else if you are full. It's not a problem at all. Honestly, how can I be so stupid?'

'Don't worry at all. It's fine, Amy. The last guests left this morning, and that is us now until the wedding. Which is actually quite exciting as I have been so on edge with everyone staying. There's a mystery inspector doing the rounds and I have had to be on my best behaviour.'

Amy giggled and began to unwind her plaits, dropping her hair pins on the table in front of her in the same way she did when she was at school. Their mum would always be telling her to take her hair stuff up to her room and she never did, instead leaving a trail of debris wherever she went. 'What's the prize?'

'Twenty-five grand — which would go so far. There's so much we want to do with this place.'

'Wow,' said Amy.

Kirsty flapped her hands dismissively. 'Anyway, it doesn't matter. I still can't believe you are *actually* here. And you're on your own?'

'Ten points for observation,' said Amy, drily.

Kirsty rolled her eyes. 'Less of the cheek, missy,' she said. 'What have you done with him?'

Amy blinked innocently.

'Are you going to tell me where Ross is?' she asked, placing a mug of peppermint tea in front of her sister. 'Is he coming on a later flight?'

Amy didn't answer for a moment and kept fiddling with her hair.

'Amy?' pressed Kirsty.

'So . . . Ross isn't . . . He isn't coming to the wedding,' she finally said. 'We broke up last week. Or maybe it was the week before. I've actually lost track of time. But don't worry it's all fine and I won't let my newly-single status spoil the big day.' She shrugged. 'I'm fine. It's really no big deal. Let's not dwell on it.'

'Hold on a minute . . . this is the first guy you have ever lived with, and you were going to bring him to meet the family? What on earth happened?'

Amy took a breath. 'Actually, I never did invite him to the wedding as I wasn't convinced I wanted him as my plus one. I'd not been all that happy for a while and my sense was that it wasn't right for me. It just took me a while to get it all clear in my head and then do the right thing and tell him.'

'Oh, I see,' said Kirsty taking a sip from her mug. 'How did he take you telling him?'

'Well, when I started to tell him that I needed some space to figure stuff out, he thought I was in a huff with him.'

'What do you mean?'

'He said he thought I was cross with him because he'd slept with his ex-wife.'

Kirsty half-choked on her drink. 'Are you kidding me? Did you know?'

'Nope, I am not kidding you and no I didn't know. Though I do now.'

She put a tentative hand on her sister's arm. 'I'm sorry, Amy. What an eejit.'

'Yip.' She shrugged. 'Don't be sorry . . . I'm fine. Really, we weren't right together and he did me a favour. Anyway, enough about me. How are you and where are the kids?'

'Are you sure you're okay though?'

Amy nodded, keen to change the subject. 'Yes. I'm fine. Anyway tell me about the kids.'

'The kids are both working at the pool and probably earning more than me, and Steve combined. Honestly to be young again, they're having a ball. They're both saving for summer holidays and uni and are hardly here. They'll be so excited though when they hear you're back.'

'And Dad? How is he?' She watched as her sister frowned.

'Okay, just a bit confused at the moment but that's maybe due to the time of year and the anniversary of Mum's death and of course the wedding. I don't think he realized he would need to make a speech and that seemed to stress him. But I've offered to help and so have Steve and the kids.'

Amy noticed that Kirsty was composed and in control as she spoke, but her face looked etched with worry and she had definitely aged. She decided it would be kinder not to share that observation with Kirsty. Instead, she said, 'I'm here now, and will do as much as I can to help you. I'm sorry you've had to do this all on your own.'

She nodded. 'It's been tough . . . that and the kids leaving after the summer and . . .'

Amy wrinkled her nose. 'You've a lot going on, sis, and as soon as I have balanced my energy from the flight you are first on my list for a reflexology session.' She yawned noisily, clamping her hand over her mouth. 'If it's not too rude, can I go and get some shuteye please and then I will go see Dad? Then we will face the rest of it together, one day at a time.'

'Sure,' said Kirsty, hugging her again. 'Off you go and get some rest. It is *so* good to have you here. Honestly, I can hardly believe it.'

Amy smiled, yawned again and pointed upstairs.

CHAPTER EIGHTEEN

'Look who's here!' said Kirsty over Facetime.

Emma almost dropped her phone when she saw Amy's face next to Kirsty's. They were outside the cottage, sitting under the sycamore tree.

'Amy, when did you get back! Did you know she was coming?' She narrowed her gaze in suspicion and shook her head at Kirsty.

'Nope. Honestly! I am as surprised as you are. She just appeared. Steve happened to be driving past the ferry terminal and saw her waiting at the bus stop.'

'My plans were a bit fluid.' Amy giggled. 'And so, I thought I would surprise everyone. You know me, I like to go with the flow.'

Kirsty laughed. 'She certainly did surprise us . . .'

'Where's Ross?' said Emma. 'Have you given him the tour?'

'Well . . . that's the thing. He's not here. We broke up.'

Emma was shocked. 'Wha-a-a-t? When did this happen?'

'I'll fill you in on the details when I see you.'

Amy didn't look particularly sad or bothered by the break-up which reassured Emma. Honestly, her sister was one of a kind.

'When are you back?' asked Amy.

'Well now that you are there, as soon as possible. I was meant to be coming on Monday, but Max is working away up north and so I'll be there as soon as I finish work. Tomorrow night if I can.'

Amy clapped her hands together in excitement. 'Seriously? That would be amazing. I can't wait to see you. I am so excited for you!'

Emma couldn't help but smile at her sister's beaming face. 'Did you tell her about the distillery?'

Kirsty angled the phone, so she had a better view of Emma. 'Yes, she knows about it. In fact, I think we may go down tomorrow and check things out.'

'I wish I could be there with you,' said Emma.

'We can wait until you're here?' suggested Amy.

'No, honestly, it's fine. Just go down and have a look and we can all go again when I'm there.' Emma paused. 'Does she know *all* about it?' she said, knowingly.

Fortunately, Kirsty clocked the question and giggled. 'She will get the tour and learn *all* about it when she goes.'

Amy looked completely bemused. 'What are you two going on about? You're being weird and talking in riddles. Just be normal, please!'

Emma loved how they quickly relaxed into their familiar roles, and she couldn't wait to hug Amy in person. 'I'm going to check ferries this minute and let you know my plans. Can't wait to see you, girls!'

Kirsty waved. 'Bye, darling.'

'See you soon, Emma.' Amy blew her a kiss.

Emma ended the call and flopped down on her bed. It had been another long day. Just one more to go and then she would put her out of office on, letting the world know she would be unavailable for a fortnight. She couldn't believe that Amy was back in Arran and hadn't told them about her plans. The thought of her sisters being there without her was strange and now she was absolutely desperate to get back.

But when she checked the ferry slots for the following night there was no availability. At least there were only two more sleeps to go, and she was definitely booked on for Saturday morning. She supposed that was better anyway just in case she was held up at work. And she told herself it was better that she didn't rush as that would mean she would most likely forget something like the wedding dress or Max's kilt. She leapt off the bed and, for the umpteenth time, went through to the spare bedroom and checked the hanging bags and her holdalls, packed with all that she would need. Yes, it was all there and ready to go.

Emma peeled off her work clothes, slid into her pyjamas and climbed under the covers, wishing Max was there. She had missed him this week. Whenever he did speak to her, which tended to be brief and snatched bits of conversation, he sounded tired and strained. He couldn't say much about the case, but she knew it was taking its toll and weighing heavily on him.

Which only exacerbated how she felt. Useless and helpless and guilty. In a bid to slow her busy brain, she reached for her phone, found her breathing exercise and focused on breathing in and out as Wim Hof instructed. *Round number one, breathe in and breathe out, breathe in and breathe out* . . . she felt muscles loosen and she soon lost count of numbers and whether she was breathing in or out.

When she opened her eyes with a jolt, she was in darkness. Emma had no idea if she had actually done three rounds of the breathing exercise or had fallen asleep in the first round which she was prone to doing. Feeling parched, she padded through to the kitchen and poured a glass of water. The clock on the oven said it was 3.52 a.m. Normally she set her alarm for 6 a.m. and she wondered if she may as well just stay up now and make a start on work so she would definitely have everything cleared by that night.

Opening her laptop, she sat at the breakfast bar and quickly scanned her inbox to work out what could be passed to her colleague, what could wait until she got back and what needed her attention now. She scowled when she saw an email from a client who had become a regular fixture in her inbox. This person had been horrible to deal with and she had really struggled to work on his behalf as his moral compass was off the scale. She had just, and only by the skin of her teeth, managed to settle his custody battle with his ex-wife which had been a complete power game from his perspective. It didn't matter she was divorcing him on the grounds of his adultery. This was a slur on his male pride, and he made it as difficult as possible for her, even challenging custody of their three children despite the fact he barely knew their names.

She scanned his email and shook her head. It appeared that he was looking to challenge the legitimacy of his deceased father's will, especially now a half sibling had emerged from the past. Normally, with her compassionate head on, she would say that he was acting like such a jerk because he was trying to hold onto his father's memory and that was why he didn't want a random person who had appeared from nowhere to now disrupt those memories.

Emma knew that grief could deeply stir many emotions and open up things that people had buried in the past. Those feelings could run very deep and if a stranger turned up staking a claim on his inheritance, then Emma could only imagine how much that would have infuriated him. She forwarded the email onto her colleague, hoping that it was something she would take care of in Emma's absence.

Honestly, families and the toxic situations they could create, were horrible. She was glad she had a relatively normal upbringing with Jean and Alex, and she absolutely adored her sisters. Nothing would ever change that.

When she noticed it was just after six, she took ten minutes to do some yoga — wait until she told Amy, who was forever telling her she should embrace it as she needed to calm her parasympathetic nervous system — and stretched out the kinks in her hunched-up shoulders. As she lay on the mat on the floor, she began to unwind and almost drifted off to sleep again. But she knew she needed to get into work for her final day. Pulling herself up, she stretched and headed to the shower.

CHAPTER NINETEEN

Amy was true to her word and had risen early to go and spend some time with their dad. Steve was out doing tasks and the kids were working again although they were a bit annoyed about that given that Amy was now in town. Somehow with them being a bit older, they were now very excited by the appearance of their cool and internationally travelled aunt.

Kirsty sat by the window in the yellow guest room, which Emma would be staying in, taking a moment to admire the blooming flowers in the garden. She loved all the seasons and the different scents and colours they brought but if she had to pick one as a favourite then it would be early summer, just as the petal blossom started to fall from the trees and the flowers in the garden were starting to thrive.

Steve loved the garden and would spend hours pottering around, assisted by Dad, who had created such a magical spot with his careful pruning and nourishing over the years. When her parents moved into Meadowbank Cottage all those years ago, the house was a little tumbledown, but they had done what they could to restore it to its best.

Sitting in this spot reminded her of the constants in her life and Steve and the kids and how this place would always be home. She was glad Tom had inherited his dad and grandfather's green fingers. He had always been fascinated by trees and plants and so the opportunity with the Forestry Commission was perfect for him. She also thought, rather selfishly, that it meant he might perhaps eventually come back one day and make the island his home again.

Not one guest had failed to remark on what a beautiful room this was and as she looked around now, she had to agree. All the rooms had been painted white to keep them fresh and clean and the white bedspreads were contrasted with bright and funky throws and cushions. The kids had christened this room the daffodil room, because of the bursts of cheery yellow including a bright yellow lamp. The space had a calming energy about it and, perhaps because it had been her mother and father's room when they were growing up, it was where she felt most connected to her mum.

Tears welled up in her eyes as she thought about her mum's twinkling eyes and calming voice. She savoured quiet moments like this.

A notification pinged on her phone. It looked like a new review had been posted. She clicked on it and gulped as she read.

I had the most fabulous stay at Meadowbank Cottage B&B. Kirsty and Steve clearly put much time and effort into catering for your every wish and there are so many personal touches which make such a difference. My room was spacious, clean and extremely comfortable. Kirsty and Steve couldn't have done enough to make me, and fellow guests, feel welcome. From meeting us at the ferry to the breakfast service. The pancakes and also the porridge are must-haves, and the homemade shortbread in the room was heavenly.

The island itself is a magical place and Steve was more than happy to advise me on walking routes and even accompanied me on some of them which went above and beyond his role as a host. The other guests were lovely too and I was so disappointed to leave. I could have stayed for another week! It was my first visit to Arran and definitely won't be my last.

It's a place that I am already looking forward to returning to soon. This B&B is without doubt one of the nicest I have stayed in and one of the best kept secrets, in my opinion. Thank you so much for looking after me. My heart has been captured by the magic of your island! Neil, Hove, June.

Kirsty's heart swelled with pride as she read Neil's review and she smiled wryly at the last line. She was quite sure that his heart had also been captured by the other guest, Alice. Time would tell if something blossomed there, she thought to herself.

She knew Steve would be delighted. He kept telling her she worried too much about what guests thought but right now she was worrying about everything especially with her sisters being back for the wedding. Now wasn't the time to offload her burden. It would have to wait until after Emma's big day. The thing was that Kirsty wasn't even supposed to know. The only reason she knew about it was when she was in the loft, just after her mother died, looking for some old photographs.

Her parents always maintained they had lost lots of their photographs over the years and Kirsty never even thought to ask them if they had properly cleared the attic. Until recently, she and Steve had never any reason to go up there as all the extra stuff they had, like Christmas decorations, were stored in one of the outhouses which was much easier to access.

Kirsty had thought she may as well have a final look up there just in case there were some photos stashed away in a box. She thought her dad may appreciate it after Jean's passing, and she wanted to find something that might offer him a shred of comfort.

She climbed up into the eaves and crouched down to avoid hitting her head on the beams. There were a couple of old and battered suitcases and when she opened them, she saw they were full of old blankets, the old-fashioned crocheted ones that the older generation used to lovingly make whenever a new baby was on the way. By the time Becky and

Tom were born, everyone used cotton and fleece blankets which could be washed and dried quickly.

She was about to give up when she spotted a couple of cardboard boxes tucked away in the corner. Coughing, as she unsettled the thick layers of dust by pulling them towards her, she sat down and opened up the first one. It looked to be stuffed with newspapers and some old receipts and she wondered if she should bring it down so it could be flung in the rubbish. Then she opened the other box. Inside were some sepia prints of her parents on their wedding day. The photographs had rounded edges and were faded but there was no doubt it was her mum and dad, smiling and very much in love. They were wonderful and she was so pleased to have found them.

Then she saw a baby picture she had never seen before. Studying it, she saw the familiar blonde curls and realized it must be her. She was smiling and looked content in a bright yellow sundress in a garden that didn't look like Meadowbank's. *That's strange*, she thought to herself. *I wonder why I've never seen it before and why it's tucked in here*. She was about to bundle the pictures up and take them downstairs to show her dad, Steve and the kids when she noticed an official looking envelope.

Kirsty reached for it and gingerly slid her finger under the rim, pulling out the yellowing and musty smelling paper. Uncurling it, she squinted, wishing she had her glasses on so she could see properly, but she could just about make out the words. She had to read it several times to make sure. Then she looked back in the box and saw a newspaper cutting. Scanning it she gasped and put her hand to her mouth. Afterwards she sat in the stillness of the attic for a while until she heard the kids calling for her.

Now, as she looked out the window, she thought about the contents of the letter and knew that at some stage she would need to share it with her sisters. After the wedding she told herself. After the wedding.

CHAPTER TWENTY

Amy couldn't help but notice that Kirsty's smile was a little more strained than usual and that she had a gentle fragility about her. She knew she had a lot on her plate, and it upset her to see her normally confident big sister like this.

'Sometimes I think I'm imagining it with Dad,' Kirsty told her after they visited him yesterday.

Amy agreed that he had seemed his usual self and was over the moon to see his youngest daughter. 'How marvellous to have you with us, darling,' he had said. 'Oh, how I have missed you, my baby girl.' He had clutched Amy close and for a moment she wondered if he would let her go. Amy had cringed slightly at his words as she was all too aware how much Kirsty did for their dad. Yet she had just arrived, after a couple of years absent, it was understandable that he was treating her like a long-lost celebrity daughter.

'He seemed perfectly fine, didn't he?' said Kirsty as they'd walked home.

Amy nodded. 'Well, yes, but that doesn't mean I don't believe what you're saying. If Dad does have signs of dementia, then it doesn't mean that he will be forgetful every day. It is different for everyone.'

Kirsty frowned. 'What do you mean?'

'Exactly that. There are no two cases the same. I think there's so much stigma around it that people automatically assume it's about memory loss, but we need to remember that everyone will be different.'

Kirsty looked at her for a moment. 'What made you so wise?'

Amy shrugged. 'I had a couple of yoga clients in my senior class who had dementia. One had Alzheimer's that affected her sight rather than her memory. The other one had early vascular dementia which meant she started to get a bit disorientated. But they were both very much in the present and knew who they were and where they were. If that makes sense?'

Kirsty sighed, her face creased with anxiety. 'I just worry about him, Amy. What happens if things get worse and he can no longer live on his own?'

'We worry about that if and when it happens. All we can do is worry about this very moment right now. I am here to support you. So, let's take one step at a time.'

'My friend Nicola did say I should make an appointment with the doctor and take him in so they can run some tests.'

'Let's do that and I can come?' suggested Amy. 'Or I can take him?'

They walked along in silence and Amy felt a lump in her throat as she thought about her dad and the guilt she now felt. She should have come home sooner. It wasn't fair to expect Kirsty to shoulder all of this on her own. In a bid to lighten the mood she suddenly blurted out, 'Kirsty, the dresses. I keep meaning to ask you about the bridesmaid's dresses. Was I supposed to buy one?'

Kirsty rolled her eyes and laughed. 'Oh Amy, you never change, do you?'

'What do you mean?' she said, giving an indignant toss of her ponytail.

'Do you really think Emma would have left it to us to sort out our own dresses?'

Amy's shoulders sagged in relief. 'Valid point. So where are they?'

'In the cupboard at Meadowbank. One for you, me and Becky.'

'Will we look like backing singers?'

Kirsty guffawed with laughter. 'No! Of course not. Do you think Emma would want us all in matching dresses for the photos? My wedding was more than enough for those kinds of shots.'

Amy laughed. 'You're telling me! What are they like then?'

'You can see when we get back. But they are lovely. You've nothing to worry about.'

Amy glanced up at the sky which had turned a deep shade of grey. 'I hope this is just a brief downpour. I thought you said the weather has been good?'

'It's been glorious. But a quick shower will do all the plants good.'

Fat rain drops began to fall from the sky. 'I'll race you back!' Amy cried, giggling as Kirsty had chased her up the hill to Meadowbank like old times.

This morning, Amy had promised she would take her dad out for coffee, and they sat in the tearoom by the golf course.

'When will we see your mum?' he said as he sliced open his fruit scone and spread thick, yellow butter on it.

'What do you mean, Dad?'

'I mean, when will she be back?'

Okay, thought Amy. *This was what Kirsty was talking about.* 'Maybe later, Dad,' she said.

'Fine dear,' he said with his usual smile.

'How is your scone?' she said in a bid to distract him.

'Okay, thanks though I don't like the wee black things. They look like flies.'

'I have to agree. I have never liked raisins either.' This was the first time she had heard him complain about them. 'In Vancouver, muffins and bagels tend to be what people have with their coffee.'

'Not scones?'

'No, I rarely saw them.'

'Your mum makes good scones.'

Amy nodded. 'Are you looking forward to the wedding? Emma will be back soon.'

His eyes lit up. 'That will be nice. Though I don't know what I'm supposed to wear.'

'Probably your kilt if you're comfortable with that? What did Emma say?'

His eyes clouded over. 'I think she said Kirsty would organize it.'

'Do you remember your wedding with Mum?'

He smiled. 'Yes. It was one of the happiest days of my life.'

Amy raised an eyebrow. 'What were the other happy days?'

'When Hearts won the Scottish Cup.'

'Dad,' she said, admonishingly. 'I thought you were going to say the birth of your girls.'

'Aye, that too,' he said, smiling, taking another bite of scone.

'Kirsty said you're going to come up to the house later on to do some gardening?'

He nodded. 'I just do as I'm told.'

'She said you've been a great help with getting things planted and making the place look lovely.' She patted his hand which was stretched out in front of him on the table. 'What are you going to be planting today?'

'Carrots,' he said, 'Though I am worried that we are a bit too late now that we're into June and I prefer getting them in the ground a bit earlier than this.'

Amy sipped her latte. 'Why is that then?'

'You should really get root vegetables planted in March. That's because the cooler soil helps them germinate. But spring was quite cold to begin with and so I thought we would wait a bit longer. Last year, we had a bumper crop.'

'Was that when the kids helped you plant them?'

'Aye. We put them in those raised beds, and they were very good and took it very seriously. At least Tom did. He had his ruler out, making sure they were exact rows three inches apart.'

'He definitely takes after you,' said Amy.

'Then we made soup. Lots of carrot soup. And courgettes,' he said. 'There were loads.'

Amy remembered the pictures on Instagram of ratatouille, courgetti, courgette cake. As she listened, she couldn't help but feel wistful. She had missed out on so much. She had always been close to her dad growing up. Perhaps because she was the baby of the family. They had a shared love of the outdoor and spent hours walking in the hills and foraging what they could. Her dad would point out the mushrooms you could eat and the ones that were deadly. That had put her off mushrooms completely.

At moments like this her dad was totally lucid and engaged and she knew to focus on these moments with him. He smiled happily as he told her about the flowers he was planning on putting in the wedding bouquet.

'Are you coming up to the house for lunch?' she asked, glancing at the clock. 'Only, I know the kids were on the early shift and will be back soon. They will love seeing you.'

'Is that okay?' He sounded apologetic. 'I don't want to get in the way.'

Amy scoffed. 'Dad! You're never in the way. Come on. Let me settle the bill and then we'll head home.'

'Okay, dear. Thank you.'

Amy went over to the till and as she reached into her bag for her purse, she felt a hand on her shoulder.

'I thought it was you. Is this you back for your sister's wedding?'

Amy's heart sank. It was their old neighbour, Anna, who was also an annoying busybody.

'Yes, that's right. How are you, Anna?'

'Och, you know. Okay. My back is giving me bother. But that's old age for you, isn't it?' She glanced over at Amy's dad and lowered her voice. 'Your sister will be glad to have you back. I hear your dad's got a wee problem.'

'What do you mean?'

'Getting a bit forgetful by all accounts.'

Amy felt her cheeks flush in anger. She knew Anna was stirring things up as she had nothing better to do, but she felt so protective of her dad and hated the thought of people talking about him.

'Aren't we all, Anna? Aren't we all. Now I'm sorry to be rude, but we are in a bit of a rush. Must dash.'

'See you around, dearie.'

There was nothing kind about the way she said those words and they certainly didn't sound like a term of endearment. Amy didn't even bother with a backward glance.

Back at Meadowbank, they settled Dad in front of the TV, which gave him a chance for a quick snooze, while she filled Kirsty in on their morning.

'She's a daft old cow,' said Kirsty. 'Always has been and I can't see her changing.'

'Why don't you go and sit with Dad, and I'll make lunch?' Amy suggested. She'd noticed her sister's pale face.

Kirsty stifled a yawn. 'Well, if you don't mind that would be nice. Thanks, Amy, I appreciate it. Just have a look and see what you can find.'

Amy rummaged in the fridge and pulled out some salad leaves, cherry tomatoes and reached for a red onion from the vegetable rack. Contemplating what to make, she saw that Kirsty had a glut of eggs. Omelettes would be perfect. She sliced up the onion, browned it in a pot with a little oil and some spices and whisked the eggs together before pouring them into the pan. Keeping a close eye on it, she then quickly set about laying the table. She lowered the heat on the pan and stuck her head into the living room. Both her dad and Kirsty had nodded off.

Maybe it was best to let them sleep for a few minutes longer while they both had peace. Her sister clearly needed it. All the stress and tension of Dad and the wedding must have been taking it out of her. As soon as Steve and the kids arrived back, she would wake them up.

CHAPTER TWENTY-ONE

Emma smiled gratefully when Joy came into her office and placed a takeaway container of soup on her desk. 'You are a star,' she mouthed, thanking the gods again for making Joy such an angel.

Joy winked at her. 'Don't want you passing out on your big day,' she whispered.

So much for Emma firing through all her tasks and getting everything ticked off her list. Sometimes, everything felt like such a fight. She had been on hold on the phone for what felt like hours, seeing if she could speak to someone, anyone, at the Crown Office. A particularly nasty domestic abuse case had come in first thing and her client needed a court order offering protection from her abusive partner who had violently attacked her and had been tracking her movements, unbeknown to her, by installing cameras in their home.

Emma sighed. Nothing in this job surprised her and she was so used to listening to similar stories time and time again. Yet these awful stories also served as a reminder to her of how lucky she was.

For a moment, she allowed herself to think about Max and how excited she was going to be to see him. The very thought gave her a glow which was then dulled by the little voice in her head which she then pushed away. She was getting better and better at compartmentalizing things and right now her priority was making sure this poor client was safe.

A couple of hours later, aside from a quick trip to the loo, Emma was still at her desk.

'Hello, hello,' said a voice. Emma looked up to see a very heavily pregnant Ruth standing at the door.

'Hi there. This is a surprise,' she said, trying to sound as kind and genuine as she could. 'Come on in.'

'I was having a massage in the spa, you know that fancy, new one on Princes Street? And I thought I must drop in and see you before you disappear.' She walked into Emma's office and collapsed on the small sofa in the corner.

Emma felt a stab of guilt that she hadn't called her friend since their curry the other week. 'How are you feeling?'

Ruth made a dramatic display of patting her very large bump. 'Shattered. You know? Who knew it would be so exhausting growing a human being.'

Emma looked at her trying to think what to say. 'Can I get you anything? A tea or some water?'

'You are just so thoughtful. A tea would be perfect thank you. Herbal — peppermint if you have it.'

'Of course. I'll be back in a minute. You just sit there and relax,' said Emma, feeling less than charitable. She went into the small kitchen across the hallway and started rooting about in the cupboards looking for some herbal, or ''erbal' as Ruth called it, tea. She quickly made two cups of peppermint and took it back to Ruth.

'You are a doll. Thanks, you. My indigestion has just been awful. I'm up all night burping.'

That was perhaps information that Emma didn't need to know right at this moment. 'How are you feeling?' she said, slightly worried at the incessant pinging of her email inbox and phone.

'Oh, you know, just utterly exhausted.'

Emma tried to make sympathetic noises and appropriate facial expressions.

'Are you all set for the big day?'

Emma couldn't help thinking that Ruth's words sounded contrived. 'I think so,' she tried to say brightly. 'I finish up today, hopefully if I can get through everything . . . then head over to Arran tomorrow.'

'To be reunited with your sisters?'

'That's right.' She didn't like the slight sneer in Ruth's voice when she mentioned the girls. Ruth had a younger brother, and, over the years, she had made it quite clear that she would have loved sisters and was envious of the close bond Emma had with hers.

'And what about Max? I hear he has been stuck up in Aberdeen?'

'Yes, how typical, eh? A full-on case. He's not due back until the start of the week.'

'Mmm,' said Ruth in a way that made Emma realize that there was more to Ruth's visit than just a friendly, I-want-to-wish-you-well-for-your-wedding, drop in. 'He's cutting it quite fine then?'

'I'm sure all will be good,' said Emma, trying to keep her tone light. 'Look, I've got a lot to get through today before I finish up. I'm sorry, if you don't mind, I'm going to have to get on with it.'

'Sure,' she said, feigning hurt. 'Well, I just hope that man of yours is back in time for the wedding. I'd hate to think of you being left high and dry at the altar.'

'I don't think it will come to that,' said Emma, resisting the urge to lose her rag at the bitchy comment Ruth had just made. She would put it down to her hormones, even though these little snide comments were a theme of their apparent friendship of late. Emma was definitely relieved she wouldn't be at the wedding.

'Sounds like it's not all work up there and a bit of play too,' said Ruth, clearly not in a rush to move.

'What do you mean?' Emma's curt tone made it clear that she'd better get to the point.

'Oh nothing, nothing . . . I just heard they had some late nights which involved drink.' Ruth's reluctance to share any details was unusual and confirmed to Emma that she was just there to cause mischief.

'I'm not surprised drink is involved, Ruth. He's working on a very highly pressured case. I think a few beers at the end of a night are allowed.' She stood up, signalling that their conversation was over.

'Okay. I get the message.' She made a dramatic display of hauling herself to her feet and kissed Emma on both cheeks. 'I hope you have a wonderful day, and I am sorry I will miss it. There is no way I could have been a bridesmaid anyway looking like this.'

'Thank you,' said Emma. There was no point in telling Ruth that she never would have been a bridesmaid whether she was pregnant or not. 'Do let us know about the baby, won't you. And take care.'

In a bid to speed up her exit, she walked Ruth out the door and to the lifts. 'There you go,' she said, hitting the button. 'You don't want to take the stairs in your condition.' Fortunately for once the lift doors opened almost immediately.

Ruth waddled in and turned round. 'Bye, Emma,' she said as the doors slid shut.

Emma breathed a huge sigh of relief. Shaking her head she walked back to the office, clocking Joy's face which made her laugh. Clearly, she wasn't a fan of Ruth.

When she got back to her desk, she saw she had several missed calls from Max which set her on edge. Her phone must have been on silent. Calling him back straight away, he picked up almost immediately.

'Hey there. How are you?'

'Up to my eyes and just had a visit from Ruth.'

He sighed. 'Let me guess, she was there to tell you I had been spotted out on the town.'

'Yip,' she said, sighing.

'Thought as much. A friend of hers is working on this case and, well, you know how the jungle drums beat.'

Emma walked towards the window and looked down below to the people milling about George Street. 'Should I be worried?'

'Not at all.'

'What's with all the missed calls then?'

'Just wanted to speak to you when I could. We are about to get back into things again and I don't know when I'll get another break. I miss you.'

'You sure you don't have anything to tell me?'

'Hey,' he said, gently. 'This isn't like you. Emma, you know I would never lie to you about anything. I really hope you know that. And I hope you know that you can tell me anything too.'

'I know,' she said, flustered. 'Look I need to go, too. Loads still to get sorted before I finish up. I could be here late as well.'

'Text me when you're home so I know you're okay. What time are you leaving in the morning?'

'I'm on the first ferry so I'll aim to leave here just after five, so I've got plenty of time in case the traffic is bad.'

Max laughed. 'That should give you loads of time, love.'

'You say that, Max,' she said with a snort, 'but let's not forget that occasion when we almost missed the ferry.' She smiled as she remembered the first time she took him home to Arran to meet her parents. She told him it would take at least two hours to get to the ferry terminal. They had accidentally slept in and then Emma had managed some heroic, *Top Gear* style, driving which involved overtaking lots of cars on single, windy roads down the Ayrshire coast. Max had later confessed that he hadn't dared ask if she could pull over as he felt so sick.

Normally the ferry staff were quite pedantic about timings and expected all passengers to be there a minimum of half an hour before departure. It was only because she happened to know the ticket inspector from school that they were allowed to drive on moments before the ferry door closed. Then, as soon as the car stopped, Max had vomited into his empty coffee cup. Now and then, she liked to remind him about it.

Her eyes widened in excitement as she thought about making the journey tomorrow. Just then her landline started to ring. 'Bollocks. I'd better go in case that's the Crown Office. Love you.'

'Love you, too. Take care,' he said.

Emma snatched up the other phone before it rang off. She couldn't wait until it was just the two of them. Surely then everything would be okay?

CHAPTER TWENTY-TWO

'I'm heading down to the distillery later if you fancy coming along with me?' said Steve. 'We could take your dad too?'

'He's in the garden with Tom sorting out the carrots and then Tom wants to take him for a walk. I think there's a fungus he spotted on some trees in the woods the other day which he wanted to show Dad.'

She smiled at the thought of Tom and her dad chatting passionately about fungi of all things. She had no need to worry when he was with Tom as they would both be absorbed in the moment of planting and then later peering closely at the mushroom and working out what type it was and whether it was edible or not.

'Ah, okay,' said Steve. 'How about you then?'

'I have a few things to do here,' said Kirsty, looking at the wedding folder on the table and wondering if she ever wouldn't have things to do or worry about. Was this now how her life would be?

'It would do you good to have a break,' said Steve, his tone adamant. 'Plus, I could do with your help in case I forget anything about the menu. You know what I'm like.' He saw her staring at the spreadsheet on top of the notes. 'Bring it with you and I'll even treat you to a coffee in the café.'

For a moment she wished she and Steve could just go for a walk deep into the forest like they used to. The dark green woods, complete with pine needle carpets, were peaceful and meditative and if you knew where to go you could see waterfalls with mossy green backdrops. It was a special place.

The island was popular with tourists all year round yet depending on the day you could walk for miles and maybe only see one person if one at all. There were so many walking trails that they used to love exploring and that was when they had their best chats, and she would confide in him and tell him what was on her mind. They had been on one of their long walks when she had told him about her discovery in the loft. Steve had been shocked but as supportive as ever and told her he was there to listen whenever she was ready. But there hadn't been much chance to talk properly lately what with the guests and the wedding.

She gave herself a shake. She was being selfish. This wasn't the time for unburdening herself. Focusing on Emma's wedding was key. 'Okay, deal,' she said. 'I'll come and make sure we're on track for the big day on one condition.'

'What's that?'

'That you buy me cake, too.'

Steve walked over and took her in his hands and gazed into her eyes. 'Are you okay, love?'

She wanted to collapse into his chest and go to sleep. 'I'm fine, honestly. It's just a bit mad around here isn't it. Always something going on.'

He nodded. 'That's why I get worried about you as you do so much for everyone.'

'I'm fine,' she said, her voice trembling. She moved forward until their foreheads touched.

'Where's Amy and Becky?' whispered Steve.

'Upstairs, I think. Becky wanted to show Amy her dress for the wedding.'

He kissed her and for a few blissful moments she was able to forget everything that had been threatening to engulf her. Then they heard Amy and Becky clatter downstairs and she pulled away.

'The kids seem to be happy she's here, don't they?'

'Yes,' she said, rolling her eyes and laughing. 'What's not to love?'

'Hey, lovebirds,' said Amy, as she followed Becky into the kitchen. Reaching for an apple from the fruit bowl on the kitchen table, she took a loud bite.

'What are you up to, sweetie?' Kirsty asked her daughter.

'I'm off paddle boarding with the gang.'

'Okay, well just be careful as there's a wee bit of swell out there this afternoon,' said Steve.

'Don't worry, I promise that I'll be careful,' she said, absent-mindedly picking away at the frayed edge of her jumper sleeve.

Kirsty took a breath, trying to ignore that familiar sense of worry that gnawed away at her whenever the kids did something even slightly risky. She needed to distract herself otherwise she'd start wittering on like a highly-strung parent.

'Amy,' she said brightly. 'Steve and I are heading down to the distillery.' Then she remembered its new manager which made it even more pressing that Amy should come along. 'I'm sure you'd like to see where Emma's big day will take place?'

Amy nodded. 'Sure, that sounds good. If at the very least to check out the local whisky.'

Kirsty clocked Steve raising an eyebrow at her.

'What?' she mouthed innocently.

'I didn't realize you were so into whisky,' said Steve to Amy.

Amy tapped her nose. 'I'll have you both know that I became very partial to a wee dram or two when I was away.'

'Really?' said Kirsty in surprise.

'Yes. Don't look so surprised. It was almost expected of me. There's a tendency to think that all Scots drink whisky, so I didn't want to let anyone down. So, I thought why not, I'll give it a go and found I actually quite liked it.'

'The Canadian whisky?'

'Some of that was okay but there was a bar specializing in Scotch whisky, particularly the island malts. So, a wee trip to check this place out sounds great and, obviously,' she added rather hurriedly, 'I will give it the once over for Emma's wedding, too.'

Steve laughed. 'Well just remember that I keep an eye on the level in my bottles.'

'Don't worry, Steve. I won't drink you dry. I'll always ask your permission before helping myself to a dram and if not, I'll be sure to add water in, so you don't think you're running low.'

Steve chuckled and once again Kirsty was reminded of how fond he was of her youngest sister. They had always got on well and he treated her as his little sister too.

He grabbed his car keys. 'Shall we go then?'

'It will be good to have a wee nosy ahead of the big day,' said Amy cheerily as Steve pulled into the car park. 'I'm actually more impressed that you managed to talk Emma into it.'

Kirsty twisted round from her seat in the front. 'It was Steve's idea as he got chatting to the new manager and . . .'

'How did you convince Emma though?'

Kirsty smiled wryly at Amy. She had been about to tell her some more about the new manager, but she hadn't been given much of a chance. 'She appointed me as her wedding planner and was fine with it. She has actually been quite low maintenance for a bride-to-be. Plus, she was busy and distracted and . . .'

'No surprise there then,' interrupted Amy.

'Are you going to let me finish?'

'Come on, girls, stop bickering,' said Steve, turning off the engine.

Kirsty pretended to scowl. 'See, I can't even remember what I was saying.'

They walked across the crunchy gravel to the entrance of the eco-friendly wooden and glass building and Kirsty watched Amy's reaction as she took in the surroundings and the incredible setting.

'Wow,' she said, turning to stare at the water stretching out before them.

'Come on. Let's go inside,' said Kirsty, tugging at Amy's arm and pulling her through the door. 'Now please don't freak out,' she said in a whisper. 'But there's someone here who I think you may remember.'

'Who—?' but Amy's question was answered for her when she saw who was behind the welcome desk.

'Hello again,' said James, smiling warmly at the group. Kirsty noticed his smile widened when he spotted Amy.

'Ow,' she said, as Amy purposefully stood on her toe.

'Amy! How are you?' James stood up and came round to greet her properly, kissing her on both cheeks. 'It's been ages. When did you get back?'

'Just the other day. Um, yesterday I think,' she said, flustered.

'It's the jet lag,' joked Kirsty, who was now very aware of the glare her sister was throwing her. 'She's not quite herself.' Now Kirsty felt bad that she hadn't given her sister the heads up.

'Come on, Amy, I'll give you a quick tour,' said James who led the way, accompanied by Steve.

The girls held back and let them move ahead and Kirsty winced, knowing what was about to come.

'I can't believe you didn't tell me he was here,' hissed Amy.

'Yes, sorry about that. I was going to but didn't quite get round to it . . .' said Kirsty who decided that Amy didn't actually look too mad. It could have been a lot worse. If she was really angry, she would have flounced back to the car. Instead, she seemed unable to take her eyes off James. That had to be a positive sign.

CHAPTER TWENTY-THREE

Amy had tried not to blush when he reached for her hand in greeting. His grip was firm and warm, and he didn't take his eyes from her face. Then when he kissed her on *both* cheeks, she could smell his warm, spicy aftershave. He had definitely become more ruggedly handsome as he'd got older, with his cropped blond hair and deep blue eyes. She couldn't believe that Kirsty had failed to mention he was back and would be a key part of next week's wedding.

'How long have you been here?' Amy said, as she followed him outside.

'Well, I've been back and forth for a couple of years now with a view to managing the distillery.'

'Where were you before that?'

'Up in the Highlands, in Beauly, near Inverness.'

'Oh, that's where Steve is from.'

'I know. Small world, eh?'

Amy wondered if that was why they had bonded. They did seem very friendly with their easy banter and the way they had embraced when they'd arrived.

'It's a beautiful spot. I loved it there and worked in a few of the distilleries, learning the trade. I always hoped to come back here one day.'

'And what a place this is,' said Amy gesturing around.

'Thank you. I'm really pleased with it, and we've had excellent feedback so far.' He glanced over at a couple of people who had arrived. 'Give me two minutes and I'll be right back.'

Amy tried not to stare at James's athletic frame as he turned and walked away, but it was hard not to. Her cheeks flushed every time he caught her eyes and there was a flutter of butterflies in her stomach. This was ridiculous. She was behaving like a lovesick teenager rather than an independent woman who had just come out of a long-term relationship and had no plans to look at a man any time soon.

'Incredible,' said Amy, in awe.

'This place or James?' said Kirsty, coyly.

Amy's cheeks flushed as he walked back towards them. 'I still can't believe you didn't tell me,' she muttered under her breath. Then turning to smile at James as he rejoined them, she said, 'The view is incredible.'

'I know,' said James nodding. 'That is what's going to get people through the door.'

'Then the whisky will make them want to stay?'

He chuckled. 'Exactly.'

'No wonder Emma chose it for the wedding.'

'Sorry guys, I just need to take this call,' said Kirsty, pulling her ringing phone from her bag. 'You go ahead and I'll catch up.'

Amy narrowed her gaze as she saw Steve hold back too. Did they think she didn't know what they were up to?

James brushed his hand against her arm as he took a step forward to open the bi-folding doors which opened onto a large decking area. 'I know the original plan was to have it at the house, but I think Steve realized Kirsty was getting a bit stressed about it and then when he saw this place he thought it may be a good alternative.'

Amy smiled as she thought about Steve and the way he knew how to step in and take charge when Kirsty got overwhelmed.

‘I just hope Emma likes it,’ said James.

‘She will.’ Amy shrugged. ‘Who wouldn’t? When Kirsty suggested it and sent her the pictures, she thought it was a great idea. Means we can all get dressed together at Meadowbank and Kirsty isn’t running around worrying about caterers and so on.’

‘Yip. That is what we are here for. To take the worry away.’

‘How many weddings have you held?’

‘This is actually our first,’ admitted James. ‘We weren’t quite sure if we’d be open in time and wanted to do a soft launch.’

Amy gasped. ‘Well, you better make sure you get it right for Emma!’

‘It’ll be fine. Let me show you around.’

She followed him through the doors, and they weaved their way between the tables and chairs. Then he led her to a small set of steps which led directly onto the beach. It was surprisingly sheltered, given the breeze in the air. The golden sands looked like crumbled digestive biscuits.

‘This is amazing,’ she said, looking around in wonder.

‘I know. Isn’t it such a glorious setting? I think this,’ he said, gesturing to the sea stretched out before them, ‘is what tempted me back.’

The sky was a perfect shade of blue dotted only with a few fluffy clouds. He spread his hands out and beamed. ‘It will be such a perfect wedding.’

‘Hopefully this weather will hold for them.’

‘The voice of doom,’ he said, laughing. ‘Even if it doesn’t, we can just move the ceremony inside; they will still have the view.’

Amy gulped in the fresh, salty air. ‘You’ve thought of everything haven’t you?’

‘Well, you know me. Always prepared.’

Amy thought briefly about their short romance in their final year of school. ‘Always prepared’ was something that he always said. She blushed as her mind took her to those heady evenings on the beach where they would stay all night with friends. They would find a secluded spot and . . .

'Penny for them?' he asked.

His eyes were twinkling, and she wondered if he was sharing the same memory. Amy blushed, thinking about the synchronicity of thoughts. 'Oh nothing.'

He turned and she followed him back up the steps and they paused to admire the view afresh.

'It really is a magical spot. And that air. It just smells like home.'

James looked at his watch.

'Oh, sorry I'm keeping you,' said Amy.

He shook his head. 'I have a meeting in half an hour but have time for a quick coffee if you fancy?'

'Sure, but only if you have time.'

'I do.' He smiled and Amy felt herself blush again. What was wrong with her?

'You take a seat and I'll go and get it. What would you like? Coffee? Tea?'

'Um, I'll have an almond latte please, if you have it?'

'Of course. Coming right up.'

James returned moments later with two mugs. 'There you go. Looks like Steve and Kirsty have found themselves a quiet spot in the café.'

'Yes, they'll be making the most of that as it doesn't often happen.' She took a small sip of the coffee. 'I can't believe that you are here, and this is what you are now doing. Who would have thought?'

He laughed. 'Funny how things turn out isn't it?'

'True.'

'Did you think you'd be living in Vancouver?'

'No, that was all very unexpected, and I suppose a bit rebellious of me.'

'How come?'

'Well, I had a very respectable job,' she said rolling her eyes when she said 'respectable'. 'I was working for a big accountancy firm, and they sent me over for a conference. Within days I had fallen in love with the place.'

He raised an eyebrow and took a sip of coffee.

'I went home and decided to move there permanently.'

'So where did the yoga come from?'

'I always loved it, and as work got more and more stressful, I turned to my yoga practice more often. It was the thing that kept me grounded and sane. I just decided to go for it and turn it into my new career.' She sighed and paused. 'It was a lifeline for me, even more so when Mum died. It helped me cope with her loss.'

'I was so sorry to hear about your mum. I know how close you were.'

She held back a wave of emotion. 'Thanks. I know. I miss her and her death has made me rethink *a lot* of things over the past couple of years.'

'It was very brave to go out there and make a life for yourself. But then you always grasped life with both hands. I always admire that side of you, Amy.'

'Really?' she said looking confused. 'I wouldn't ever say I was brave. I tended to go with the flow.'

He tipped his head to the side. 'Mmm, you never did anything you didn't want to though and you always seemed to follow your heart.'

Amy wasn't quite sure what was happening to her, but she seemed unable to pull her eyes away from James's. She needed to deflect. 'You could say the same thing about you though. You followed your heart, too.'

'Maybe we are quite alike after all,' he said, shrugging.

Amy's mind again drifted back to when they had decided to split up and go their separate ways. 'We are too different,' she told him at the time, his eyes pooling with tears when he realized she was breaking up with him. 'We want different things and that's okay. But we need to do what is best for us.' Amy realized now that she needed to do what was best for her. That had always been the case and she felt a pang of guilt as she thought about Ross back in Vancouver.

'Did you ever settle down?' she asked.

'As direct as ever,' he said and smiled.

'You know me,' she said, realizing that he didn't anymore. It had been about sixteen years since they had last seen each other. But Amy had always asked questions, sometimes very direct questions, thanks to her parents who had encouraged all the girls to be curious.

'I did when I was in Australia,' he now said.

'I didn't know you were there. What did you do there?'

'Bar work, mainly. Surprising, eh? I loved it. I lived in Sydney for a while and there was a girl, but she wasn't for me.' He paused. 'And you? Did you settle down?'

She shook her head. 'A bit like you. Not really. There was someone in Vancouver. In fact, he was meant to come to the wedding. But it wasn't right.'

'So a relatively new break-up then? I am sorry.'

Amy reflected for a moment. She had barely given Ross a second thought since she'd left. She definitely wasn't sad or heartbroken. 'Don't be. It just wasn't meant to be.'

'When do you head back there?' He held her gaze.

'I don't quite know. Haven't decided yet. Sometime after the wedding probably . . .' Time to change the subject, she thought. 'I've kept you long enough, James.' She stood up. 'Thanks for the tour and for the coffee.'

'Anytime,' he said. 'Hopefully we can catch up again before you leave. Here's my card,' he said, pressing it into her hand. 'Give me a call. Come on, I'll walk you out.'

'No need to,' she said, panicking at the butterflies in her stomach. 'I'll make it to the door and anyway,' she said, pointing at the reception, 'looks like your next meeting is here.' A striking woman stood by the desk, looking around.

James beamed when he saw her. 'Amanda!' he cried. 'How are you? Good to see you.'

'Oh, James. Isn't this place just epic,' she enthused, just a bit *too* loudly.

'I'll leave you to it,' Amy said, scrambling to get away and annoyed at the stabs of jealousy she felt.

'See you soon, Amy. Come down and see me any time.' He bent down to kiss her cheek and then turned to the other woman.

'I will do,' she mumbled as she walked past Amanda who looked at her curiously. Amy smiled at her as much as she was able then breathed a sigh of relief when she got outside.

Who was that? And why was James so pleased to see her? Had Amy imagined the lingering gaze or the connection between her and James still there even after all these years? She shook her head. He had clearly moved on and was just being friendly. He had to be; he was hosting her sister's wedding. She exhaled and then realized Steve's car wasn't in the car park. Glancing at her phone, she saw a message;

Thought we would leave you to it. See you at home xx

She shook her head and then started the walk up the hill to Meadowbank, her head spinning with thoughts of James.

CHAPTER TWENTY-FOUR

As expected, Emma made it to the ferry terminal with plenty of time to spare and she sat in the car dozing in the morning sunshine after her early start. She thought about all the times she had made this ferry crossing over the years and how she had always taken her wonderful upbringing for granted. As a child you never paused to reflect on how much your parents did for you and all the sacrifices they made. Yet now, as Emma sat reflecting about her lovely childhood, she wished she could thank Mum for all that she had done, it had shaped who all three of them were today.

When the sisters were growing up, they all had their own jobs to do at home. Amy helped her dad in the garden. Kirsty was in charge of pegging out the laundry on the line and helped in the kitchen. Emma always insisted that she should be the one to assist with the baking, much to Kirsty's annoyance as she loved to bake, too. Mum had always called her Em. It started when she was a toddler and then the rest of the family would call 'Em' in a singsong voice if they wanted something, or scream 'Em' if they realized she'd borrowed an item of clothing without asking. Except her father, he had always called her Emma and since their mum had passed, her sisters had reverted to calling her Emma again as though Em was a painful reminder of their loss. Max had never called her 'Em'. It had always been 'Emma' or 'Emmy'. Sometimes she missed 'Em'.

It was a gorgeous morning and Emma noticed the holidaymakers, kayaks on their roofs, and bikes strapped to the back of caravans. It was a magical place to go on holiday and a special place to grow up with summers spent mainly on the beach, dipping in and out the sea, picnics with sandy sandwiches and ice cream cones. It didn't matter that the ferries arrived packed with tourists over the summer months, you would always find a quiet spot to think and just be.

Despite the island being small, it had so much to offer and was rich in history. There was even evidence of Viking activity. The island hadn't escaped the clearances of the nineteenth century when alternative land and accommodation was promised to every adult male if they emigrated to Canada. Whole villages were displaced, and the Gaelic culture of the island changed forever. They had done a project on in at school and Emma often wondered if Amy's fascination with Canada took root when she learned about what had happened. There was even a memorial to the displaced families on the shore at Lamlash paid for by the Canadian descendants of the emigrants. As a child, Amy could often be found looking at the world map on her wall telling her sisters that she would live there one day. They never actually believed that she would.

A ticket inspector knocked on her window and jolted her from her daydreams. They were getting vehicles on board. She smiled and mouthed, 'Thank you', started the car and followed the line snaking ahead of her. Once on board, she sat outside, glad of the blasts of fresh air. Emma hadn't been home since Christmas, when it had looked a lot bleaker than it was now. Back then, the sky was a heavy grey and the air was cold and damp. This morning, the water sparkled in the summer sun and the flashes of golden beach were a welcome sight. Looking around she spotted a few tourists, transfixed by the view. How she loved watching the reaction of visitors arriving on the island for the first time.

'Isn't it beautiful?' a man with an Australian accent said to his partner. She nodded, seemingly spellbound.

Emma smiled. It really was magical.

'Well, hello there, is that you, Emma?' said a voice from behind.

She turned to see Edie smiling at her.

'Oh, Edie. How are you? It's so nice to see you.'

She leaned forward to hug Emma. 'I'm very well, thanks. But more importantly, how are you? Is this you back for the big day?'

Emma nodded, genuinely pleased to see Edie, who always brightened up anyone's day with her warm smile, twinkling eyes and brightly coloured clothes. Today she wore a cerise linen dress with orange and yellow beads. Edie had been really kind when their mum died. The women had played bridge together at the church hall in Lamlash, and Edie had been a good friend to the family, dropping off soup and dishes of lasagne and casseroles in the dismal days after her death. 'How are you doing, Edie? You look so well. I love your dress; it really suits you.'

She smiled, clearly pleased by Emma's compliment. 'I am great, thanks. I have just had a lovely few days visiting a good friend of mine in Pitlochry.'

'How nice,' said Emma. 'I do love it there.' Pitlochry was one of her favourite places. It was a small and very pretty town in Perth and Kinross, lying on the River Tummel. In fact, it was where Max had unexpectedly proposed to her right by the famous salmon ladder which was specially constructed to help salmon bypass the dam and make their way upstream to Loch Faskally above.

'Are you all set then?'

'I think so, although fortunately Kirsty has it all in hand. Amy is back and it will just be nice to have some time with them.'

Edie nodded. 'Your dad will be pleased to have you all back.'

Just then an announcement came over the tannoy asking passengers to return to their cars. 'Lovely seeing you, dear. You take care and enjoy every minute of your special day. I am so looking forward to it.' She hugged her again before adding, 'Don't hesitate to let me know if you need anything.'

'Thanks so much.' Emma watched as Edie deftly nipped between the crowd in front and made her way to the car deck. She was glad they had invited Edie to the wedding. It was going to be hard enough getting through the day without her mum and it reassured her to think that Edie would be there. She knew she would keep an eye on things in the same way that her mum would have.

Kirsty had offered to meet her off the ferry, but Emma reassured her she would be fine, and would make her own way to Meadowbank Cottage. There was something about the short drive home that she always found quite reassuring. She texted Kirsty to let her know she had made the ferry and to expect her just after nine. She smiled as she thought of seeing her sisters which she hoped would help settle her nerves.

Emma normally prided herself on her organizational skills. She could have held a first-class degree in efficiency yet almost left the flat without her wedding dress and kilt that morning despite all her checks. She had left them hanging in the hallway in a white protective carrier and managed to walk right past them, actually ducking to avoid them. It was only as she was about to pull away that she remembered and dashed back up to get them.

Steadying her hands on the steering wheel, she took a breath; this was all normal. Everyone felt like this before they married, didn't they? The little voice reminded her that not everyone found out that they were in early menopause just days before their wedding.

There was a clunk as cars started to slowly drive off the ship and over the metal ramp. It was a feeling that always made her feel at home and when she drove round the corner and out of the terminal she could have cried. It was all so familiar, and she felt that sense of belonging, and a bit of her tension slowly start to ease off.

She was so glad that Kirsty and Steve had decided to buy the family home and run their business from it. It would be so weird not to have a place to return to when she did visit Arran. She knew she was lucky that their home was still in the family. There was no way she would ever have wanted to buy it or stay there permanently, but rather selfishly she always wanted to know she could come back if she wanted.

She felt a twinge of guilt that Kirsty was the one who had borne the brunt of everything with their mum and now their dad these past two years. Then she felt even worse when she reminded herself that she hadn't seen Dad for six months. Her parents used to visit her in Edinburgh all the time as they loved the museums and art galleries and visiting the theatre. However, she didn't think Dad had left the island at all since Mum died.

Pulling into the driveway, she sat for a moment looking at the blonde sandstone building in front of her which was so homely and meant everything to her. Then she watched the door swing open and Amy and Kirsty run out to greet her. Jumping out the car, she grinned.

'Hello bride-to-be.' Amy threw herself at her older sister and hugged her close.

'You look tired, Emma,' said Kirsty, stepping forward to give her a quick hug.

'Jeez thanks, Kirsty. You sound *so* like Mum.'

Kirsty frowned. 'Sorry.'

'What I mean is that's not what a bride-to-be wants to hear,' she said, trying to lighten the moment. 'I should be luminous and glowing and dewy.'

'You're all of these things too or you will be after a few days of yoga and massage,' said Amy, rubbing her hands together. 'I've got plans for you.'

Emma stifled a yawn. 'Sorry. It was an early start and work has been . . .'

'Hectic,' said Amy and she and Kirsty burst out laughing.

Emma rolled her eyes at them.

'Come on, let's get your bags and get settled,' said Kirsty and she set about starting to unload the boot.

'Here, Amy, you can take the dress,' said Emma.

'Are you sure you trust me with it?'

'Absolutely.'

Emma glanced about briefly as they walked through the back door into the kitchen. Things were as pristine as ever. She smirked when she saw Amy catch her eye.

'I can't help it,' said Kirsty, throwing her hands up. 'I know, I know, I have become Mum. It's official. I'm just used to having guests around and keeping the place tidy.'

Amy giggled as she grabbed an apple from the fruit bowl and followed her sisters upstairs. Emma smiled affectionately at her. She never changed and didn't age either.

'We are going to put you in the hen suite,' said Amy.

'Have you renamed the rooms?' said Emma, slightly confused.

'It's the room where you can hear the hens in the morning.'

She turned to Kirsty in shock. 'You got hens? You didn't tell me!' She could feel her cheeks flush. Hens? Noisy hens? How would that work? She didn't want noise. That wasn't part of the plan. She just wanted some peace and quiet.

'It's okay,' said Kirsty clocking her reaction and frowning at Amy. 'She's just winding you up. Come on, we're putting you in the daffodil room.'

Emma followed Kirsty into the yellow room and watched as she hung the dress carrier on the wardrobe. 'Everything that you need is in here and there are plenty of towels in the bathroom. Just make yourself at home, my lovely, and shout if you need anything.'

Emma felt herself choke up with emotion. What was wrong with her? Why was she so unreasonably annoyed at Amy's hen comment? 'Thank you and sorry for being grumpy. I am sure if you had hens that would have been fine.' She shrugged. 'Sorry I am quite tetchy at the moment.'

'If you can't be tetchy with us, then who can you be with?' said Amy kindly, putting an arm on Emma's shoulder.

Her sister's kindness was too much, and Emma promptly burst into tears.

CHAPTER TWENTY-FIVE

Kirsty shot Amy a look of despair. This was not quite how she had imagined her sister's homecoming. She had been expecting smiles and laughter and excited chatter. She was looking forward to spoiling Emma with a special breakfast and had stocked the fridge with all her favourites: thick Greek yogurt, berries, bacon and she had planned to make fresh pancakes with maple syrup. Instead, poor Emma was an emotional wreck, which didn't bode well at all. What on earth had happened?

'Let me just hang this safely out the way,' Kirsty said, carefully putting away Emma's dress in the thick oak wardrobe. Emma perched on the edge of the bed, and Kirsty sat next to her and clasped her hand. She grabbed the box of tissues from the dressing table, pulled one out and passed it to Emma who took it gratefully.

'It's okay, Emma,' Kirsty said in a soothing voice. 'You're home now and it will all be fine. Getting married is one of the most stressful events in your life. And you've had an early start.'

Emma noisily blew her nose and tried to force a smile.

Kirsty was quite shocked by Emma's emotional outburst as it was so very unlike her. She was usually calm and very much in control which made this more than a bit unsettling.

'Take a breath,' said Amy, sitting on her other side. She gently rubbed Emma's back until her shuddering sobs subsided. 'We are here, and you are okay, Emma. We're not going anywhere. You are safe and everything will be okay.'

Kirsty sat there watching and quietly wondering if this was a delayed reaction to their mum's death and maybe finally Emma was realizing she wasn't coming back? Emma hadn't cried much in front of her sisters at the funeral or at any time since then, as far as she knew. It was as though she didn't want to let herself show her emotions.

'How does that feel now?' said Amy when Emma's breathing was less ragged.

'Better. I'm sorry . . .'

'There's no need to apologize,' said Amy.

'It's . . . it's just that . . .' Emma's voice trailed away. 'It doesn't matter. Look, thank you for that.'

Kirsty could now see why Amy was so good at what she did. She was so calm and reassuring. Kirsty even found herself feeling calmer and grounded from the sound of her voice.

'Look, why don't we tuck you up in bed so you can have a rest? We'll bring you up a cup of tea. Then we can chat later. Okay? Remember what Mum always said? Sleep is the best medicine and everything will feel a bit better after a good rest.'

'Thank you both.' She sighed. 'I'm mortified. I haven't even had a chance to ask after the kids or Steve or Dad? How is he?'

'Don't you worry, there's plenty of time to see them,' said Kirsty, standing up from the bed. 'Steve is out on errands just now and the twins are both at work. Dad is just fine. We can go and see him later on.' Her voice was curter than she intended, and she tried to soften it when she spoke again. 'Have a rest,' she said, astonished to see Emma actually pulling back the cover and curling up underneath it. That was a sign she was definitely exhausted. Emma never went to bed without putting up a fight. 'I'll come and check on you in a bit.'

She pulled the cover over her, kissed her gently on the forehead and glanced at Amy, who stood up. Kirsty pulled the door quietly behind them, and she and Amy made their way downstairs. 'When did you become so calm?' she said, turning to look at Amy.

'I guess someone has to be and it seems to come naturally to me,' she said. 'It's probably because I don't have anyone else to think about other than me. That is until Ross and Caleb,' she said. 'Anyway, being on my own suits me. It helps me stay very tranquil and Zen. You're not so bad yourself, Kirsty.'

Kirsty felt far from calm and wished she could bottle some of her sister's tranquillity. She knew they would need to get to the bottom of whatever Emma was upset about. She wondered what was really wrong. Sunlight flooded in through the kitchen windows and lit up the room making it warm and welcoming. Kirsty boiled the kettle and made a fresh pot of tea and placed it on the table in front of Amy who had sat at her usual spot.

'Thanks, sis,' she said. 'You really don't stop do you?'

'I will when I have taken this up to Emma,' she said.

A few minutes later Kirsty returned and sat down in the chair opposite, suddenly feeling exhausted. She exhaled through her mouth slowly. 'She's already asleep. I wonder what's going on with her?'

'She'll tell us when she's ready.' Amy's voice was firm. Wrapping her fingers around the mug she eyed her sister, 'Anyway why don't you tell me what's on your mind?'

Kirsty frowned. 'What do you mean?'

'You look tired and stressed out, as though life is taking its toll.'

Kirsty's shoulders slumped. She was so used to being the big sister and keeping an eye on her siblings. Even more so now their mum was dead. But she didn't mind admitting that she was torn. 'Everything is just getting a bit much. The guesthouse, worrying about the mystery inspection, the kids leaving, sorting the wedding and now . . .'

Amy reached over and clasped Kirsty's hand. She noticed the tears sliding down her cheeks and pulled a tissue out her pocket. 'I think we could perhaps buy stocks and shares in a tissue company. Go on. Have a good cry. It's no wonder you're fed up.' Amy paused as Kirsty collected her thoughts.

'It's Dad.'

'I know, I agree, he is a worry,' said Amy.

Kirsty looked at Amy wishing and wondering if she should tell her what was *really* on her mind, aside from Dad. Could she just tell her? Would it make her feel better? No, she said firmly to herself, she couldn't do it to them. Not when the wedding was just days away, it wasn't fair.

'I'm worried about what happens next,' Kirsty said, her words nuanced on several levels. This wasn't just about their dad.

'We do as Nicole suggested and take him to speak to the GP.'

Kirsty nodded. That was all fine but then what happened after the wedding? She knew Amy meant well, but she would just fly off to Vancouver and not have to worry about it.

'You don't have to do everything yourself. It is okay to ask for help.'

Kirsty blew her nose. 'I know. I guess I've just always been used to being the big sister and looking after everyone.'

'We will plan to take Dad to see the doctor and get him checked out. But I think we should probably focus on Emma for the moment and get to the bottom of what's going on with her.'

'I know, sorry and here is me making this about me. Just ignore me.'

Amy frowned. 'It's all relative, Kirsty, so don't apologize.'

'You are right, though. It's so unlike Emma. She's usually the one who never cries and has everything under control. What's going on?'

'Let's see how she is after a nap. Knowing her, she will have been burning the candle at both ends and not eating properly or sleeping much either. I didn't want to say but she does look like she has lost a bit too much weight. Her face is quite drawn and pale.'

'Yes, I agree. Hopefully, a few days of fresh air and home cooking will get some colour back into her cheeks.' She poured some tea into their mugs and took a sip.

Amy clicked her fingers. 'I know,' she said with a flash of inspiration, 'I've got a brilliant idea. The weather is so lovely so how about later on we take a picnic over to Blackwaterfoot? We can watch the sunset later, like we used to do. It will be like the good old days.'

'Brilliant idea,' said Kirsty springing to her feet and going to the fridge. 'Let me just start rustling up a few bits and pieces so we are organized.'

Amy rolled her eyes. 'I meant just let's keep it simple. It doesn't have to be a banquet. You don't have to do it now. Drink your tea!'

Kirsty turned, her hands on her hip. 'It's what I do. I look after people and feed them, so just let me do it, please.'

'Okay,' said Amy, her voice light as she rose from the table. 'Well, if you don't mind, while you do that, I am off to do some yoga practice. I need to try and stay calm and grounded if I am to be the calm one around here.'

Kirsty looked at her sister with affection. 'I hope some of your positive energy rubs off on me while you're here.'

'I've been quite gentle with you so far, Kirsty — I haven't quite forgiven you for not warning me about James — but I am going to have you doing downward dogs and butterflies before you know it. In fact,' she said, her eyes widening in amusement, 'Come and join me now if you want to? I think I'll go and do it in the garden seeing as it's so sunny out. It will do you some good to stretch yourself out. Come on, Kirsty, I can tell you're all out of alignment and could do with some time to balance your chakras.'

Kirsty thought for a moment and looked at her sister eyeing her with anticipation. 'Okay. You're on,' she said. 'The falafel can wait. Let me just go get changed and I'll see you outside.'

CHAPTER TWENTY-SIX

Amy chewed her lip as she waited for Kirsty to come out and join her. She had already unrolled her mat on the stretch of lawn in front of the house and she sat, crossing her legs and looking ahead at the sea which today was a deep azure. There wasn't a cloud in the sky, and she so hoped it would stay like this for the wedding.

Getting married on the beach would be amazing — like being on a tropical island in the middle of the Caribbean, rather than off the west coast of Scotland. Her heart thumped a bit faster as she thought about yesterday and the distillery. Seeing James again after such a long time was surreal. In fact this whole trip home felt kind of strange and as though she was experiencing everything differently. She took a deep breath in, counting to four slowly, then held her breath for four counts before exhaling for four counts and then holding again for four counts. Square breathing, as it was known, was one of her favourite methods when she was in need of grounding herself.

Although she always tried to leave her mobile well away from her yoga practice, she had brought it outside and she couldn't resist reaching for it. These were views that had to be photographed. Capturing a couple of shots of the sea ahead, she sent them to Josh. He'd been in touch most days on Messenger, checking how she was and how she felt now that she was home. She always felt so comforted by his messages and his little anecdotes about classes and her clients. She watched as the little dots started to move, showing he was typing.

Wow! Are you really in Scotland? Looks amazingly tropical! I'm on the next flight!

She laughed and typed a quick reply.

Yip, the motherland has its moments! All good and I'll message later with some goss. You're up late!! x

Dangling that carrot wouldn't land well with him and she knew he wouldn't want to wait.

Tell me now!!

She shook her head, smiling and quickly typed. *Good things come to those who wait! I will be in touch x*

She quickly refreshed her inbox and took a sharp breath when she saw an email from Ross. Tentatively, she clicked it open.

Dear Amy,

I hope you are enjoying time at home with your family and that your sister has a wonderful wedding.

I thought I should write to tell you that I am sorry about the way things ended. It didn't feel like a very nice way to part, especially when you were such a support after the breakdown of my marriage. Caleb was a bit sad that he didn't get a chance to say goodbye. I explained that was my fault and that you had wanted to speak to him but I wouldn't let you. I hope he will understand one day.

The other thing I need to tell you is that Lucinda and I have begun relationship counselling together and are hoping to make a go of things again. I didn't want you to hear from anyone else. I also thought I owed you the truth. It probably won't come as a surprise to you to hear that I had never stopped loving her. She has and always will be the love of my life. We are both trying to put our marriage back together again for each other and for Caleb.

Thank you for being brave enough to end our relationship. You deserve to be loved properly. You are an incredible human being and I hope you find the happiness you are so worthy of.

I will always be grateful for what you brought to my life and for what you did for me and Caleb.

I wish you lots of love for the future.

Ross x

As Amy digested his words, she felt only relief and a sense of calm. There was no anger or sadness or frustration. She silently wished him well and exhaled. Then she switched her phone off and pushed it to one side.

She took a few deep breaths in and out thinking, again, about James and how random life could be. Ross's email had just confirmed that to her again. Meanwhile James was absolutely the last person she had expected to bump into here, never mind that he would now be a part of Emma's big day. There would be no escaping him, which was actually quite a nice feeling and she had to admit to herself that seeing him had made her day.

It had been years since he'd gone completely off radar. Most people could be tracked down on social media or you could find out where they worked if you entered their name into Google. Not James, though. Over the past few years, she had tried looking him up a couple of times but there had been nothing, no trace of him at all which made her wonder if he'd not wanted to be found. Then he had drifted from her mind entirely as life happened, and she became settled with work and other boyfriends and then had left Scotland completely. As far as she knew, his family had moved away from Arran too so there was no connection linking him there anymore and the few friends she kept in touch with from school didn't know where he was either. He always had been very unassuming as a teenager and hated any kind of attention. It didn't particularly surprise her that he wanted to keep a low profile as an adult.

'I'm ready,' said Kirsty, appearing next to Amy.

'Oh, hello. Sorry, I was miles away.'

Kirsty glanced at her, raising an eyebrow. 'You look kind of dreamy. Can I guess who you were thinking about?'

'Nice to see that you do actually use the mat that I got you. Nice leggings too,' said Amy, trying to change the subject though secretly quite pleased to hear the fun tone that had crept back into her sister's voice. 'You look quite the pro.' Kirsty's hair was scooped into a topknot, and she wore leggings with a tiny daisy print and a navy-blue, loose-fitting vest. Amy always thought her big sister was extremely pretty but today she looked stunning. 'You look like you could take the class,' she said with a grin.

'Hardly. Wait until I sit down, and you hear everything start to crack and creak. I'm as stiff as a board.' She threw Amy a knowing look. 'And I would just like to say that I know exactly what you're doing . . . with your deflections.'

Amy ignored her and kept talking. 'The garden looks fabulous by the way. I love the yellow flowers over there.' She pointed at the flower beds, crammed with bold daisy-like flowers and proving popular with butterflies and bees who were creating a low drone of buzz.

'I know, they're lovely, aren't they? Their technical name is *Inula hookeri*.'

'*Oooh* get you,' said Amy, impressed, nonetheless.

'I just listen to Dad telling me what he's going to do when he goes into the garden. Apparently, you've got to be quite careful with them and make sure they have enough space otherwise they spread like wildfire. He's forever splitting and dividing things in the autumn in preparation for summer.'

'Is he putting them in the bouquets?'

'I don't think he has finally decided yet. I heard Tom asking him about it the other day and he said it would be better to wait until the morning of the wedding and go with what looks good that day. Hopefully there will be some yellow flowers in there though as they are so cheery and brighten things up.'

'I have to say that Emma is being incredibly blasé about not being involved in the wedding preparations. I'm not quite sure I could be so hands-off if it were me.'

'The focus for her is being with Max. It's quite romantic if you think about it. She never wanted a big wedding with lots of fuss and attention.'

'I guess so,' agreed Amy. 'That's what it should be about. The person you are marrying rather than the stuff that goes with the day. Is that how you felt?'

'It was a bit different then. I was younger and the first one to get married and I suppose Mum and Dad were keen that I had a big bash. Not sure if we were to do it again that we'd do the same. I admire Emma for keeping it low-key.'

Amy nodded thoughtfully. She glanced back over at the flowers. 'I've missed gardening, you know. I used to love those times in the garden when I was a kid and Dad would tell me all of this.'

'I'm guessing there wasn't much time for gardening in Vancouver?'

'Nope,' she said. 'Talking of which, I have also just had an email from Ross.'

'Saying what?' said Kirsty, her eyes widening.

'Basically telling me that he is getting back with his wife and that I was right to finish things as she has always been the love of his life.'

'Nice,' said Kirsty sarcastically. 'Are you okay?'

'It's fine,' said Amy. 'It *was* nice actually and he was being honest. He said I deserved to be happy.' She couldn't resist a cheeky laugh.

'Well, I would agree with that,' said Kirsty and winked. 'I have a feeling things could get very interesting around here'.

Kirsty seemed a bit more relaxed now and Amy was glad. 'Right, let's get started,' she said, trying her best not to sound flustered at what her sister was insinuating about James. 'Let's get you started in the Dandasana pose.' Amy stretched her legs out in front of her and watched as Kirsty followed.

'What's this good for?' she asked as she gracefully copied the pose.

'It will help to stretch your hamstrings, strengthen your muscles in the lower back and is also good for your abdomen and your pelvis.'

Kirsty sniggered. 'That may come in handy for you, then?'

Amy shook her head in mock disgust. 'If you were in one of my proper yoga classes, I may have to ask you to leave for being such a disruptive student.'

'I'm sorry, I'm sorry. I promise to behave. I won't say another word.'

Amy looked over at Kirsty fondly and realized how content she was right here in the garden at Meadowbank. She had a sense that everything was going to work out absolutely fine.

CHAPTER TWENTY-SEVEN

It was after 2 p.m. when Emma woke. For a moment, as she looked up at the pale lemon ceiling and saw the yellow cushions next to her, she wondered where she was then felt a sense of relief settle over her when she remembered.

She was safe and she was at home at Meadowbank Cottage. This room always felt so peaceful. Stretching, she did a quick body scan. Her head had a dull ache, which always happened when she cried, and her mouth was dry. The girls had left a glass of water on the bedside table, alongside a mug of tea that had gone cold. Gratefully she leaned over and took a gulp of the water. Then she felt a slight stab of shame when she thought of her emotional outburst earlier. Fear welled up inside her.

Why did she have to burst into tears the minute she arrived? Couldn't she have held it together for a bit longer? Her sisters would be wondering what on earth was wrong with her. It was as if she had arrived back to go to a funeral and not a wedding. She was acting so out of character, and they certainly weren't used to seeing this unhinged version.

Emma didn't like the way in which her emotions were making her act so strangely. When her clients had broken down in front of her at work, she always passed a tissue and said the right things. If she was quite honest, she was always a bit bemused by other's emotions and their inability to reign them in. This was certainly giving her fresh insight and perspective which, she told herself, wasn't necessarily a bad thing. Perhaps it would make her a bit gentler and more understanding at work?

She reached over to check her phone and saw a missed call and voicemail from Max. She clicked to listen.

'Hi, love, just thought I'd give you a quick call. We're just having a break for lunch. Hope you're there with your sisters now and busy catching up. I'll try you later. I love you so much.'

Emma smiled and quickly sent him a text message reassuring him she was safely there, and all was fine. There was a gentle knock at the door.

'Come in,' she called, hauling herself up and rearranging the pillows behind her. The bed was particularly comfortable.

'How are you, sleepyhead?'

'I'm okay, thanks. Had a good sleep,' she said, yawning and rubbing her eyes. 'I didn't realize I was so tired.'

Kirsty raised an eyebrow at her and folded her arms. 'Emma, you do work very hard. Too hard.'

'Just the same as everyone else, though. Everyone works hard and juggles stuff. Look at you and all that you do, Kirsty, and you have the kids and Dad too.'

'Don't change the subject, Emma,' said Kirsty, shaking her head. 'You are such a lawyer! No wonder you're in demand.'

Emma took a deep breath and looked up at her older sister. 'It's so good to be back. I don't tell you enough but thanks for looking after me and for organizing the wedding.'

Kirsty frowned. 'Oh Emma, you definitely are out of sorts as this is so unlike you. You don't have to thank me.'

'I do and I don't say it enough, but I really appreciate you. Now I really need to get up,' she said, pushing back the covers. 'Where is everyone? What have I missed?'

'Steve and the kids are in the garden with Dad and, no pressure, but they're desperate to see you . . . and Amy has been hatching a plan.'

Emma surprised herself by laughing. When was the last time she chuckled? 'That sounds ominous. Do I want to hear more?'

'It's okay. It's a good plan. She wants us to go over to Blackwaterfoot later and watch the sunset.'

'And take a picnic?' Emma said hopefully, feeling positively enthused by the prospect. They used to do that all the time when they were younger and would spend hours lounging on the beach there, picking on food Mum had packed, swimming and then cosying up together, with a flask of tea and blankets, to watch the sunset. As they got older, the three of them would head down alone and Kirsty was always the driver, which she insisted she didn't mind about, and so Amy and Emma would take rosé wine. Now whenever she was in a restaurant, even on a warm summer's day, she couldn't order rosé wine as it made her feel so homesick.

'Don't you worry, we are on it. And Amy has even nipped off to get some rosé wine and salt and vinegar crisps.'

'Sounds heavenly,' said Emma, feeling so much better than she did earlier. 'Let me go and wash my face quickly and then I'll be right down.'

'Okay. I'll go and tell your fans, and get the kettle on.' She reached over and hugged Emma tightly and as she leaned back, a look of determination flitted across her face. 'I'm your big sister and I'll always be here for you. *Always.*'

At that moment, Emma felt more love for her sister than she ever had before. She was so grateful she was here with her. Maybe telling Kirsty what was really on her mind would be easier than she thought.

CHAPTER TWENTY-EIGHT

A few hours later, Kirsty was driving across the String Road that joined the north and south of the island and took them to the village of Blackwaterfoot.

'Did you drive much in Vancouver, Amy?' she said, glancing at her sister in the rearview mirror.

'No, not really. Other than the times I hired a car to explore. Ross had a car and he drove, but he wouldn't let me behind the wheel. It was his pride and joy.' Amy rolled her eyes. 'And before you completely deride him, I have to be fair by saying it wasn't all bad. He's not a terrible guy, just not right for me. It didn't really bother me to be honest. I tended to prefer using public transport or walking. I always think that's how you get to know a place.'

Kirsty listened with interest and silently agreed that it sounded like it had all worked out for the best. She was just a bit worried about what would happen when Amy went back. Would she be lonely? She gave herself a little shake. That was none of her business. It was Amy's decision and she needed to learn to keep her nose out of things that didn't concern her. 'It has been sooo long since we did this, girls,' she said.

Sunset trips used to be one of their favourite things to do together. Brodick, where they lived, had the most beautiful sunrises and their mum could often be found up early watching the fiery, orange glow on a clear morning. However, the sunsets were best from the other side of the island, and they used to spend hours on the gentle, sloping beach at Blackwaterfoot scrambling about in rock pools, waiting for the sun to go to bed — that's what Dad always used to say. Even though Kirsty lived here she still didn't make the time to go over and do this. It never seemed the same without the girls or the kids who were much happier doing their own thing now they were older.

It only took about twenty minutes to get to the car park by the beach, which was always much quieter than the other beaches nearer Brodick. Kirsty switched off the engine and they smiled as they looked ahead at the clear waters over Kilbrannan Sound and towards the Kintyre Peninsula.

'Come on, let's go,' said Kirsty, leaping out the car in excitement. The girls followed her, grabbing the picnic bag and blankets and made their way down the sloping sands towards the water. All of them were lost in their own thoughts as they went down memory lane, remembering joyful times as kids, filled with excitement and hopeful times ahead.

'Remember the sandy sandwiches? And the bashed bananas?' said Emma.

'Yuck and Mum's egg sandwiches which nobody liked apart from Dad.' Kirsty chuckled. 'Then she started going the opposite way and getting all posh, making mini quiches and Scotch eggs?'

'I hope you've got all of that in there.' Emma pointed at the cool bag that Kirsty had dumped on the sand.

'I don't have egg sandwiches, but I do have other things that you like. Maybe not as fancy as Mum . . . but . . .'

'Did you bring your tomato and feta salad?' asked Amy.

'Yes . . . and the falafel and some pitta bread and dips.'

'Amazing,' said Amy, turning to Emma. 'You know if it was left to me, it would be wine and crisps?'

A seagull dived over their head and squawked. 'He thinks that sounds good, too,' Emma said smiling.

'Isn't it a lovely evening and still so warm? I can't believe how still the water is,' said Kirsty, gesturing at the glass surface ahead. 'We should have brought the paddle board.'

Amy's mouth twitched with excitement. 'Let's just go for a swim instead. I have been *dreaming* of being back in the sea here.' She kicked off her flip-flops and pulled her floaty summer dress over her head. 'It was on my bucket list of things to do when I got home. I can't believe I have been back for a couple of days and not ticked it off yet.'

'Don't you swim a lot though, in Vancouver?' said Kirsty, who bent down to take her sandals off.

'Yes, but there's something about being in the water here. It's just different. Maybe it's the air or something . . . but isn't it crazy to think too that the water temperature isn't that different to what it's like in Vancouver.'

'Seriously?' said Emma. 'That seems very weird. I would just have assumed it was warmer there.'

'I know,' said Amy. 'It surprised me, too.'

'I can safely say it's been ages since I've been in the sea.' Emma frowned, clearly trying to think when she had last been to the beach. 'Maybe North Berwick last summer with Max and his sister?'

Kirsty was now pulling off her shorts and T-shirt until she stood wearing just her bathing suit. 'I'll race you in,' she said, pulling her hair into a high ponytail. She watched as Emma shrugged off her clothes too and ran behind her, splashing them as they shrieked at the cool water landing on their warm skin. They all floated on their backs and took a few moments to let their bodies get used to the water.

'Remember to breathe calmly and slowly,' called Amy.

Soon after they began swimming further out. 'Don't go out your depth,' said Kirsty, feeling very much like the parent of the group.

Amy giggled. 'You're always such a mum, Kirsty. Have you appointed yourself as the group's lifeguard?'

Kirsty shook her head and laughed, used to her sisters teasing her about her constant health and risk assessments.

She had always been the same. 'I just don't want to have to come and save you. I'm too hungry for that.'

It was hard to think that it was late on a summer's evening as the sun was still high in the sky and the air was a perfect temperature. Kirsty let her imagination relax and she tried to focus on the present, noticing the colour of the sky and the bubbles on the surface of the water as they pushed their arms through it. She looked at the birds overhead and then flipped onto her back and let herself float and stare at the sky above again. It was lovely to be in the moment and not think about anything but being in the cool water and watching the faint streaks of clouds above.

Eventually she decided that she'd had enough. She didn't want to sit shivering on the beach for hours afterwards. Flipping onto her stomach, she began swimming towards the shore and Emma and Amy followed behind. They all dressed quickly and pulled on extra layers to keep cosy.

'I think Mum would be glad we were doing this,' said Amy wistfully as she lay back on the blanket.

Kirsty nodded. 'Definitely. She would want us to be having fun and looking ahead.' She had started to unpack the picnic and there were Tupperware tubs of feta and tomato salad, some cold meat, hummus, carrot and celery sticks, falafel, a baguette, some cheese and olives. 'I hope you're hungry!'

'Don't worry, Emma,' said Amy, reaching into her own bag. 'I've got the most important bit — the crisps and the wine!'

'Oh, Amy, you are a star. This is amazing. Thank you.'

'Think of it as a kind of hen night, though I know you hate the concept and didn't want one.' Amy poured some wine and handed her sister a glass. 'You sure you don't want a small glass, Kirsty?'

'Thanks but I'm fine. This,' she said, clasping both her hands together, 'is what it's all about and me driving and being chauffeur to you two is part of that memory.' She gulped as she looked at her younger siblings who had always looked up to her when they were younger and come to her if they had problems. Kirsty just hoped that they always would continue to do that even though their lives were now so different, and they were all doing very separate things. And then there was what she had to tell them . . .

Emma was now half-lying back on the blanket, glass of wine in one hand and sunglasses perched on her head. She still looked a bit pale, but Kirsty would make sure she got a good dose of fresh air and vitamin D over the next few days. 'How do you feel now?' said Kirsty, aware that she didn't want to start grilling Emma quite yet. She hoped she would share what was on her mind in due course.

'Ready to eat,' said Emma, reaching for a plate and beginning to fill it with bits of everything. 'I love this kind of eating when you just graze on lots of different things.'

'Is Max still doing the cooking mostly?' said Amy, tearing off a chunk of baguette and cutting a slice of cheese.

'Yes, he is, though he is so busy with work. We have a loose agreement that whoever is home first will cook so I try to walk home very slowly . . . but it often doesn't work. He's been doing a lot of late nights these past few weeks. Unfortunately, that has meant a lot of basic salads and pasta for dinner. Or crackers and cheese if I can't face cooking.'

'Do you think Max's long hours are likely to change?' Kirsty was well aware of the hours they both put in and wondered if it was sustainable, especially if the couple wanted to have a family. However she thought it better to keep quiet on that, aware that it was none of her business.

Emma shrugged. 'I don't know. I see him getting tired and a bit worn down by it and I know he wants to open his own restaurant one day.'

'In North Berwick?' asked Amy.

Emma nodded.

'How do you feel about that?' Kirsty wondered what her sister's ambitions might be. For as long as she could remember it had all been about the law and helping people who faced social injustice.

'I'm fairly relaxed about it as I could still work in my practice and commute in or work less or from home. There are always options aren't there?'

'Yes,' said Kirsty. 'The main thing is that you do what is right for you.' She reached for an olive and popped it in her mouth, noticing that Amy was listening intently to their conversation. 'That goes for you as well, Amy. We are all different and we need to follow our own path and it's testament to Mum and Dad that we are all leading very different lives.'

'How did you know you wanted children, Kirsty?' said Amy, suddenly taking a gulp of wine.

'Erm, I just knew. From quite an early age. It was something Steve and I were always clear about.' She cocked her head to the side, thoughtfully. 'Why do you ask?'

Amy took a bit of bread and chewed for a moment. 'That's the thing. I don't think I actually want kids. Is that bad?' She glanced at her sisters. 'That was perhaps part of the reason it didn't work with Ross — the 'stepmum' part and he kept hinting that he wanted more and that made me want to run for the hills.'

'Who says you have to have kids?' Kirsty was aware Emma had gone quiet and was also watching Amy.

'Nobody,' Amy shrugged, 'but sometimes I feel it's an expectation.'

'Well it's not,' interjected Emma suddenly. 'It should be a choice. People make far too many assumptions when you get to a certain age, or you are living with someone or getting married. She sighed noisily. 'I wasn't going to tell you this tonight, girls, but . . .'

'You don't have to tell us anything you don't want to, Emma,' said Kirsty, concerned at the change in her sister's tone.

'I know . . . but seeing as we're talking about it then I need to tell you. I was going to tell you anyway and, well, I don't know if there is ever a perfect time, is there?'

Kirsty took a sip of water, waiting and wondering what on earth her sister was going to say. Then she was reminded of Emma's earlier emotional outburst. Was she about to tell them she was pregnant?

CHAPTER TWENTY-NINE

It was now or never and, seeing as Amy had brought it up, she could hardly just sit there and say nothing about the thing that had been weighing so heavily on her mind for the past few weeks. Kirsty and Amy were waiting for her to speak, and she picked up some sand and let it fall through her fingers as she thought about the best way to tell them. 'I don't quite know what to say or how to tell you this girls but . . . a few weeks ago I had some tests done because I had been feeling a bit under the weather.'

Amy's face paled. 'Are you ill?' she asked in a whisper.

Emma reached over and squeezed her hand. 'I'm not ill but there's a chance I could be infertile.'

Kirsty gasped. 'Oh, Emma. That must have been a shock. Tell us what's been going on.'

Emma took a breath. 'I just thought it was stress with work and the wedding — though the whole point in keeping it small was so that it didn't become a huge thing. Thanks to you,' she said looking at Kirsty, 'it's not even like it's caused me much stress at all.'

Emma focused on the horizon ahead as she told her sisters about the hot flushes, waking in the night drenched in sweat. 'I lost track of when I had my last period and then wondered if I might be pregnant. That was a shock as I definitely wasn't ready to have a baby. But then of course I wasn't, and I was devastated. I went to the GP, and she took some blood. When she called me back to discuss the results, I thought she was going to tell me I had cancer. She looked so serious when she told me I could be in early menopause. For some reason, I thought she was joking.'

'When did you find this out?' Kirsty asked gently.

'A couple of weeks ago.'

'What did Max say?'

Emma shook her head and wiped away the tears pooling in the corner of her eyes. She gratefully accepted a tissue from Kirsty. 'Here we go again,' she said, trying to make light of crying again. 'He doesn't know. How can I tell the man I am about to marry that I might not be able to have children?'

'Oh, Emma,' said Kirsty, reaching to put her arm around her.

Amy moved closer and the two of them hugged her as she allowed the tears to freely fall. 'I'm sorry', she said, wiping her face with the tissue. 'I thought I had done all my crying. I didn't think I had any tears left.' She exhaled. 'I feel sick about it and dreadful that I've not told him, but I know I need to, and I must speak to him before the wedding.'

The sisters sat in silence for a moment, watching the sun begin to dip in the sky in front of them, the colours changing rapidly.

'This is better than watching TV,' said Amy, trying to lighten the mood but her comments fell on deaf ears.

'Is there anything else the doctor can do?' said Kirsty, with her practical head on.

'Yes, she said she will refer me for further tests to find out what's going on . . . I know we can go to a fertility clinic and explore our options. But I just don't know if that's what I want to do. We have watched so many friends go through IVF, and it's been so stressful for them and has put a huge strain on their relationship. Look at Ruth and Oliver. There's no guarantee that it would work either. We always said we wouldn't do it.'

'So you've had the "what if" conversation with Max, then?' Kirsty asked.

Emma nodded, her voice deflated as she said, 'Yes, we have. A while ago . . . but he may now think differently when he realizes it's not a "what if" conversation but a highly-unlikely-to-happen situation.'

'Oh, Emma,' said Amy. 'From what we know about Max, that doesn't sound like him at all.'

Emma gave a sad smile. 'I love him so much and I can't imagine my life without him. But,' she said, her voice wobbling, 'I really think I've got to give him the option to walk away if he wants to.'

'No wonder you've been feeling so emotional,' said Kirsty. 'That's *a lot* for you to have been carrying around on your own.'

'I suppose so. But you just do what you need to do, don't you?' It was starting to grow colder, and Emma reached for her hoodie and pulled it on.

'Come on,' said Kirsty. 'Let's get everything packed up and get you home for a warm shower. It's been a long and emotional day for you.'

'It has,' agreed Amy. 'I think you should have an early night.'

Emma nodded, aware her sister was trying to be helpful, but no amount of sleep would fix the predicament she was now in. At least she felt a sense of relief that she had shared this with her sisters. There was a lot of wisdom in the saying that a problem shared is a problem halved.

'It won't feel like this forever,' said Amy. 'I promise.'

Emma smiled at her. 'I can feel another Mum saying coming on.'

Amy laughed. 'Yip. This too shall pass . . .'

The sisters hugged and there was something magical about the moment, almost as though their mum was beside them. They gathered up their belongings and slowly walked back up the gentle slope of the sands towards the car.

'It will be okay,' said Kirsty, reassuringly.

Emma smiled sadly. 'I hope so.'

She looked back towards the horizon just as the sun started to dip. The sky was awash with shades of deep pink and orange. 'I will tell Max. When he gets here, I will tell him everything.'

CHAPTER THIRTY

The past few days had passed in a bit of a blur as the girls rallied together to make sure everything was ready for the wedding. Amy was relieved that their dad seemed to be quite focused on Emma's big day and he was spending more time in the garden with Tom as they discussed the most likely flower choice for the bouquets. She had really enjoyed getting to know Becky more, who was loving having both aunts in the house at the same time.

Emma had decided against having an official make-up artist to do her wedding face and instead had asked Becky to do some trial runs. This morning, Amy had watched as Becky deftly and expertly applied the lightest of make-up to them all, which transformed them, giving them luminous complexions. Emma had even agreed to do some yoga with Amy and the previous day had let her do a reflexology massage on her feet which definitely seemed to relax her.

Amy noticed Emma becoming increasingly pensive as the day went on and Max's arrival drew closer. She knew her sister had plenty to think about and the sooner she was able to speak properly to him, the better. She could understand why Emma was nervous, but she had a feeling everything would be okay.

Amy had been tasked with accompanying Emma to the distillery to check all was in hand. 'I can go alone if that would be easier,' said Amy, trying to be helpful. She saw Kirsty smirking at Emma.

'No, I'll come,' Emma replied. 'I feel like I've hardly done anything. It will keep me busy and anyway I want to check out the new manager. I hear he's quite easy on the eye. She grinned.

'He is *hot*,' said Kirsty, her eyes twinkling in amusement.

Amy shook her head in disgust at both of them and could feel her cheeks flush. 'I can't say I've noticed. Anyway, how shallow of you to suggest that he's like eye candy. He's in charge of Emma's wedding. That's all. And a friend from the past.'

'A *special* friend,' said Emma.

Amy ignored her, just pleased that she could hear some lightness in Emma's voice again. If winding Amy up helped her mood, then she was welcome to keep going. 'Come on, we'd better make a move. I have lots to get through this afternoon.'

Emma and Kirsty began giggling again at their younger sister, but Amy turned her back on them, grabbing her sweater and handbag.

As they walked through the glass doors of the distillery, Amy felt all her senses heighten as she became aware of James standing at the reception desk. He was dressed in navy-blue shorts and a pale-blue polo shirt with the emblem of the distillery etched on the front pocket in gold thread. When he looked up, a smile slowly spread across his face. She was unable to drag her eyes away from him and a slow flutter of nerves started to gather in the pit of her stomach.

'Hey!' he called to them. 'How are you?' He walked over. 'It has been a long time, Emma. It's good to see you. Congratulations on your engagement.' He leaned in to kiss her cheek. 'We are so glad you chose us to host your wedding.'

'No,' said Emma. 'Thank *you*. It sounds like you have been amazing in handling everything.' She threw Amy a meaningful wink.

'Everything is in hand and the forecast is looking great for the big day which is brilliant.'

'I know,' said Emma, 'I've been obsessed with checking the weather.'

'Yip,' Amy said, rolling her eyes. 'On the hour every single hour.'

'That's fair enough though,' said James. 'I would be doing the same if it was my wedding. It's a special day . . .'

Amy briefly imagined how she would feel if she was the one getting married today . . . to James. Then she gave herself a shake. What was the matter with her? When she looked up at him, he was looking curiously back at her.

'Shall I give you the quick tour?' he said.

Amy followed and listened as James guided Emma around the distillery, showing her where the ceremony would be and where they would serve the BBQ. 'If it rains, which it won't, but just to reassure you that if it does then we'll just move things inside here and that way you still get the view,' he said, showing her the spot right in front of the floor to ceiling windows. 'The ceremony at 4 p.m. is the perfect time as it means we can serve fizz straight afterwards with canapés and there is plenty of space to mill about outside on the terrace and down on the beach. How does that sound?'

Emma's eyes shone with happy tears. 'It's absolutely perfect, James. Thank you so much. It's even better than I imagined.'

Amy reached for her hand and squeezed it.

James grinned. 'I'm just glad you're happy. But I do have another very pressing question for you,' he said in amusement. 'How do you feel about fairy lights?'

'Fairy lights?' said Emma, bemused.

'Yes, fairy lights. I have ordered some and thought it would be nice to string them up around the terrace. I know you want to keep things simple, but I do think they add a little bit of romance to things.'

Emma sighed. 'That sounds marvellous. Thank you.'

'Great!' He smiled and gestured inside for the two women to go ahead of him, but Amy misunderstood and as he shut the door behind him, her body was suddenly pressed close to his.

There was a suspended moment of *something* when they looked at each other and then Amy gently stepped inside. She could sense him watching her and she wondered if he was feeling the same connection that she was. She noticed Emma give her a questioning look.

'Erm, I'll just nip to the ladies if that's, okay? I would quite like to check them out,' said Emma, leaving Amy and James alone.

'It sounds like you have everything under control,' Amy said, desperately trying to make small talk.

'It will all be fine. The weather looks good, the bride is here and it's a small gathering. What could possibly go wrong?' He grinned at her and tilted his head to the side. 'How long did you say you were staying?'

'Oh, I didn't,' said Amy, slightly flustered. 'Er, a couple of weeks at least.'

'Let me know if you fancy a drink then? Either before or after the wedding? It would be good to have a proper catch up.'

Amy clocked Emma walking back towards them. 'Any time would be great,' she said. 'Any time at all. In fact, how about tomorrow night?' She could have kicked herself for blurting that out and sounding so desperate. 'I mean, I was just thinking aloud . . .' She groaned inwardly. She sounded like a twit.

Amusement danced in his eyes, and he smiled lazily at her. 'Tomorrow night is fine. How about 8 p.m. at the Ship Inn?'

'Sound good,' she said, trying desperately to sound non-chalant. 'See you there.'

He nodded. 'Great.' Turning his attention to Emma, he said, 'Remember what I said, don't worry about a thing and call me if you need anything. The food is all under control and you're happy with the final menu?'

'Absolutely,' said Emma. 'Thank you again for making this all so stress-free, James.'

He smiled. 'I aim to please. Now you will have to excuse me, but call me anytime.' Rather formally, Amy thought, he shook both their hands and headed back to work.

Amy's hand tingled from his touch, and she snorted when she saw Emma staring at her. 'What?'

'As if you didn't know,' she said. 'He *has* got a lovely handshake. Firm and commanding but gentle too. He's certainly aged well. And just how charismatic? What an absolute catch.'

'*Sssssh*,' said Amy brusquely. 'He might hear you.'

Emma smiled knowingly at her.

'Anyway, I think it's time we got back.' Glancing at her watch, she saw that the ferry would be due in soon. 'Come on, let's go. Max will be here soon.'

Emma sighed. 'Oh God, so he will.'

As they walked back up the hill towards Meadowbank, Amy noticed Emma had gone quiet. 'Are you okay, sis?'

'Mmm. I love the spot. What a beautiful place to get married . . . I just hope, well I just hope that it's all going to be okay.'

Amy stopped in her tracks and looked at her. 'Emma, can I ask you a frank question?'

'Of course you can.'

'Do you want to get married?'

Emma stared at her in horror. 'What do you mean?'

'I mean when you went dress shopping did you feel excited? Or did you have a nagging feeling in your gut that you were doing the wrong thing?'

'No, not at all. I smiled that whole day and when I picked it up the other week and tried it on again, I was happy. Until I remembered . . . But I love him. I love Max with all my heart.'

'And he loves you, too,' said Amy.

'But . . .' Emma began to protest.

'Look, what is the worst thing that can happen? You tell him and . . . ?'

'I tell him, and he decides he doesn't want to marry me.'

'Exactly. You tell him and he walks away and there is no wedding.'

Emma shook her head at her sister. 'Don't mince your words, Amy. Just tell me how it really is.'

'Don't sound so surprised. You know I don't like sugar-coating things. I'm trying to help you and there is no point in tiptoeing around this. I'd rather be honest with you, and it would seem that this is going to go one of two ways. If he walks away from you then he is wrong for you, and you're not meant to be together.'

Emma winced at her words.

'But — if you don't tell him — then you are living a lie and that's not fair either. Especially as Kirsty and I know what is going on. When he gets here, take him for a walk and talk to him. I can almost guarantee that he will be more supportive than you think. He's marrying you for you, Emma, and not because of your womb and your ability to provide him with offspring. This isn't the eighteenth century.'

Amy crossed her fingers behind her back, hoping that she was right.

CHAPTER THIRTY-ONE

Kirsty pulled up outside her dad's house and sat for a minute, giving herself a chance to collect her thoughts. The past couple of days since Emma's arrival had been busy and she yawned, realizing just how tired she was. She now just really hoped Emma would get a chance to talk to Max. Looking up, she saw Dad standing at the window. She waved but he didn't respond and just kept looking out beyond her. She frowned and got out the car.

'Hi, Dad,' she called, opening the door.

'Hello, dear.'

Kirsty walked into the room, but her dad remained where he was and when she went over to hug him, she noticed the glassy look in his usual warm, brown eyes. 'Is everything okay?' she said noticing the tear that slid down his cheek.

'I couldn't find her earlier.'

'Who?' said Kirsty, fearing she knew exactly what he was going to say.

'Your mum. I was looking for her and I couldn't find her anywhere and then I remembered that she's gone . . .'

Kirsty wrapped her arms around him. 'Oh, Dad. Why don't you sit down, and I'll make you a nice cup of tea?'

'That would be lovely, thanks, dear. I don't know what I would do without you.'

Kirsty felt a tightening around her heart as he followed her through to the kitchen. Glancing around she saw the post-it notes that he had stuck to the cupboards to remind him what to do when he woke up in the morning. It was a plan they had devised a few months earlier when they realized he was starting to forget to do things, including eating breakfast.

Dad sat down at the breakfast bar, his hands clasped together, his head bowed. Kirsty filled the kettle and flicked it on, reaching for two pottery mugs, in shades of red and blue, from the cupboard. 'I love these mugs,' she said, dropping a tea bag in each and filling them with water.

'I know,' said her dad. 'We got them just before your mum became proper poorly. Edie made them, didn't she?'

Kirsty nodded. 'That's right. I remember that day we went out for lunch and stopped in at the gift shop afterwards. She is a talented lady, isn't she? Remember, we couldn't decide which ones to choose and so I bought some as well for the B&B.'

Each one of Edie's mugs was different and she made them in shades of red, orange and blue as she said they reminded her of the changing colours of the sky. Visitors to Meadowbank always commented on them and so Kirsty would send them off in the direction of the gift shop so they could buy their own to take away. At times Edie found it hard to keep up with the demand.

He smiled as he remembered, then his face clouded over. 'Edie will be at the wedding, won't she?'

'Yes, she will. Emma bumped into her on the ferry. She had been away for a few days in Pitlochry and was on her way home. She said she was looking forward to seeing us all.'

He nodded, still looking worried. 'The flowers and the talk on the day. Those are the only things I have to remember — is that right, dear?'

'Yes, that's it and Tom will help you with the flowers. Becky has a copy of your speech just in case.'

'They're good kids, you know,' he said wistfully.

'Yes, we are very lucky.' She passed his tea to him and looked inside the biscuit tin. 'Looks like I need to restock this?' she said, raising an eyebrow. 'You've either developed a very sweet tooth or Tom has been in to see you?'

He smiled and put a finger to his lips. 'I can't give away secrets.'

'You will have to do without a chocolate biscuit then as he's cleaned you out. Do you want a digestive?'

He shook his head. 'No thanks.'

They sat in companionable silence, sipping their tea. 'Dad, did you and Mum always want to have children?'

He looked at her in surprise. 'Yes, we did. Why do you ask?'

'I just wondered why there was such a big age gap between me and Emma.'

He frowned and took a deep breath before answering. 'Your mum had a stressful time when you were little with various things going on. She actually lost a few babies early on.'

'She had miscarriages?'

'Yes, several.'

'I didn't know that,' said Kirsty in surprise. 'Why did she never say anything?'

'Your mum always wanted to move on and leave negative things in the past,' he said, looking around for something to dunk in his tea. 'She never liked dwelling on things, as you know.'

Kirsty jumped off the stool and reached into the back of the cupboard where she had spotted a packet of digestive biscuits earlier. 'There you go.'

'Thank you, dear.'

'You were saying . . .'

'Your mum didn't like going over the past. She was grateful she had you all and didn't see the point in raking stuff up.' He focused on dipping the biscuit into the tea.

Kirsty watched him until she knew the biscuit would end up at the bottom of his mug if he didn't pull it out. 'That's probably enough, Dad.'

He laughed as it crumbled into his tea. 'Oopsie.'

'I'll get you a fresh cup.'

'No, don't worry, it's fine. It doesn't bother me.'

'How was she when she was pregnant with me? Did she have any bother?' She watched her dad's face closely as he answered.

'You were a dream. A beautiful gift,' he said, adjusting his glasses. 'You always were and always have been. I don't know what we would have done without you.' He suddenly reached for her hand. 'You, my precious girl, were the best thing that happened to us,' he said firmly. 'You truly were.'

Kirsty felt quite taken aback. It was the first time her dad had ever said anything like that to her and she was lost for words.

'Your mum adored you and she maybe didn't tell you enough, but she was so proud of you when you came back to Arran to make a go of the business at Meadowbank. She knew out of the three of you that you would be the one to make it a success. You've not always had it easy, my love, especially with her illness and now me being a burden.'

'Dad,' she said, shocked. 'You're not a burden. Please don't ever think that.' Kirsty felt gutted he thought of himself that way.

'I forget things and it scares me,' he admitted sadly.

'That's understandable, Dad, and you're doing a brilliant job of taking steps to do things that will help — like the sticky notes on the cupboards and things like that.' She paused. 'How about we make an appointment to go and speak to the doctor after the wedding?'

He nodded. 'Sure.'

Kirsty knew that the wedding felt like a watershed in lots of ways for all of them. Because no matter what happened, things were going to change one way or the other and their lives as they knew them would change for ever.

CHAPTER THIRTY-TWO

Emma was waiting anxiously at Lilybank Cottage for Max to arrive off the ferry with his mum, sister Lauren, and her partner, Milly. The cottage was just minutes from Meadowbank Cottage, and it was a clever conversion of an old stone steading, beautifully refurbished throughout with an open plan layout and sunken sitting room with lots of different seating areas.

Dependent on your mood, you could curl up on a love seat in the corner, on the large squishy sofa, or lie on the chaise longue by the window and admire the view. The spacious kitchen was bright and airy and had French windows opening out to the decking area. The three generously-sized bedrooms all had ensuite bathrooms with walk-in showers and baths. Kirsty knew the owners and had managed to secure it as soon as she and Max had settled on a date for the big day.

Emma ran through all the rooms once more to check everything was in hand then gulped as she heard a car pull into the driveway. They were here. She ran out to see Max climbing out of the car, his smile widening when he spotted her. He ran over and threw his arms around her. Her mother-in-law-to-be, Helen, was also beaming as she looked around.

'Oh, Emma, this is such a beautiful spot. And the weather! You couldn't have picked a better time or place to get married,' said Helen, leaning in to hug her tightly.

'It is amazing, isn't it? And we have been so lucky with the weather. It looks set to hold, fingers crossed.'

'Hey, Emma,' said Lauren, smiling shyly. 'Nice to see you. This is Milly.'

Emma was very fond of Lauren, who was so different to her brother. She was petite and blonde and much quieter and more reserved, definitely the introvert of the family.

Milly stepped forward to shake her hand.

'Thanks so much for inviting me,' she said smiling. 'This is just amazing. I can't believe we've never been here before.'

'Well, you're here now, and have plenty of time to go and explore. It is a beautiful place. Come on in though just now and get yourself settled.'

Max was already at the boot, grabbing the bags and suit carriers and Emma helped them ferry everything in. There were lots of appreciative gasps and oohing and ahhing as they looked around the cottage which would be their home for the next few days.

'Now who would like a cup of tea?' asked Emma. 'Or something stronger?'

'Tea is great thanks, dear,' said Helen.

Emma walked into the kitchen, leaving them to go outside to explore and admire the setting. She felt Max's hands snake around her waist from behind.

'I have so missed you,' he said, kissing her neck. She giggled and swatted him away, before turning to face him.

'I know. It feels like weeks since we last saw each other, doesn't it? I thought you were never going to get away from Aberdeen.'

He rubbed a hand over his jaw. 'I know, don't joke. It was touch and go for a while, but I said there was no way I could miss my wedding and that I would have to resign.'

Emma's eyes widened. 'Really?'

He flapped his hands. 'Anyway, it doesn't matter. I am here now and that is all that matters. Let me help you with this, then we'll leave them to acclimatize. Maybe we could go for a walk?' He dipped his head to kiss her, slowly to begin with then deeply . . . until they heard someone clearing their throat.

'Sorry guys,' said Lauren. 'We're all parched out here.'

'Honestly,' said Max, shaking his head at his sister. 'I can't even get two minutes peace away from these guys.'

'How was the journey over?'

'I have never heard three women talk so much. I don't think they stopped for breath.'

Lauren shook her head at Emma and gave her a conspiratorial wink. 'He is, of course, exaggerating that completely. We are all just quite chatty whereas my brother is silent and has no chat.'

'Oi,' said Max lightly. 'I am here, and I can hear what you're saying about me. I just don't witter on for the sake of it. I choose my words carefully.'

Emma laughed. 'I'll whisk him away for a while and give you all a break from his sarcasm.

'Hallelujah,' said Lauren gratefully.

'Kirsty is doing dinner later on for everyone so we will meet there at about seven. It's just up the road so nice and handy,' said Emma.

'Perfect, that is so kind of her.' Lauren glanced at her watch. 'That means Milly and I can go for a wee walk down to the beach and explore. Maybe dip our toes in the water and get a bit of sunshine.'

'Yes, you can compare the water to the east coast and see which is colder?'

'I think it will be the east coast. It looks like you've been getting all the warm weather these past few weeks,' said Lauren.

'Okay, let's have a cuppa and then we can all do our own thing,' said Max, gesturing at the kitchen. 'What do you all want?'

‘Tea for me please, bro,’ called Lauren. ‘Milly, honey, what do you want?’

‘The same please. With two sugars.’

Emma followed Max out onto the decking. ‘Here you go, Helen,’ she said, taking her mug from the tray Max was holding. Helen was sitting with her eyes closed, enjoying the warmth on her face.

‘This place is incredible,’ said Helen. ‘Thanks so much for organizing it.’

‘You are very welcome. I just hope you have a good time.’

‘I am sure I will. I’m so happy for you both and I know you are made for each other.’

Emma smiled at her, hoping she was right.

An hour later she and Max walked down towards the beach towards the distillery so he could see where their big day would be.

‘How did things go in Aberdeen, then? Sounded stressful?’

‘It was a bit hairy at times. But to be honest I was more worried about getting here on time, Emma. Thankfully, everything is now in place for the trial.’

Emma knew how important client confidentiality and discretion were so didn’t ask him anymore. She was just thankful that the trial wouldn’t take place until they were back from their honeymoon.

He slung his arm around her shoulders, pulling her close. ‘For the record though, there was no way I would have let work get in the way more than it already has. Just in case you have any doubts. As I said, I would have quit rather than miss our big day.’

Emma’s heart soared as she listened to him and she knew she needed to open up and tell him what was on her mind, but she couldn’t. It was as though the words were stuck inside her. As they walked, she thought about how wonderful he was and how much she loved him. *That is why*, the voice in her head said, *you need to be honest with him*. He deserves to know the truth.

'Mum is so excited about the wedding and it's great seeing Lauren happy too.'

Emma nodded. It had been a tough few years for them all. Max's father had died suddenly, the victim of a hit and run car accident in Edinburgh. Not long afterwards, Lauren finally found the strength to tell Max and her mum that she was gay. Neither were particularly surprised about it, and were just pleased she was able to be herself. Around about that time she and Max met and started dating. At the time, his mum told him it was great to remember that life had pockets of joy and that she was able to start smiling again because her kids were happy.

Emma was in awe of her mother-in-law-to-be. She was always so kind, graceful and diplomatic and admitted to Emma that the last thing she wanted to be was a burden or overbearing to her kids. But Emma knew she was delighted that Lauren and Milly had recently moved to North Berwick, and she was always so happy to welcome Max and Emma when they visited. 'Lauren does look fab and so happy, and your mum is always so great too, isn't she?'

Max kissed the top of her head. 'Yes, I mean she misses Dad, but I know she is so excited for us and about the wedding. The only thing she gave me a lecture about was the lack of honeymoon.'

Emma rolled her eyes. They had agreed to make the most of their time on the island, especially as Amy was back for such a short time. After the wedding they planned to enjoy a couple of days with their family and friends before spending two nights at a boutique hotel on the other side of the island. After that they would return to work with plans to have a longer honeymoon in Asia in the winter months when they both tended to crave sunshine and a break from the bleak and very cold Scottish winter. 'Did you tell her our plans, though?'

'Yes, but she thinks we both work too hard. She's just looking out for us,' said Max. 'Anyway the main thing is that we will be married, and you'll be my wife. It will be great having some time with family and friends and then we have our days away at the end of the week to look forward to.'

'Yes,' bristled Emma. 'You may find by then you are ready for some peace and quiet.'

Max laughed.

Emma felt so secure and loved as they strolled along together and despite the voices in her head, she knew now was not the time to tell him her news — not now they had just been reunited and were in this lovely bubble. The clock was ticking though. She promised herself that tomorrow was another day.

CHAPTER THIRTY-THREE

The next night, Amy sat on the terrace of the Ship Inn pub, enjoying the spectacular views across the bay. She had to pinch herself. Who would have thought her life could have changed so much in a matter of weeks? She couldn't quite believe that she was here.

In some ways so little had changed on the island, yet so much had. She needed to work out what to do. Could this really become her home again? Is that what she *really* wanted? Or should she return to Vancouver?

It was so good seeing Emma and Kirsty and she was glad she could be here for them both, especially when she'd been so absent for the last few years.

She was also worried about Emma and really hoped she would find time to talk to Max soon. The wedding was just two days away, yet Emma admitted earlier that she was trying to find the right moment to talk to him . . . Amy wondered if there ever would be a right time.

She could also tell Kirsty was harbouring some stress over something other than just Dad. Perhaps she was worried about the thought of the kids leaving and her empty nest, but Amy's intuition told her it was more than that. And she also felt bad about Dad and all the challenges he was facing, but also grateful she was here and able to spend time with him.

Could she *really* just pack up her belongings and head back to Vancouver again without a backward glance? She'd left some of her belongings with Josh, but if truth be told she didn't really need them. It was just a few items of clothing and books which could easily be donated to the charity shop. Amy had always preferred to travel light and, whether consciously or subconsciously, had packed with a view to not returning. Josh's daily messages to her reminded her that although he missed her, she had to do what was right for her.

Amy jumped as she suddenly realized James was in front of her.

'Hello there,' he said, leaning over to kiss her on the cheek. He smelt of citrus aftershave and wore a crisp white T-shirt with dark jeans. 'Sorry,' he said gently. 'I didn't mean to startle you.'

'Hi!' she said. 'Sorry, I was miles away.'

'Well, I don't blame you. The view is amazing isn't it and what another glorious night. You'd think we were living on a Greek island in the height of summer.'

She nodded and stood up. 'What can I get you?'

James looked as though he was about to argue but thought the better of it. 'Just an Arran blonde please,' he said.

She laughed and put her hands on her hips. 'It's lucky that I know what you're talking about, James. Others may have taken that the wrong way.'

He laughed. 'That is very true.'

She returned with two bottles of the pale ale and watched as he poured them into glasses. 'Cheers,' she said, clinking her glass against his.

'Cheers. To old friends and happy memories.'

Amy took a gulp of the cool beer.

'So,' he said, placing his glass on the table. 'I can't believe after all these years you've come back and here we are.'

'I know. Although I could say the same thing about you.'

'Tell me what's been happening then, apart from what you filled me in on at the distillery.'

Amy wasn't even sure where to begin. It must have been at least fifteen years since she last saw him. She gave him a brief version of the waypoints of her life and where she had been since leaving Arran to go to university in Glasgow. 'And then, as I told you, I've been in Vancouver for the past six years.'

He cupped his chin in his hands and focused his gaze on her. 'I love Vancouver.'

She was puzzled. 'What do you mean? When did you go?'

'It must have been about the time you moved there.'

'Really? So, you were there about six years ago?'

He nodded.

'Why didn't you look me up?' she asked, narrowing her eyes.

'Because I didn't know. I'm not on social media. I can't stand it — so I never kept up with what folk from school were doing. I'd actually left by the time you arrived.'

'Wait a minute. What were you doing in Vancouver?'

'I was travelling across North America then ended up in Seattle and made friends with a bunch of guys who were heading up to Vancouver in their camper van. They invited me to join them, and I did.'

'How long were you there for?'

He took a sip of beer and frowned. 'It must have been a few weeks. We went all over and saw the sights; the suspension bridge, the parks — Stanley Park was amazing — and did the islands too, which were sensational. It's a beautiful part of the world.'

Amy was surprised and pleased that James had also experienced the beauty of Vancouver. Neither of them spoke for a moment. They sat in a comfortable silence as they contemplated another sliding doors moment.

'What happened after you had been there?' said Emma, curious to know where he went next.

'By then I was running out of cash, so I went back to Edinburgh and got an office job but to be honest my heart was never in it. That was when I quit and went back to working in bars and learning everything I could about whisky. Then I moved up north to the Highlands and started working in a distillery there.'

'Ah, I see,' she said.

'Then when I heard about the role back here, I got in touch with the owners and decided that it was time to come home.'

Amy was mesmerized by his blue eyes. She had forgotten just how much of a spell they could cast. She quickly swigged another mouthful of beer. 'Timing is everything, isn't it?'

He smiled. 'Indeed.' His voice was gruff, and he held her gaze.

Once again, Amy found herself remembering the good days when their teenage love was full of hope and exciting times. Being here now with James felt surreal and every time she looked at him, she felt herself melt a little. She stood up abruptly, keen to change the dynamic between them. 'Another drink?' She didn't wait for him to answer and turned to walk to the bar, aware that he was watching her every step.

CHAPTER THIRTY-FOUR

It was the day before the wedding and Kirsty was just unloading the dishwasher when Emma walked into the kitchen. She was dressed in her leggings, a T-shirt and trainers and had a hoodie tied around her waist.

'Hi there,' Kirsty said, resisting the temptation to ask *again* if she had spoken to Max about what was on her mind. 'What are you up to this morning?'

Emma looked at her and sighed. 'I am going to tell him today. Don't worry. I know it's awful that I haven't spoken to him yet, but the timing just hasn't been right, especially with everyone constantly hovering about.'

Kirsty was about to speak but Emma waved her hand at her to hush her.

'I know, I know. You are right. There never will be a right time. I need to bite the bullet and be honest. Otherwise, there's no point in having a wedding, is there? I don't want to start out our married lives by lying to him. That's not fair.'

'Yes, I agree,' said Kirsty, relaxing her shoulders slightly. 'I will be thinking of you, Emma.' At least Emma sounded a bit more confident about her intentions to tell him, though Kirsty didn't envy her one bit.

'Any advice?' asked Emma anxiously.

The kitchen window was open and the scent of lavender wafted in. Kirsty took a deep breath. 'All I can say is be yourself and be honest and . . . remember it's Max. He loves you and he'll be so sad that you've been carrying this burden alone for so long.'

Emma gave her a small smile. 'Thanks, Kirsty. I'll do my best. See you later.'

Kirsty waited until she heard the back door close, then glanced out the window. She watched Emma's forlorn figure walk down the driveway. Sighing, she continued to unload the dishwasher, jumping when Steve put his hand on her shoulder.

'Oops, sorry, I didn't mean to scare you,' he said with a cautious smile.

'I was miles away, again,' said Kirsty. 'Just thinking about Emma.' Kirsty had filled Steve in on the basics and sworn him to secrecy. 'She's off to see Max now and tell him . . . I just wish I could wave my magic wand for her and sort it all out.'

'I know, love, but you need to leave them to figure it out.'

'You're right.' She smiled at her husband, who looked earnestly back at her. Would he think less of her for withholding a huge secret too? Though she couldn't imagine ever keeping anything from him. 'Hopefully he will understand why she hasn't told him.'

He cupped her face in his hands and kissed her. 'She has her reasons for keeping it to herself and that is understandable.' He paused. 'I hope you know you can always tell me anything, love?'

'Of course,' she said lightly. 'Now come on, let's just check we've done all the things on the spreadsheet.' She kissed him gently on the lips again and then backed away.

He groaned. 'Okay, but how about a walk first? If everyone is busy doing things and we are all organized for tomorrow, we could do the coastal path over to Lamlash. It's ages since we did that, and I would quite like some time with you; tomorrow will be manic and I can't remember the last time we had some quality time together.'

Kirsty had to admit that the thought was appealing. She smiled at him, quickly glanced at the spreadsheet, then looked out the window. Although it was a bit cloudy, she could see patches of blue in the sky, a sign that it would soon be fine, especially as the weather outlook was sunshine for the next seven days. The thought of fresh air and time chatting with Steve outside was really welcome.

'That sounds like a great idea,' she said softly. 'It looks like we're up to speed with everything for today, anyway.' She looked up at him. 'I love you, Steve.'

'Hey, are you okay?' he asked, looking at her closely.

'I'm fine. Honestly. It's just all been crazy around here since Emma and Amy came back and you're so patient with us all. I probably don't tell you how much I appreciate you, but I really do.'

Steve chuckled. 'There certainly is never a dull moment with those two around. Now come on, let's go while we can and while the coast is clear. I'll go and grab my shoes.'

The kids were working and, as far as she knew, Amy was still in bed asleep. She had heard her come in late last night and was keen to find out how her date had gone with James. But there would be plenty of time to hear about that later.

Life seemed very exciting all of a sudden, in a change from her usual mundane day-to-day life of laundry and breakfasts. She couldn't quite believe both sisters were home — and facing potential romantic challenges. She had better make the most of it because she knew this time would go in a flash and then everyone would be away back to their lives and the twins would leave to start the next chapter of theirs. Then it would just be her and Steve and, of course, Dad.

Her phone pinged with an incoming message. Picking it up she read the message out.

'Kirsty, the mystery inspectors have just left me. Just thought I should give you a heads up. I inadvertently saw some paperwork they had left lying out in their room. They are heading to Arran today and will be there for the next few days. Good luck! Angela x'

Kirsty's heart sank. She was grateful for Angela's tip off, but it wasn't the news she had hoped for. Angela ran an Airbnb in Troon, and they had kept in touch after meeting at a tourism conference held a few years ago in a top Ayrshire hotel. They'd both felt a bit out of their depth with their smaller establishments and so had immediately hit it off.

Kirsty could have screamed in the here and now though. The inspectors were on their way to the island — just when they were closed due to the wedding party. They couldn't even take part! Bang went the chance of winning any of the cash prizes on offer that would have gone towards the upgrade and renovation of Meadowbank. But what could they do? There was no point in crying about it, she told herself sternly. Emma's wedding came first, and the renovations would just have to wait.

'It's not the end of the world, love,' said Steve, reading the text too. 'Look on the bright side. At least we don't need to spend the next couple of months worrying that an inspector is going to pitch up.'

Kirsty shrugged and rolled her eyes. 'I know, you're right. It's just annoying.'

'Come on,' said Steve. 'Let's get out and enjoy the sunshine while we can.'

Kirsty filled a couple of water bottles, quickly buttered some rolls and filled them with cheese salad then popped them in a small rucksack along with some suntan lotion and a hat.

She knew a walk would be a welcome distraction and take her away from the swarm of buzzing thoughts going round and round in her head.

CHAPTER THIRTY-FIVE

Emma walked slowly towards Lilybank Cottage, deliberately taking deep breaths, taking the time to slow down her mind and notice what was around her. She counted five things she could see and said them out loud. 'The sea, the hedge, the path, the clouds in the sky, the roses,' then four things she could feel, 'my trainers on the ground, the breeze on my cheek, my hoodie around my waist and . . .' She thought for a minute and did a quick body scan, 'the butterflies in my stomach.' What could she hear? 'The chirping of the birds, a car engine and a buzzy bee.' Emma thought about what she could smell which took her longer as she tried to focus her sense on what was around her. 'Salty air and paint.' She nodded at the elderly man touching up his garden fence with a fresh coat. Things she could taste? 'The mint from my toothpaste.' This was one of her favourite techniques for calming herself down at work when she felt stressed and overwhelmed. It helped to pull her into the present moment and connect with herself. It was proving pretty essential today when she was about to drop an emotional bombshell on her fiancé.

She knew that what needed to be said wasn't a conversation that should be rushed, but the clock was ticking, and she simply had to tell him. She just hoped everyone else had gone off to do some sight-seeing as planned. Helen, Lauren and Milly were keen to explore Brodick Castle and its grounds and Max had said he would be in the cottage alone if she wanted to join him for breakfast. He had said it rather suggestively, she knew that orange juice and croissants were not what he had in mind.

When she arrived at the gate of the cottage, she pushed it open and heard him call her name. When she rounded the corner, she saw him sitting on the terrace with a coffee.

'Good morning,' he said, jumping to his feet and striding over to kiss her.

The butterflies were still there but they began to settle as she kissed him back. It was so tempting to fall into his arms and let him take her to inside, but she knew she had to tell him what was on her mind. He looked surprised when she took a step back.

'Everything okay?' he asked in concern.

'Yes and no,' she said, crumpling into one of the chairs.

Max raised an eyebrow and looked at her questioningly. 'Can I get you a coffee?'

She shook her head. 'No, thanks.'

'What's up?' he said, reaching for her hand.

'I don't quite know how to tell you this . . .' Her voice was thick with emotion.

Max looked worried. 'Just start at the beginning.'

'I am so sorry I haven't told you this until now. I just didn't know how to break it to you, Max.' She focused her eyes on the decking, noticing the smooth grooves of the wood and the small dark circles dotted up and down the planks.

Max grabbed her hand. 'Are you having an affair?'

'No!' she cried in horror. 'How could you even think that?'

'I don't but the way you are setting this all up is making me think the worst, Emma. What on earth is wrong? If you're not having an affair then whatever it is, please just tell me. We will work it out, I promise.'

Emma gazed at the man who she loved more than anyone in the world and sighed. 'I might not be able to have children, Max,' she said quickly. 'I had some tests, and the GP has told me that I'm most likely having an early menopause.' She realized the words were flooding out of her in a torrent. She paused, steeling herself for his reaction, and watched as confusion and then relief flitted across his face.

He exhaled loudly. 'Oh, darling, I am so sorry to hear that. When did this all happen and why didn't you tell me?'

'I couldn't find the right time. Work and life have been so busy,' she said and shrugged. 'You were away in Aberdeen. There has been so much going on. I missed a period and then another one and thought I might be pregnant. But I wasn't and then I was having hot flushes and my mood . . . well I don't need to tell you how snappy and emotional I've been.'

He squeezed her hand. 'I had noticed but I put it down to work stress and the wedding . . .'

She nodded. 'And so did I, but then the GP ran some tests and when I went in a few weeks ago to get the results she told me the *good* news.' She knew her words were harsh, and she didn't mean to sound bitter, but she couldn't help it. Glancing up at him she was relieved to see the kind expression on his face hadn't changed. 'I understand if this changes things, Max.'

'What do you mean?' He sounded confused.

'If you want to back out of the wedding then I will understand. I know you want children, and I don't want to be the one who stands in your way.' She couldn't meet his eye.

'Emma,' he said looking completely taken aback. 'I'm marrying you for you. I don't see you as some potential mother or children carrier.'

'But you always said you wanted children,' she replied, unable to hide the sadness from her voice.

'Yes, with *you* and if that's not possible then I would rather have just you, Emma. I love you and you're what matters most to me.'

'I mean I know we could look at IVF or surrogacy or adoption . . .'

'Yes,' he said calmly, 'but we have also seen friends go through that and it's been really stressful for them.'

'I don't want to become fixated or obsessed about it. It all terrifies me,' she said, realizing that was the first time she had admitted it. Emma had read about the drugs she could take that would pump her full of oestrogen so her eggs might still give her a chance of conceiving. She knew there was only about a twenty per cent chance that IVF would work. However, it all seemed costly both emotionally and financially and it wasn't a journey she wanted to embark on. She was only aware of the tensions and rows it had caused friends.

'How do you feel now that you have told me?' Max asked.

'Relieved,' she said. 'I was so numb when I found out but also a bit relieved as I thought I was going crazy. I had no idea why I was behaving in the way I was. That night we went out with Ruth and Oliver was a prime example. I felt like such a bitch, but I couldn't help myself from saying what I did.'

He nodded, smiling. 'I did think you were particularly intolerant that night. Mind you, I couldn't really blame you. Ruth annoyed me, too.'

'I think it also made me realize that work has always been my priority and that I need to have more of a balance. But . . . I don't even know if that means with kids.' There, she had said it.

He moved closer to her, and they sat staring ahead at the horizon. 'I'll let you in on a little secret. That's exactly what I think, too . . . though obviously if it did happen, I would be delighted as well.'

Emma's heart soared with relief, and she wiped her eyes.

'I love you and that is the most important thing in all of this. Being married to you and spending the rest of our lives together is what matters. Not whether we have children or not.' He looped his arm around her shoulders, pulling her closer. 'We are a team, and I can't wait to start this next chapter of our lives with you.'

Emma's lip wobbled as she thought about the guilt she also felt. 'I feel so bad for you, though.'

'But Emma — what if our roles were reversed?'

'What do you mean?'

'What if I told you that I couldn't have kids and that I was infertile. Would you walk away and go and find someone who could father a child with you?'

Emma looked horrified at the suggestion. 'No,' she gasped. 'That would be awful. Of course, I wouldn't.'

'There you go. So why would I want to do that?' He tipped her chin up so she was looking at him then gently kissed her on the lips. 'I don't want to live without you. I love you and I can't wait for you to be my wife.'

Emma felt overcome with emotion as the pent-up stress from the last few weeks washed over her. 'I'm sorry I didn't tell you straight away,' she said, shuddering in between sobs.

Max held her close. '*Shhh,*' he said soothingly, over and over. 'It's okay. I love you and everything will be okay, Emma.'

'It was awful not being able to share with you what was going on. I'm so sorry.'

'Don't apologize. Just promise me that you will let me know if anything ever worries you again so I can be there for you. Life can be tricky, but we are in this together. We are a team.'

She let him hold her and stroke her hair until her breathing calmed. Then she felt a sense of peace and serenity wash over her and a sense of hope that things would maybe be okay. She looked up at Max with overwhelming love. He was all that mattered, and she knew then that their love for each other would transcend the challenges that would arise in the future. Emma smiled through her tears. Now Max knew and was accepting, she could finally allow herself to look forward to tomorrow.

CHAPTER THIRTY-SIX

Last night, after her evening at the pub with James, Amy had slept fitfully and had ended up sitting for a while watching the moonlight reflecting on the still water. She was in the smaller guest room, at the front of the house, with views over the bay. The calming and still waters looked like the perfect place to escape. But she didn't think Kirsty or Emma would thank her if she went swimming in the early hours of the morning. Especially when the sun hadn't yet risen.

She looked out over the garden and thought about all the happy times they had spent their as kids playing rounders, having picnics under the tree and camping over in the corner. She missed that sense of belonging somewhere. She knew she would always have a home here, but it wasn't the same since Mum died. She felt her loss more acutely when she was here in Arran.

She thought about all that Kirsty had done over the years, especially to support their dad. She needed a break and Amy intended to suggest to Steve that he take her away for a few days. She was sure she could manage the B&B for them, especially if the twins stepped up and helped too.

She always assumed she would never want to return home permanently to live on the island. The grass always seemed greener elsewhere. But now she could imagine herself living back here, which surprised her. She could understand why Kirsty and Steve had moved back when the kids were little. Their upbringing had been idyllic, and it was the best thing their parents could have done for them, but she had neither kids nor a partner.

She must have drifted off because when she opened her eyes, Kirsty stood in front of her, in pyjamas, with a cup of tea. 'Hey, sleepyhead.'

Amy yawned. 'Oh dear, I must have nodded off. I couldn't sleep, so was admiring the view. The moon was huge last night and lit up the bay.'

'I love sitting there,' said Kirsty, squeezing in beside her. 'Even if it's just for a few minutes here and there in between stripping the beds. It's like a live picture frame. Always changing and never the same.'

'I was just thinking that you don't appreciate things until they're not there and you miss them.'

She placed a hand on Amy's shoulder. 'That sounds a bit melancholy. Are you okay?'

She shrugged. 'Yes. Just thinking about Mum and the perfect childhood we had.'

'We were very lucky,' she said, nodding. 'There was always a real warmth about our home which I took for granted.'

'That was all we knew,' she said. 'Our friends always loved coming over, didn't they?'

'Yes,' said Kirsty. 'Mum and Dad had that magical ability to always whip up something tasty to eat, from nothing.'

'I've definitely not inherited that,' said Amy, laughing. 'Seriously, though, you have done such an amazing job with this place and with the kids. They are brilliant.'

Kirsty smiled brightly at her. 'Thank you.'

'I know it's not been easy, but do you ever regret leaving London and your jobs there?'

Kirsty shuddered. 'Not for a single moment. I have never regretted leaving that behind. This is what we both wanted, and it was important for the kids to have the freedom we had as kids.'

'I envy you. I hope that doesn't sound bad. But you seem so content and together.'

Kirsty grimaced. 'That's all a front. I can assure you I am like a swan. Perhaps calm on the outside but there is a lot of flapping about going on under the water.'

Amy giggled.

Kirsty tipped her head to the side. 'Coming back to where you're from is always emotional. Especially just now with the wedding and Mum not being here. Don't forget that you also had a break-up before you came back so you're bound to feel unsettled.'

Amy nodded thoughtfully. 'You're right. I think I lost a sense of who I was when I was with Ross. It was as though I was going through the motions if that makes sense?'

'I know things will sort themselves out for you, Amy,' Kirsty advised. 'You will be absolutely fine.'

Amy smiled, grateful that her sister was saying exactly the right things to lift her spirits. 'I know — things do have a way of working out. Look at all the worry Emma has been holding these past few weeks.'

Kirsty nodded. 'I am so glad they've spoken, and everything is okay for the moment. They may have a few challenges ahead of them but it's so clear they love each other and that is the most important thing.'

Amy loved how wise Kirsty was. She really was a perfect big sister. Grabbing her for a hug, she whispered fiercely in her ear, 'Thanks for all you do. I love you, Kirsty.' She was surprised when she felt Kirsty suppress a sob and clutch her tightly. 'Don't cry, come on sis, we can't have puffy eyes today of all days, can we?' she said, trying to lighten the mood.

Kirsty cleared her throat, pulling away. 'Changing the subject completely, then, I've not had a chance to ask how things went with James at the pub?' She grinned.

At the mention of his name, Amy couldn't stop a smile from spreading across her face. However, she didn't answer straightaway but instead contemplated for a moment. 'Lovely,' she said, her voice soft. 'When I'm with him it's like being with someone I know really well. I feel . . . comfortable if that makes sense?'

Kirsty nodded as she watched her sister.

'He's a good listener, he's funny and smart and *gets* me and I can't actually believe that we lost touch for so long.'

'Sometimes life can be funny like that, can't it? Who would have thought that the time you come back for your sister's wedding is when he would be back here and involved in organizing the big day.' Kirsty smiled wryly at her.

Amy nodded, ignoring her sister's nuanced words. 'Especially when we haven't seen each other for so long. I was a bit worried there might be a bit of an atmosphere between us, but it's been absolutely fine. I suppose we were teenagers when we last saw each other and a lot has changed.'

Amy wanted to tell her about the connection she felt with James and the spark of electricity that buzzed between them whenever she was near him. That she loved the smell of him, the way he moved his hands when he spoke to her and the way he looked like she was the only woman on earth. She pushed away the memory of his hand lingering on hers as they walked back from the pub. She had the sense that he wanted to kiss her. She definitely wanted to kiss him, but she'd held back, too.

Today wasn't the right time to share this insight with Kirsty or anyone. She would have to try and hold herself together for the wedding. The last thing any of them needed was any more drama, especially after the week they had all had.

'Right then,' she said, springing up from the window seat. 'We have a wedding to prepare for. Isn't it a beautiful morning?' she said, pointing outside. The sky was now clear blue, the sea was still and the sun was casting a warm golden glow on the garden.

'Just perfect and exactly what we ordered,' said Kirsty. 'It's almost like Mum is smiling down on us all.'

'Let's hope she continues to smile at us all day then and that the rain doesn't make an unexpected appearance.'

Amy flapped her hands dismissively. 'Stop worrying, sis, it will all be fine. Now tell me what the plan is for waking up the bride-to-be?'

Kirsty reached into the pocket of her pyjama bottoms and pulled out a crumpled piece of paper.

'The spreadsheet?' asked Amy.

'Indeed. Although it's becoming a little bit tatty. If I'm honest I will be glad to get rid of this!'

'You will be reaching into your pocket looking for it forever more,' said Amy laughing. 'What is on the agenda this morning?'

'Yoga in the garden and a light shoulder massage for the bride-to-be. Then I will run her an aromatherapy bath. Steve is going to make sourdough toast with avocado and eggs for brunch . . . oh and some fizz. I better remember to put that in the fridge.'

'Then it's hair and make-up time?' Amy rubbed her hands together excitedly. 'What time are we supposed to wake her up?'

'Mmm,' said Kirsty frowning. 'That must be an oversight. I haven't factored that in.'

Amy couldn't help shaking her head at Kirsty. 'That's shocking,' she said. 'What a failure you are.' She laughed. 'Do you think we should see if she is awake?'

Kirsty laughed at her sister's dig. 'It's up to you but she's not really a morning person.'

'Okay, first things first. Let's take her some coffee and remind her she has a wedding to get ready for!'

CHAPTER THIRTY-SEVEN

Kirsty watched as Becky expertly applied a light base of foundation to Emma's face. Having a confident teenager in the room was rather reassuring — nothing seemed to phase her which was great as her sunny mood was rubbing off on Emma.

'Wow, I look like I have perfect skin,' said Emma, admiring herself in the mirror.

'You do,' answered Kirsty quickly. 'You look positively radiant.'

Becky stepped back, hands on hips, to admire her work. 'Not bad at all, Aunt Em, if I do say so myself.'

Kirsty felt tears sprint into her eyes and looked at Emma who was fiddling nervously with her make-up bag. She looked up and managed a small smile. Becky was the first person to call Emma, Em, since Mum had died. It felt like another sign that their mum was watching over them.

'Knock knock,' said Steve, opening the door with his foot. He came in with a tray of champagne flutes and a bottle of champagne.

'Fantastic, thanks, love,' Kirsty smiled. 'Now is everything under control?'

'Yes it is.' He kissed her on the top of her head. 'Your dad and Tom are finishing off the bouquets and pinholes and then I will make sure they are clean and presentable. All you ladies need do is focus on your grooming and drinking fizz.'

Emma glanced around. 'Where is Amy?'

That was a good question. Kirsty had sent her down to do a final once over of the distillery and drop in to Lilybank Cottage with a bottle of fizz for Max and his family, but that was ages ago. 'She's just doing a last-minute errand. She'll be back soon.'

Emma's phone buzzed. Snatching it up she opened a message and Kirsty watched her, feeling a ripple of panic as a frown of concentration formed on her face. Then she looked as though she wanted to cry. Oh no, what had gone wrong?

'Emma what is it? What's happened?' Kirsty urged. Emma had seemed so happy after speaking to Max, and he had been so sweet. She thought everything was going to be okay. Had he changed his mind? 'Emma, you are starting to worry me . . .'

'It's good news!' she said, her voice almost a whisper. 'Honestly, don't look so worried. Max has just messaged me to tell me that Ruth went into labour in the early hours . . .' She zoomed in on the photo on her phone and turned it round to show everyone. 'And she and Oliver had a little boy called Rex. Look, isn't he gorgeous?'

Kirsty sighed a huge breath of relief and looked at the picture of Rex. He was indeed adorable with his huge brown eyes and smattering of dark hair.

'He just looks like all other babies,' said Becky, her voice quite matter- of-fact. 'Quite cute, but also let's be honest, more like a shrivelled-up wee man. I don't see the attraction at all.'

Kirsty chuckled loudly and Emma roared with laughter. 'You are absolutely right, Becky,' said Emma.

Kirsty loved her daughter more than ever at that moment for making her aunt laugh in what could have been a potentially tricky moment. 'And thank goodness she didn't come over for the wedding. Can you imagine? Knowing Ruth, she would have gone into labour during the wedding ceremony and that would have been that.'

Emma pulled a face. 'It would have been *horrendous*. There would have been so much drama and we would *never* have heard the end of it. I am so pleased all is fine and he has arrived safely. But I agree, Kirsty. Thank goodness she isn't here.'

Just then, Steve popped the champagne open and poured three glasses, handing one to Kirsty, Emma and Becky. 'Sounds like there's lots to be grateful for?'

'Indeed. Cheers,' said Kirsty, clinking the glass against Emma and Becky's. 'Here's to a wonderful wedding day with lots of happy times ahead.'

'Cheers,' said Emma, beaming.

'I'm going to leave you in the capable hands of Becky for a moment,' said Kirsty, draining her glass. 'And go and check on Dad and Tom and see what's happening with the flowers.' She also wanted to check where Amy was and if everything was going to plan.

Downstairs in the kitchen she checked her phone for missed calls or messages but there was nothing from Amy. She caught her breath though when she spotted the bouquets sitting on the kitchen table.

'Wow,' she said, gazing at the bright blooms in yellows, oranges and creams. They had also included a few bluebells which she knew was a nod to Mum. Each posy had been hand-tied with a natural raffia bow. 'They are just stunning.' Emma would love them. Looking outside, she saw Steve now chatting to Dad and Tom, and she ran outside to congratulate them on their beautiful selection. 'The flowers are amazing. Well done both of you. I love the bluebells.'

Tom looked bashful and kicked the stones on the driveway. Dad smiled proudly. 'It was a team effort,' he said. 'I couldn't have done it without this young man's help . . .' His voice trailed off and he linked his arm through Tom's. 'It was also his idea to put the bluebells through it.'

Tom blushed, embarrassed that the attention was now on him. 'I managed to find a few still flowering in the woods,' he said, bashfully.

Kirsty looked at her dad and son lovingly and pulled them in for a group hug. Steve cleared his throat. 'I don't like to break up the party, but I think we need to watch our time. I need to make sure these guys are cleaned up and looking dapper in time for the ceremony.'

'Of course,' said Kirsty, looking at her watch and feeling worried when she realized the time. Where on earth was Amy? She couldn't help feeling a terrible sense of foreboding. Had something awful happened? She caught Steve looking at her in concern and she forced a smile. 'Thanks, Steve. If you can get yourselves organized that would be great. I just need to find out where Amy is. I'll go and give her a call and find out if she'll be back soon.'

Just then Amy came running through the door.

'There you are,' said Kirsty. 'I was about to send out the search party.'

'Sorry,' she said, trying to catch her breath. 'I lost track of time.'

Kirsty knew there was more to it but this wasn't the time or place. 'Come on, we'd better go and get ready. Emma is waiting for us.'

CHAPTER THIRTY-EIGHT

Emma had done her very best to stay calm and pretend she wasn't nervous at all, but nerves were starting to flutter around in her stomach. Becky had done a marvellous job of her hair and make-up, and she gasped as she saw the final result in the mirror. She barely recognized herself. Her hair was pinned up with a few loose tendrils framing her face which had been kissed by the sunshine these past few days. Kirsty and Amy had just given her a beautiful petal pendant which Amy gently unhooked and draped around her neck. It was silver and delicate and suited her perfectly. Then Kirsty handed her another small gift box. She popped the lid off and her spirits lifted when she saw what was inside — Mum's pearl stud earrings, a present from Dad on their own wedding day. 'Oh, girls,' she said. 'I always wondered where these were but didn't like to ask.'

Kirsty smiled warmly. 'I know how much you liked them, Emma. You always wanted to touch Mum's ears whenever she wore them. And so, when I helped Dad clear out some of her things, I made sure they were put away safely for the right time. I think we can safely say that there is no better time than today for you to have them . . .'

Emma carefully took them out of the box and put one in each ear, feeling comforted that the something old was an item belonging to her mum. 'Thank you, Kirsty,' she said, her voice catching. 'They are beautiful.'

'Now we just need something blue, don't we?' said Becky. 'I mean, who even invented this tradition anyway?'

'Well,' said Kirsty knowingly. 'That is a very good question. It actually dates back to the nineteenth century and comes from a Lancashire rhyme about what a bride must have on her wedding day — something old, something new, something borrowed, something blue, a sixpence in your shoe.'

'Oh yuck,' said Becky. 'Who wants an old coin rattling about their shoe?'

Emma looked over at the row of jewelled flip-flops sitting underneath all the dresses and nodded in agreement. 'Certainly not me. I don't have the right shoes for that for a start. It would fall out within seconds.'

'You have something old from Mum, something new from us, and I believe the other things are sorted?' said Amy, jumping about from foot to foot.

'Amy, you look super stressed,' said Emma, frowning. 'Is everything okay?'

'Yes, fine,' she insisted. 'I'm just excited.'

Emma caught Kirsty throw a look at Amy and wondered what was going on. 'Are you sure everything is okay?'

'Yes, it's fine,' said Kirsty, 'now, don't change the subject. What we need to do now is get something borrowed for you.'

'I have the perfect thing here, Aunt Em,' said Becky, sliding a pearl-studded clip from her own hair and carefully fixing it so that it held some of Emma's hair out the way.

'Oh, Becky, thanks so much. It looks lovely — but what about your hair?' She pointed at a curl that had now come loose.

'I've got loads of grips here, so don't worry about that.' She quickly fixed her hair again.

'Okay, so just something blue now.' Amy shot a panicked look at Kirsty and looked around the room.

'Don't worry,' said Kirsty, 'I'm sure we have that covered.'

'The sky is blue,' said Amy, pointing at the window.

Emma nodded. 'I couldn't agree more. The blue sky will be with us all day and I will feel extra supported by it as it holds us all together. It feels like Mum has painted it blue for us. It was always one of her favourite colours, wasn't it?'

'It was. Right,' said Kirsty. She went over to the wardrobe and unzipped the dress carrier, spreading the folds of material over her arm. 'Are you ready to put this on?'

Emma motioned to her to bring it over. 'Yes. I just hope I still like it.'

'Of course you will. It's stunning,' said Becky gazing at in awe.

They all watched as Emma stepped into the dress and pulled it up over her shoulders. She turned to let Amy pull up the zip and then turned back to show everyone.

'Oh wow, you look gorgeous,' said Becky.

Kirsty and Amy clutched each other, unable to speak for a moment. 'Just beautiful. You look perfect,' said Kirsty, her voice ragged with emotion.

'Let me get some more photos,' said Becky, who had been happily snapping shots all day.

Emma bent down to slip on her flip-flops. 'These are so comfy,' she said. 'There's no way I could have worn heels. Can you imagine how uncomfortable it would have been?'

'I know, I have to say that I don't know if I could have come to your big day if you'd been expecting us to wear heels,' said Amy, grinning. 'I can't remember when I last wore them. It's always trainers or flip-flops.'

'Me too,' said Kirsty. 'The last time I wore heels, I ended up with sciatica and hobbled about like a cowboy for several days after.'

Just then there was a sharp knock at the door. 'Can I come in?' It was Steve.

'No! Please wait,' yelled Kirsty. 'Don't you dare come in.' She opened the door a tiny creak and slipped out into the hallway.

'You girls had better get your dresses on, too,' Emma said. 'The clock is ticking.'

'Yes, look at the time!' shrieked Amy. 'We don't want to be late. Let's hurry.'

'Where has the Zen Amy gone to? Please can we have her back?' said Emma laughing. Her sister was definitely up to something as she had been acting very strangely since she rushed upstairs to get ready earlier on. Kirsty slipped back into the room.

'Is everything okay?' asked Emma.

'Yes,' she said, unconvincingly. 'Steve is about to take Dad and Tom to the distillery. Dad seems fine and quite happy, and Tom will keep an eye on him until we get there. Then Steve will come back and get us. So, we had better all be ready . . .'

'I'm waiting for you,' said Emma. 'I'm good to go.' She stood watching as they all reached for the dresses that were hanging in protective carriers and perched on the picture rail on the wall. She had spent ages sourcing dresses that would suit them all for today and was very aware that they all had different tastes. Amy had told her several times that she didn't want them to look like backing singers from the eighties. She said she had PTSD from being a bridesmaid to Kirsty all those years ago. Emma smiled in quiet contentment as Amy pulled her dress on first. It was cornflower blue, with a plunging V-neck and delicate ruffled sleeves. The back was open and had a delicate sash which tied in a bow just at the base of her spine.

'Oh, you look gorgeous!' said Emma. 'It is perfect on you.'

Amy beamed as she admired herself in the mirror, looking over her shoulder at her back. 'I do have to say you have done a great job of choosing these dresses, Emma. I love this even more today than when I first tried it on a few days ago. It's not something I would normally wear — obviously — but I feel like a million dollars.'

'You look cool,' said Becky, reaching for her gown. It was also long but sleeveless and slightly slinkier and lower cut than Amy's. Emma had hoped that would appeal to her teenage side and when she'd first tried it on Emma had been thrilled with her niece's reaction. It was made from pale-blue chiffon, and she looked like a film star.

'Oh, Becky,' said Kirsty, fussing around her. 'You look so grown up and so sophisticated. Almost too grown up and sophisticated,' she said with a groan.

'Mum, I am almost eighteen . . . come on,' said Becky. 'Time for you to get yours on.'

Kirsty untied the cord on her dressing gown and reached for her dress which was also blue, but a slightly darker shade than Becky's, and as she pulled it over her head it fell around her as though it had been made just for her. It was open like Amy's dress at the back, and had a loose fishtail finish. The fabric had a light shimmer to it. Kirsty looked radiant.

'Girls,' said Emma, her voice cracking. 'You have done me proud. You look amazing. Thank you for being my bridesmaids.' She was so glad that they felt as wonderful wearing their dresses as she did hers.

The car horn honked a few times. 'That will be Steve,' said Kirsty. 'Are we all ready?'

Becky quickly hair-sprayed everyone's hair again and Emma dabbed some perfume on her wrists and behind her ears. 'Okay. Now we are good to go.'

'Oh, not yet!' cried Emma. 'I almost forgot. Here, this is for you.' She ran to the wardrobe, reached in and brought out three small gift bags. Handing them to the girls, she shook her head in disbelief that she had almost forgotten to give them out. 'These are for you to wear today,' she said, watching as Kirsty, Amy and Becky opened the small boxes and took out a silver knot bangle with a heart-charm.

'Look!' said Becky, pointing at the charm. 'They've got our initials on and today's date. I love it! Thanks, Aunt Em.'

They all quickly slipped on the bracelets, hearing Steve honk the horn again.

'I'm supposed to be a bit late anyway,' said Emma, her mouth now becoming dry with nerves.

Their excitement was palpable as they proceeded down the stairs and Steve whistled as they walked through the hallway. 'You all look absolutely amazing,' he said grinning.

'Thanks,' said Emma with a nervous shiver.

'Is all okay at the venue?' asked Kirsty.

'Perfect. It is beautiful out there. This is going to be an amazing wedding.'

'Is Max okay?' asked Emma tentatively.

'He is grand,' Steve reassured her. 'Just desperate for you to get there.'

'Okay, are we ready to go?' said Emma, taking a deep breath in. Amy handed her a water bottle and she took a grateful sip.

'Oh look!' Amy said, squealing as she saw Kirsty walking towards her with the flowers. They are incredible.'

Kirsty handed Emma the bridal bouquet.

'I couldn't have asked for anything more perfect,' Emma whispered. 'Thank you.'

'Okay,' said Kirsty. 'I've got everyone else's flowers and I'll hand your posy to you when we get there, okay?'

'You are so bossy,' said Amy. 'What do you think we're going to do with them? Drop them or sit on them?'

'I'm not even going to answer that, Amy. You're not exactly known for your grace, are you?' said Kirsty affectionately.

'Yes, that's true, you do have a point.'

Becky ushered everyone out of the door and took another quick photo as they stood in front of the car.

Emma's smile spread even wider as she looked up at the beautiful sky above her and silently thanked her mum. Then she focused her grateful gaze on her family who were waiting for her to get in the car.

'Come on, then,' she said. 'Let's do this. Let's go and get married.'

CHAPTER THIRTY-NINE

Amy sat quietly in the car, holding Emma's hand and sending out positive vibes for the rest of the day. She was so happy to see Emma looking radiant and relaxed, especially after the last few days when she had seemed so vulnerable. In less than an hour she and Max would be husband and wife and drinking champagne in the sunshine.

It had been a weird morning to say the least. Amy had led her sisters and Becky in a relaxing yoga session and then given Emma a soothing neck and shoulder massage in preparation for the big day. After their delicious brunch, cooked by Steve, Kirsty had asked her to go down to the distillery to check everything was okay, that the cake had arrived from Cèic and that there were no last-minute panics. She had been happy to assist, especially as she might get a chance to see James.

However, when she arrived at the distillery, he was nowhere to be seen and instead, his assistant, Rachel, was in charge. She was very reassuring and insisted everything was in hand, but Amy was completely thrown, wondering where James was. He was supposed to be in charge of Emma's big day. 'Is James going to be in later?' she had asked, trying not to frown.

'Yes, he should be,' said Rachel vaguely.

'I see,' said Amy, though she didn't at all but could hardly start quizzing Rachel about her boss's whereabouts. 'Do you know when?'

Rachel muttered something about him having to deal with 'an issue'. Amy felt she couldn't probe any further without causing suspicion and so had smiled, thanked Rachel for everything and given the place a quick once over — checking that the seats would be put outside in time for the ceremony underneath the thatched gazebo which had been brought in especially for the service.

'Of course, please don't worry,' said Rachel, calmly. 'It will all be sorted. I have the guest list here and everyone has a seat. Honestly, you go off and get ready and don't worry. I have your mobile number and will ring if there are any problems.'

'Okay, thanks,' said Amy turning to go, still frantically scanning every nook and cranny for James. The place didn't feel right without him there and she had a niggle in her stomach. Where was he? Did she even have a right to know? Was it any of her business? She was in such a flap that she forgot to check the cake had been delivered and had to dash back to ask Rachel, who confirmed it had, but who surely thought she was unhinged as her eyes scanned the building *again*.

As she walked along the road that was parallel to the shore, she pulled her phone from her pocket and checked it for messages. There was nothing from James so she quickly typed one to him.

Is everything okay? I've been at the distillery and Rachel said you're dealing with something x

She deliberated over the kiss, put two then deleted them both, deciding on one. What was wrong with her? She was behaving like a lovesick teenager.

She left the distillery and walked out to the main road and began winding her way along the street. She wondered if she should walk past his flat which was nearby. Would that be weird? Would he think she was stalking him? Could she really say that she had just been passing and thought she'd call in to check all was okay? As she tried to decide what to do, she kicked a stone along the pavement for a few metres then looked up and gasped.

James was walking towards her, arm in arm with Amanda, the woman who had been at the distillery that first day Amy was there. She felt a jolt of jealousy, watching as they stopped next to a parked car and James embraced the woman who wiped her eyes, stared at him lovingly and then got into the car and drove away. Not wanting him to see her, she quickly darted across the road and ran up a side street.

Amy stopped on a bench to catch her breath and process the emotional impact seeing James with someone else was having on her. Amy was completely deflated. She had clearly misjudged him and their situation. He hadn't been flirting with her, he had just been friendly. It was then she realized the time and ran home to get ready for the wedding.

Now, as Steve swept into the car park of the distillery, she had to remind herself to hold things together for the sake of Emma. Today was about her sister and not about her and the crush that she had on James.

Amy, Kirsty and Becky were clambering out of the car, ready to help the bride get out, when Amy felt a light touch on her shoulder.

'Hey, you,' said James, his eyes widening as she turned round, and he saw how she looked in her dress. 'You've scrubbed up well,' he said with a grin.

'Thanks,' she said with a shrug and turned away.

'Hey . . . Is everything okay?' he said hesitantly.

She was silent for a moment. This was not the place to start discussing what she had seen earlier. It wasn't even any of her business. 'Yes,' she said, decisively. 'We just need to get the bride out of the car and ready to walk down that aisle.' She knew there were questions in his eyes but ever the professional, he smiled kindly then indicated to the party that he would escort them inside where their father was waiting for them.

'Emma, you look absolutely stunning,' James said, swivelling round to compliment Kirsty and Becky too. His gaze lingered on Amy, but she looked away, refusing to look back at him. 'Come on, let's go.'

Amy was confused at his reaction to her. He seemed genuinely pleased to see her which she was strangely and secretly pleased by. Amy also sensed that connection between them. But how could he look at her in the way that he was when he was clearly with Amanda? Had he turned into some kind of player? She reminded herself that she hadn't been in his life for years and didn't really know him. Why was she even wasting time thinking about this!

She beamed as widely as she could, took Emma's hand in hers and looked towards the reception area where their dad was standing waiting in his kilt. His face lit up when he saw his three daughters and granddaughter walking toward him. Right now, her family was all that mattered.

CHAPTER FORTY

As they followed James towards the door to the terrace, the haunting sounds of a lone piper began to echo around them.

Emma stopped and looked at her sisters in disbelief. 'I don't believe it,' she whispered.

Kirsty wasn't quite sure what to make of her reaction and whether she was pleased or not. Judging by the look of shock on her face it was the latter which was not good at all. Emma was always so tough, and Kirsty wasn't yet used to this new, softer version which they had been exposed to these last few days.

'It's okay, Emma. Seriously, this is all my fault,' said Kirsty, putting her hands up. 'I am so sorry. I know you said you wanted everything to be low-key and simple, but we forgot to talk about the music for when you arrived and . . . well, I thought I would arrange this as a surprise. But it's fine, we don't have to have it.'

'Shall I go and ask him to stop?' asked James, discreetly.

'No!' exclaimed Emma. 'No, please don't. Oh, girls. I can't believe you organized all of this for me . . . This is just the icing on the cake. I couldn't have planned this any better. You remembered how much I love the sound of a lone piper.'

Kirsty allowed herself to breathe again. So, she had got this right after all?

‘What is it about bagpipes?’ said Amy with a sniff, her eyes glistening. ‘They get me every time. Whenever I heard the sound of bagpipes in Canada . . . well let’s just say there were tears. The sound always stirs something deep inside. It’s the sound of . . .’

‘It’s the sound of home and family,’ Emma said with a huge smile. ‘And I love it. Thank you, Kirsty.’ Emma threw her arms around her sister’s neck.

‘You are very welcome. The piper is one of Tom’s friends from school. He’s excellent and actually quite hard to get so we are lucky to have him. I’m so glad you’re happy.’

Emma grinned at her. ‘I’m over the moon. It was so thoughtful of you.’

Kirsty smiled gratefully at James who in turn glanced across at his colleagues to give them a reassuring smile.

‘Group hug,’ demanded Amy. ‘Though a quick one. Otherwise, Max will think you’re not coming.’

‘Honestly you lot,’ said Becky. ‘Even I feel teary. But Amy’s right, Max will think you’ve done a runner at this rate. Let’s compose ourselves or there won’t be a wedding. They’ll all think we’ve called it off.’

They all laughed, and Kirsty glanced over at their dad, aware that he might be feeling very vulnerable with all of his daughter’s emotions running amok. He was staring out of the window to the sea, while listening quietly to the music.

‘Dad,’ she said, touching his arm gently. ‘It’s time to go down the aisle. Are you ready?’

He looked at her, his face relaxed. ‘Oh there you are. Look at you. Look at all of you,’ he said, turning to look at the girls. ‘You are all beautiful, and I am so proud of you. Your mum would love this,’ he said. ‘She loved you all so much.’ He walked towards Emma. ‘Emma, my darling, you are stunning. You make a very pretty bride.’ He reached for his hankie and dabbed at his eyes. ‘Shall we?’ he said, offering his arm.

Kirsty leaned forward and kissed him gently on the forehead and stepped back, smiling at Emma. ‘We’ll see you at the front, sis,’ she said.

Amy reached forward to squeeze Emma's arm. 'Break a leg or something like that,' she said.

Kirsty rolled her eyes. 'That's what you say to actors when they're about to perform.'

'Och,' said Amy jovially. 'She knows what I mean don't you, Emma?'

Just then the gentle strains of 'Highland Cathedral' began, and James led the party through the door that led outside. Kirsty clocked the way he was smiling reassuringly at them all, his eyes lingering again on Amy. She noticed her sister's cheeks flush and gave her a conspiratorial wink. Amy tried to glare back at her but Kirsty just tutted and rolled her eyes. 'Come on,' she said to Emma. 'Let's not keep Max waiting any longer.'

Kirsty, Amy and Becky led the way across the terrace and down the few steps to the gazebo as the guests stood up, turned around and smiled, waiting for the bride's arrival.

With the clear blue sky and glistening sea, it was the perfect backdrop for an island wedding.

CHAPTER FORTY-ONE

Emma's eyes widened as she took in the thatched gazebo with the blue ribbons streaming gently around it in the breeze. It looked amazing and wasn't part of the plan either, but she didn't mind at all. She was beginning to like all of these surprises that her sister had arranged for her.

'Shall we?' said her dad, offering his arm.

'Yes, let's do this, Dad.'

Emma and her father followed the bridesmaids across the terrace and down the few steps onto the beach. She focused her eyes on Max, waiting at the top of the aisle with his best woman, Lauren. He turned to look at her, and she saw Lauren reach for his hand and squeeze it. Right then, as Emma's gaze locked with Max's she knew everything would be okay. This all felt right as though the planets had aligned for them and offered them this perfect day.

I must remember every single minute of this, she thought to herself, as a very gentle breeze blew in the late afternoon sun. She was annoyed that she had decided not to have it recorded, but then she spotted a friend of Becky's at the corner of the gazebo, filming it on her phone. She smiled, again grateful that Kirsty had the sense to ignore her calls for keeping everything super simple. Glancing around, she was heartened to see all her close friends. Edie, who was dressed in a lavender linen kaftan, gave her a huge wink and a little wave which made Emma grin and eradicated any last -minute nerves.

The family minister, the Rev Gary Donaldson, stood reassuringly at the altar — a simple wooden plinth — smiling kindly at her. Emma leaned slightly into her dad, feeling grateful he was there and silently thanking Mum for watching over her today. She could feel her presence and loved that her family had been so thoughtful to include the small things to remind her that although Mum had passed she was very much part of their lives today and their futures too. Dad gripped her hand one last time and then went to sit down next to Amy, Kirsty and Becky in the front row.

The service was short and simple, and they both said their vows without hesitation. When Max slid the ring onto her finger he gazed at her lovingly. 'I love you so much,' he whispered. 'You look beautiful.'

When Gary pronounced them man and wife, there was a cheer from the guests and some tears of happiness too. Emma glanced at Kirsty who was furiously dabbing at her eyes. Then she turned back to look at Max who leaned forward to kiss her.

James and his colleagues were waiting for the bridal party to arrive on the terrace where they were served flutes of champagne and delicious canapés. Emma felt so happy and relaxed, and she and Max mingled with their guests, thanking them for making the journey over.

'Oh, darling, Emma,' cried Edie. 'What a wonderful ceremony. It was so romantic. Congratulations to both of you.'

'Thanks, Edie,' she said, hugging her tightly. 'Thank you for being part of our special day.'

'I wouldn't have missed it for the world,' she said, her eyes twinkling.

Later, with the faint smell of the BBQ lingering in the air and the stars beginning to shimmer in the sky, it was time for the speeches. Emma wondered whether her dad would still want to make his father-of-the-bride speech. He had been on great form all afternoon, relaxed and mingling with the other guests and cracking jokes.

'Of course,' he said instantly, when she asked. 'Just tell me when.'

Kirsty walked towards them and gave Emma a nod to check they were ready. The staff then made sure everyone had a glass of fizz as Kirsty tapped a fork against a glass to get everyone's attention.

'Thanks everyone for coming today,' she began, smiling. 'I'm sure you will all agree it's been an incredible day. Now many of you will know that Emma and Max wanted to keep everything as simple as possible which I think we have just about managed to do. At one point they were even debating having speeches . . .' Kirsty rolled her eyes dramatically. 'However, we managed to persuade them to keep them short and sweet.' There was a ripple of laughter from the guests. 'Dad, I think you'd like to say a few words first of all?'

Dad nodded and walked towards Kirsty. 'Thank you, dear.' He tapped his glasses and then pulled out his notes, carefully unfolding them. 'Hello, everyone. As Kirsty said, I would also like to thank you all very much for coming. It means a lot to Emma and Max and to Kirsty, Amy and me too. As many of you know I am a man of few words and so I will try and stay true to form.' He smiled. 'Emma and Max, congratulations on your wedding today. I wish you every happiness for your future together. I know your mum would have loved to have been here today . . .'

Emma held her breath, feeling Max wrap his arm around her.

'And when I wrote this, with some help from Tom and Becky, I did wonder what she might say about you. You were always such a determined wee girl, Emma, stubborn but kind and gentle too.'

'No change there then,' called a guest.

Dad chuckled. 'Indeed.'

'I am so proud of the woman you have become, and I am proud to be your dad. You are very special to us all,

Emma, as are you, Max. Take care of my girl and be happy together. Life is so short, so hold each other close.' He paused to compose himself. 'Now if you will all join me in a toast, I would like us all to congratulate the bride and groom.' He held his glass high in the air and grinned. 'To the bride and groom,' he said again, and the words were echoed around the room as the guests clinked glasses together.

'Thanks, Dad,' said Emma, kissing him on the cheek, deeply moved by his words. 'That was wonderful. Thank you.' Although Emma hadn't been planning to make a speech, she made her mind up in that instant that she should also say a few words before Max made his speech. She squeezed his hand and stood up and thanked all the guests for being part of their special day. Emma was still blown away by the romantic setting and all that James and his colleagues had done to make it extra wonderful. She thanked her dad and her sisters and Max and his family. Most of all, she wanted to pay tribute to her mum who she wished was with them all. She stopped to catch her breath. 'But I truly believe she is and has been watching over us all.

'So, I would like to raise a glass to Mum, who made me the woman I am today. That is something I will be forever grateful for, and I hope her spirit always lives on in me.' Max handed her a glass of champagne. 'To Mum,' she said softly, her voice hoarse with emotion. 'Thanks for being you.'

CHAPTER FORTY-TWO

'Amy,' said James, gently tapping her on the shoulder. 'Have you got a moment?'

'Sure,' she said on a shrug, excusing herself from the guests she had been speaking to at the outside bar.

'I just want to check that everything has been okay, today?'

Amy had a feeling his question was loaded, and he wasn't referring to just the wedding. 'It's all been great thanks. I mean, what could be a more romantic setting?' She took a deep inhale of the salty sea air. 'The weather couldn't have been better, could it? It felt like we were in the Caribbean.'

He nodded, looking at her intently. 'Good, I'm glad to hear you've been happy with it. Are you sure everything is okay?'

'And the food . . .' Amy began, but James didn't let her finish.

'I'm not talking about the food, Amy . . .'

She tried to hide her frown, but it was too late.

'Have I done something wrong?' he asked.

She shook her head. 'No, why would you think that?'

He eyed her carefully. 'It's just that you have been a bit off and I wondered if there was a problem . . . I had such a great night out with you at the pub. I'm sorry if I overstepped the mark in any way?'

Amy rolled her eyes. 'I just think you might have told me.'

'Told you what?' he asked puzzled.

'Well, I thought, or maybe I imagined that we were getting on well too. I mean . . . it kind of felt like old times when we were together . . .'

'You're right,' said James. 'I agree.' He looked upset as though she had said something to make him doubt himself.

Amy looked around at the fairy lights which had started twinkling now the sun had set.

'What went wrong, then?'

'Look,' said Amy, folding her arms across her chest. 'I saw you . . . with Amanda.' There, she had said it. She wasn't one for mind games.

'What do you mean?'

Amy flicked her hair over her shoulders. Was he being intentionally stupid? 'Earlier today. I came here to do last minute checks for the wedding and Rachel said you were dealing with something and was very vague about whether or not you would be back.' She searched his face, looking for any signs of guilt or remorse.

But James grimaced. 'I had to nip out. Of course, I was coming back. Today was always really important to me and there was no way I would have missed it.'

Amy waved her hands dismissively. 'That doesn't matter. It's not about that, it's about the fact that you're with someone else.' She looked at him questioningly and waited for him to reply. But instead, he gave a small, sad chuckle. 'Okay, well that wasn't exactly the reaction that I had hoped for,' she said tensely.

'Oh, Amy, I am genuinely so sorry that you thought that when you saw us.'

Amy's gaze drifted over to Kirsty, standing a few metres away, and who looked at her with a raised eyebrow. She returned her attention to James. 'But I saw you walk her to her car and it looked like quite a hug.'

James reached for her hand. 'I can understand why you would get the wrong idea.' He looked around, seemingly back in professional mode as he scanned the area before returning his focus to her. Grasping her hand, he said, 'I was comforting her. She's had a really hard time of things these past few months.'

'How so?' said Amy, unsure of what he was getting at.

'Her wife was diagnosed with breast cancer.' James kept his voice low. 'She's been trying to stay strong for her but this morning it all got too much, and she just needed some friendly support.'

'Oh,' said Amy quietly, suddenly feeling like the most horrible person in the world. 'I am so sorry to hear that . . . and for jumping to conclusions.'

'I just needed to remind her that I am there for her when she needs a friend.'

Amy gazed at his kind face and those eyes that had the ability to capture her. Could he be any more thoughtful? And how awful of her to immediately think the worst. 'I'm sorry.' She shook her head. 'That was stupid of me and extremely insensitive. I should know better than to make assumptions.'

'Amy, please stop apologizing. Really, it's fine.' He put a hand on her arm. 'Please, it's fine,' he reassured her.

'Hey,' said Kirsty, appearing at Amy's side. 'I am sorry to interrupt but we have the first dance in a minute . . .'

'I thought Emma didn't want one,' said Amy.

'She didn't, but then she also didn't want a piper, or a gazebo and she seems happy so far.' Kirsty smiled and pointed over at Emma who looked radiant as she stood next to Max.

'No worries,' James said. 'I'll get the music sorted if you go and get the bride and groom primed and ready to take the floor.' He leaned over to Amy and whispered in her ear, 'Let's pick this conversation up later?' Then he kissed her gently on the cheek and walked away towards his colleagues.

'What was that all about?' said Kirsty, fanning her cheeks. 'Honestly, the chemistry between you two is outrageous.'

Amy tried to brush off Kirsty's comments, but she looked over at James who had glanced back at her, and her cheeks began to flush.

'You should definitely ask him to dance with you later,' said Kirsty, twirling the stem of her wine glass. 'Nothing like a wee holiday romance to help you move on from Ross . . .'

Amy wasn't quite sure how to respond to her sister. 'What music did you choose for the first dance?' she said, changing the subject.

'"You are the Sunshine of My Life",' she said drily. 'A song that would also suit you and James perfectly. Who would have thought this island was such a hotbed for love . . .'

CHAPTER FORTY-THREE

It was the morning after the wedding and Kirsty and Amy were sitting on the bench underneath the sycamore tree, slightly bleary-eyed, with their mugs of coffee in hand.

'You never tire of this view, do you?' said Amy.

'Nope, never. It doesn't matter what the weather is like. This is constant yet always changing too.' Kirsty took a sip from her mug, reflecting on what a lovely day it had been. 'It was such a spectacular day, wasn't it?'

'Absolutely. I can't quite believe it's over. It flew so quickly, didn't it? Part of me wishes we could do it all again. That was a great idea of Becky's to get her friend to film it. I know Emma was thrilled about that.'

'Yes, it was a genius move on Becky's part. It might not be the best wedding film in the world but at least it captured special moments through the day, and it was so nice that she went around asking people to share a personal message for the bride and groom. Anyway,' she said, 'did you enjoy it?'

'I did,' said Amy. 'Especially the dancing.'

'What's happening next then?' said Kirsty in a conspiratorial tone.

'What do you mean?'

'With James . . . ?'

Amy smiled. 'I don't know but I *did* invite him to come to lunch today.'

'I'm glad to hear it. I mean Amy, he couldn't take his eyes off you last night.' She watched her sister's eyes widen in excitement.

'Really? You noticed?'

Kirsty nodded. 'Yes, really. Mind you, I would say that you were just as bad.'

Amy giggled.

Emma and Max weren't due to leave for their mini honeymoon until later that day and Kirsty and Steve were hosting a simple lunch for any of the guests who wanted to come up to Meadowbank.

'And . . . come on — what are *your* plans?' She watched as Amy's brows knitted together in a frown. 'How does he fit with Canada?'

'I'm not entirely sure. I mean . . . I've been thinking about coming back for a while now. I didn't want to tell you until I was sure . . . but I think I'd like to stay here,' she looked up at Kirsty.

'In Arran?' said Kirsty in disbelief. 'You mean you don't want to go back to Vancouver?' She squealed in excitement as she reached to hug her.

'I love it there but it's not home,' she said shyly. 'And now I've been back here and seen you all and what Dad is going through . . . It doesn't feel like returning to Canada is the right thing to do.' She clasped her hands together and chewed her bottom lip.

Kirsty felt a flutter of excitement at the thought of having her sister back on a permanent basis. Then she felt cold when she realized that Amy might not feel the same once Kirsty had shared the secret, she had been carrying for so long.

She took a deep breath. 'Look, Amy, it would be fabulous to have you back here for good. But you need to think this all through very carefully before you make any decisions.'

Amy looked at her in confusion. 'I thought you'd be pleased that I wanted to stay on.'

'Of course, I am,' said Kirsty, 'But I am just urging you to think it through properly and remember it's not always like this with the blue skies and sun and the . . .' She stopped mid-sentence. 'Is James influencing this decision? I mean how would you feel if *he* wasn't on the scene?'

Amy looked annoyed and Kirsty couldn't blame her. 'What's with all the questions, Kirsty? You should know me well enough to know that I wouldn't make a rash decision like this based on a bloke. This has been something I've been mulling over for a while. That's why I asked Josh to take over my classes indefinitely, so I wasn't under any pressure to decide.

'It's since being back and seeing how much pressure you're under with Dad that has made me decide. That and seeing how much I've missed out on family stuff over the past few years. Who knows what is around the corner, Kirsty. I don't want to be away should something happen to Dad. It was hard enough to fly back and try and pick up the pieces after Mum died.'

Kirsty nodded, understanding where her sister was coming from.

But should she tell her now or should she wait until Emma returned from her days away? She suspected she would need to tell Amy sooner rather than later in case it should colour her decision to stay or not. She had a responsibility to be up front and honest with Amy. Finding the right time though when there were so many people around was going to be tricky.

'Promise me one thing,' she said, pleadingly.

'What is that?' said Amy.

'Keep this all to yourself for a few more days until you have thought carefully about it. I just want to make sure you're not being influenced by anyone or anything.'

'Okay,' she said warily. 'Is there something you're not telling me, Kirsty? You're acting strangely.'

'Let's have a proper chat when all the wedding stuff is out the way. Just think about what I said. Make sure you are doing this for all the right reasons. I want to make sure you are being true to yourself and that you're happy. You deserve to be.' She looped her arm around Amy's shoulder and pulled her close, hoping that the closeness they had would never change regardless of what happened later.

CHAPTER FORTY-FOUR

Emma opened her eyes and smiled, then she rolled onto her side and saw Max fast asleep. She traced her finger over the contours of his face, admiring every inch of him. He opened his eyes and grasped her hand, pulling it to his mouth and kissing her fingers one by one.

'Good morning, my beautiful wife,' he said with a wolfish grin. 'What a sight to wake up to.'

'You're not too bad yourself,' she said, 'considering you hardly slept.'

'I would have to argue that my time was very well spent, I think.' His dark eyes danced in amusement.

'It was,' she said, moving towards him to kiss him again . . . just as his mobile started to ring. He ignored the buzz to begin with until it started again.

Groaning, he reached for it. 'I'd better take this,' he said when he saw the number. 'Hello. Yes, this is Max.'

Emma rolled over, used to work interruptions like these and not in the least bit bothered by it. She understood completely as she had been rung plenty of times on days off and on holidays too. Standing up, she pulled on her silk dressing gown which Kirsty and Amy had thoughtfully left for her in the room last night along with matching pyjamas. Walking over to the window, she opened the blinds and let the morning sunshine flood the room.

Glancing back, Max had the phone clamped to one ear and his other hand raked through his dark hair, a sign he was stressed. What happened if he was needed back in Aberdeen? Had there been some terrible news that he was going to have to deal with? There was no point in even trying to guess what might be wrong. She gestured that she was going to have a shower, walked into the bathroom and closed the door behind her.

Standing under the warm water, she thought about the rollercoaster of emotions she had been through in the past few weeks and her worries that she wouldn't actually have a wedding day. She wished she had confided in Max earlier and told him what she had been going through. She still felt so much relief she felt knowing they were being honest with each other, and he loved her regardless of her fertility status.

Shuddering, she thought of the texts Ruth had been sending her over the past twenty-four hours. There had been some lovely pictures of her and Rex but accompanying them had been an undercurrent of *woe is me* which was so Ruth. Rex was feeding all the time, Ruth was shattered and said Emma could have no idea how tired she was as it was something she had never experienced before. Emma had given a wry smile. Ruth wasn't exactly selling motherhood to her.

As she rinsed the shampoo from her hair, there was a knock at the door. Max stuck his head around the door.

'Are you okay, love?' she said, turning off the water.

His face fell and he looked regretful. 'I don't know how to tell you this.'

'You've got to go to Aberdeen,' she said matter-of-factly.

'Just for the night. It's urgent otherwise I wouldn't even entertain it. But I promise I'll be back tomorrow for our couple of days away,' he said.

'Do you want me to come with you?' said Emma.

He hesitated, evidently tempted to say yes, but instead shook his head. 'Thank you, but you have this time with your sisters while you can.'

'I've had this week with them. It will be fine — honestly, I can come with you.'

'I would love that but seriously, when will you get a chance like this again with the girls, Emma? Amy could be leaving soon and it's not often that you get to see each other. And anyway, if you did come you would be stuck in the hotel room just waiting for me.'

She sighed. 'Sure, okay, I suppose you're right.' Emma did a double take as he slipped his T-shirt over his head and pulled off his boxer shorts. 'I do need to have a shower first though, so stay where you are. That is unless you have somewhere better to be?' he teased.

His smile made her heart do a little flip. Emma pretended to think about it before flicking the water on again and pulling the screen back so he could join her.

CHAPTER FORTY-FIVE

Amy knew Kirsty was right and that her advice was well-intentioned, but she couldn't help feeling annoyed as she walked down towards town to collect Dad for the lunch.

Was she making a rash decision? Based on very little and a bit of a brief fling, if it even was that, with James? Nothing had even happened with him. Yet. She had a feeling that it was just a matter of time. Especially after last night and the dance they had together. He had pulled her close and she daren't look up at him as she knew that if she did, she would want to kiss him. When she left the reception, he had dropped a playful kiss on her cheek. Every nerve tingled from his touch, and she had lain awake most of last night thinking about him. A voice calling from behind jolted her out of her daydream.

'Hey, Amy, wait up.'

She turned round to see Steve jogging towards her. 'I didn't realize you were heading this way, or I would have waited.'

'I needed to stretch my legs and we're out of milk, so Kirsty sent me. I think she maybe wanted to get me out the way,' he said smiling. 'She's a *bit* tetchy. I think she's tired from the wedding.'

They walked together in companionable silence for a few minutes, both enjoying the late morning sunshine.

'I've been a bit worried about her,' Amy said with a sigh. 'I get the feeling there's something on her mind . . .' When Steve didn't respond, she continued talking. 'It's been a busy time for you both with the wedding, hasn't it? And Dad? And it will soon be business as usual! When do the next guests arrive?'

'The day after tomorrow,' Steve said, scratching his chin thoughtfully.

'Here's an idea. I think Kirsty could really do with a break and a couple of days away from everything. She always has a lot to juggle, and she seems tired. It could do her no end of good?'

Steve hesitated, slightly distracted by his thoughts. 'She does need a rest. I know she has a lot on her mind . . . but I don't know. Leaving Meadowbank might stress her out. You know what she's like about the guests.'

Amy waved her hands dismissively. 'Just tell me what needs doing. I can easily hold the fort for a few days and I'm sure Becky and Tom can lend a hand. What could possibly go wrong?'

Steve chuckled. 'Oh Amy, don't even ask that. Thanks for the offer. Let me think about it and make a plan, okay. In the meantime, don't say anything to Kirsty as she'll fly into a panic and make excuses as to why it's not a good idea.'

'True. Okay, the offer is there if you would like it. I mean, perhaps James might help too if I asked him. Seeing as he is Mr. Hospitality . . .' she added hastily.

Steve gave her a sideways look. 'Mmm and so how are you feeling about James? Seems like you're getting along fairly well?'

She paused before answering, gathering her thoughts. Even hearing his name being said made her pulse quicken. 'It feels like I've met a long-lost friend . . . like we have never been apart, and I feel the same way I did for him all those years ago which seems weird. Except it's more than that. It feels right.'

Saying those words out loud made it all seem real. With the heady feelings she had of excitement and anticipation, it was as though she was a teenager again. 'However, James aside . . . I did say to Kirsty I was thinking of staying on. Not for him but to give a hand and also help support Dad. He was great yesterday but that doesn't necessarily mean he'll all of a sudden be back to his "normal" self . . .'

Steve looked at her quizzically. 'Is this something you've been considering for a while?'

'Yes,' she said, 'even before I came back. Things didn't feel right anymore, and I started feeling a bit restless again. A lot of that was to do with Mum dying. It just didn't feel the same when I went back after the funeral, and I tried to get on with things and build a life . . . but . . .' Her voice trailed off. A cool breeze had sprung up which she was grateful for as her cheeks were flushed in the heat.

'It's a lot to think about and a big decision, Amy. One that only you can make. We would love to have you here, but you need to do what's right for you.'

Amy felt her shoulders sag in relief. Steve was right and she appreciated his supportive words. She was glad he wasn't trying to tell her to do one thing or the other. However, her gut instinct told her that staying on Arran was the right thing to do, regardless of James being there.

* * *

Amy arrived at her dad's cottage, having parted ways with Steve who carried on towards the shop. She wondered when the best time would be to tell Dad she wanted to stay on in Arran and ask if she could lodge in his spare bedroom for a while. She knocked at the door and waited for him to answer but there was no reply. That was strange; he was usually up and about early in the morning, and it must now be near midday.

Rapping the door again, she noticed that the curtains around the side were still drawn. Perhaps he'd forgotten to open them? He was usually so meticulous about letting the daylight flood into the house . . .

Her heart started to thump in panic. What if he'd fallen and couldn't get up? Maybe something had happened to him, and he'd been lying on the floor in agony all night? That was the sort of thing that happened to pensioners all the time. She tried to remember who took him home last night and couldn't. Surely, they didn't leave him to make his own way back from the wedding? Typically, she hadn't brought the spare key with her, even though Kirsty had reminded her to do so; she'd left it on the kitchen worktop. Why was she so useless?

She dropped to her knees and pushed the decorative piece of driftwood out of the way so she could check under the doormat in case another key was there. It wasn't. *Think Amy, think*. She pulled her phone from her pocket and dialled Kirsty's number.

'Kirsty, you need to come now. It's Dad, he's not answering the door. I think something is wrong.'

CHAPTER FORTY-SIX

Kirsty dropped what she was doing, jumped in the car and arrived at their dad's within a few minutes of Amy's frantic phone call.

'Hurry!' Amy cried. 'I'm so sorry. I can't believe I forgot the key.'

'Don't worry,' said Kirsty, feeling quite the opposite. 'I'm here now and I'm sure everything is fine.'

Fortunately, when she opened the door with the spare key and called, 'Hello,' their dad came stumbling through to the hallway, bleary-eyed.

'Good morning, you two,' he said, scratching his head. 'Did I miss something? Have I slept in? Where is Emma?'

Kirsty pulled a face. He was clearly exhausted. Usually, he would be energetic and cheerful in the morning. The wedding must have taken more out of him than they could have anticipated. 'Emma's at Meadowbank with Max,' she said. 'We're going to have a small lunch for them before the guests start to go.'

His face drained of colour. 'I think I'll stay here, girls, if that's okay. I'm tired. *Really* tired.'

'Do you remember getting home last night, Dad?' Kirsty gently asked, feeling a flicker of guilt that she should have been the one who brought him back.

He stifled a yawn. 'Tom brought me in and got me settled. I think?'

She glanced at Amy who looked wary. 'That's right, Dad. He and Becky walked back with you. Everyone was talking about what a great speech you did.'

He smiled sadly. 'Oh, that is nice, dear.' As he stood there in his pyjamas, he looked a bit forlorn and lost.

'How about we get you back into bed for a rest, Dad? And Amy will go and make you some tea and toast.'

Amy gave her a thumbs up sign and turned to go into the kitchen.

Once Dad was settled, Kirsty came into the kitchen to find Amy doing the dishes. 'I tidied up just the other day,' she said.

'He's maybe just not done any for a couple of days after being out of his usual routine,' said Amy.

Kirsty rolled her shoulders back, trying to ease the growing tension that she could feel. 'That's a good point. I don't think we should make him come to the lunch — what do you think? He's clearly exhausted.'

Amy nodded in agreement. 'Let me take this cup of tea through and we can see what he says.'

Once Dad was settled and happy to have a quiet day at home, the girls left him, promising to return later with some leftovers from lunch.

'This,' said Amy, 'is why I need to stay. I could live with Dad and keep an eye on him which would take the pressure off you.'

Kirsty sighed. She was beginning to think that Amy was making a lot of sense. He was such a worry.

'I could keep an eye on him and then look at doing some yoga classes in the community hall . . .'

Kirsty nodded but was quiet on the way home. Amy had really been thinking about this, it was clear to see. When she pulled into the driveway, she turned to face Amy. 'Let's chat properly after the lunch,' she said.

The lunch guests started to drift off just after three, some keen to explore the island and others needed to catch the departing ferry back to Ardrossan. Emma had already told her sisters that Max would be going to Aberdeen and was leaving for the night. Kirsty was relieved that she didn't seem upset. And it would give her the opportunity to talk to both the girls at once.

Kirsty noticed James had barely left Amy's side and she wondered how she could politely ask him to give them some space, so she could talk to Amy. Steve offered to take some food down to their dad and gave her a knowing look. 'I'll have a quick word with James and get him to make a graceful exit now too. I'm assuming you want to take the chance to speak to Emma and Amy?'

'Thanks, love.'

He kissed her on the forehead. 'Just be honest and tell them, my love.'

She was so glad she had told him when she had done and he was right. There was no point in putting things off any longer. It was time to tell her sisters the truth.

CHAPTER FORTY-SEVEN

Kirsty knew she wore a look of intense concentration on her face as she led her sisters to the bottom of the garden, away from the house. She had wondered about taking them for a walk along the beach but decided it was too risky. There was too much likelihood of bumping into someone they knew and losing the chance to have a proper chat. She spread a blanket out on the grass and motioned to them to sit down beside her.

'This is a bit ominous,' said Emma cautiously, lowering herself to the ground.

Amy sat gracefully with her legs crossed and back tall, fiddling with her plait which hung over her shoulder. 'What's the matter?' she said, perhaps worried by the look on Kirsty's face. 'I hope this isn't an intervention.' She looked suspiciously at Kirsty and then at Emma who looked none the wiser as to why Kirsty had gathered them together at this moment. 'Is it?'

Kirsty exhaled. 'Look, there really is no way to break this to you gently and I don't know if there ever will be a good time for what I'm about to say. Let me just say that you will be shocked.'

'Just tell us,' said Emma. 'I have heard most things so I am probably quite shockproof.'

Kirsty looked at their faces, looking slightly nervous and waiting for her to talk. She just hoped they wouldn't think of her differently or distance themselves from her once they found out.

'Where should I even start . . .' She took a gulp from her water bottle.

Emma smiled reassuringly. 'Just start at the beginning.'

'Okay,' she said, taking a deep breath. 'A few months ago, I was up in the attic looking for some photos. Dad was getting upset as he couldn't find their wedding picture and Steve suggested I take a look in the loft in case it had been left there when they moved out of Meadowbank.' Her cheeks flushed as she remembered. 'There are a few bits and pieces up there.'

'And . . . ?' said Amy, trying not to be impatient.

Emma threw her a look.

'And I discovered . . . I discovered that I am not actually your sister. I'm adopted.'

There was stunned silence as the girls stared at her in shock. Amy clapped a hand to her mouth and Emma looked at her, totally nonplussed. Kirsty knew it was important to give them a chance to process what she had just said so she didn't speak for a moment.

Amy finally broke the silence. 'Oh, Kirsty. But how? What do you mean? I don't understand. How can you be adopted?'

Kirsty tried to smile kindly at her in a bid to lessen the tension, but instead grimaced. 'I know, believe you me, I didn't understand any of it either. I found out by complete accident . . .' Her voice broke as she tried her best again at a wobbly smile.

Emma reached over to touch her hand. 'Tell us everything. Just take your time.'

Kirsty told them about that afternoon when she discovered the documents in the box and her shock at seeing the baby photo and then finding the certificate of adoption.

Amy blinked and shook her head in dismay. 'I don't understand. Why did Mum and Dad never say anything? Why did they never tell you? Or us?'

Kirsty shrugged. 'I thought about that for a long time, Amy.' She looked up as she saw a couple of tourists who had clearly taken a wrong turn and were now heading down the lawn towards them. 'Terrific,' she said sarcastically. 'Just what we need.'

Amy jumped to her feet. 'They'll probably be after coffee and might not understand that the closed sign means that we are actually not serving . . . leave it with me.' She ran to meet them, pointed at the sign on the van and then down to the bay and shrugged apologetically. Then she walked back to the girls, shaking her head. 'You were saying?'

Normally Kirsty would have been worried about turning away prospective customers but today she didn't care at all. 'Well, I thought about nothing else for ages . . .'

'Did you tell Steve?' asked Emma curiously.

'No, not to begin with and then he found me crying and I had to tell him. But he has been sworn to secrecy. I'm sorry,' she said sorrowfully. 'I felt I owed it to you both to tell you first, but it was a struggle to carry alone and then with the wedding . . . well I thought it was better to wait until it was all out of the way.'

'So, you didn't say anything to Dad?' said Amy.

'No, I didn't know where to start. He was so upset about Mum and now with his memory starting to affect him, I didn't think it was the right thing to do. I thought I'd speak to you both first.'

'I'm glad you've told us,' said Emma with a sympathetic smile. 'I just wish we'd known sooner, and could have shared the burden.'

'I didn't want to do that though,' said Kirsty, 'especially with your wedding. I feel bad for telling you today.'

After a long pause, Emma said, 'Well maybe Max being called away was fate stepping in, so that you could tell us today.'

'What about your birth parents?' said Amy.

Kirsty was so relieved that she hadn't said *real* parents because to her that was who Mum and Dad were and that would never change. 'Well, this is where things kind of get weird . . .'

'What do you mean?' said Emma.

'Once I worked out who my birth parents were, things fell into place and it made sense.' She looked away for a moment, thinking about the moment she saw the names on the birth certificate.

'Who? Who were they?' Amy was evidently getting impatient again and had begun to fidget with the corner of the blanket.

Emma put a warning hand on her shoulder.

Kirsty's voice softened as she looked at Emma and Amy. 'Sarah and Michael Thompson.'

Emma frowned. 'But . . . I know those names.'

'That's Mum's sister and husband,' said Amy, incredulous.

'Yes,' said Emma sadly. 'They died before we were born.'

'Well, before *you* were born . . .' said Kirsty.

'All we were ever told was that they were killed in a car crash and Mum was devastated by it . . .' Emma's voice trailed away.

'And she didn't want to talk about it as she found it too painful,' said Amy, finishing her sentence.

'It turns out that I was only a couple of months old when they died so was an orphan and Mum and Dad obviously decided to adopt me.'

'Oh, Kirsty, how have you managed to carry this alone for so long?' said Emma.

Kirsty closed her eyes, trying to calm herself from the emotions threatening to overwhelm her again. She felt as though she was still in that attic, crouched in confusion over the box. 'I needed time to process it all. There was a lot to get my head around.'

'It sounds like they must have adopted you and then moved to Arran to avoid the questions?'

Kirsty nodded. 'Yes, I agree and I can understand. It was probably easier that way. Mum always said they came here for a fresh start after her sister died and to raise a family. They wanted a quiet life.'

'Wow,' said Amy, her throat sounding tight with tears. 'I guess the next question is, do we talk to Dad?'

Kirsty looked at Emma who shook her head at what Amy was suggesting. 'I don't think that's a good idea. Do you? It may just upset and confuse him even more,' said Emma.

'I think you're right,' said Amy, nodding her head in agreement.

'That's a first,' said Emma drily.

Amy continued, her brows furrowing together as she spoke. 'I mean, it's not like it's going to change anything, is it? I mean, I suppose technically we are cousins. But you're our sister, Kirsty and you always have been. That will never change.'

Emma handed her a tissue. 'Oh, Kirsty, we will always love you regardless of this. Even if you told us that Amy and I were also adopted that wouldn't matter one wee bit. We are sisters and always will be.'

Kirsty wiped away tears as she listened to her sisters. She was so grateful that they felt like that. Yet she was also so sad that she had never got to know anything about her birth parents other than the very rare mentions of her deceased aunt and uncle that her mum would sometimes make. This was something that she would never be able to ask her mum now.

The girls huddled together, arms around each other and holding each other tightly.

Kirsty didn't think there had ever been favouritism between the girls as they grew up. She was the oldest which perhaps meant they hadn't all been treated the same because of the age difference. Kirsty had just turned eight when Emma was born and then nine when Amy came along. However, she never felt that she'd been cast aside or loved less because she wasn't her parents' actual child. She had always felt truly loved by them. She just wished they had told her and couldn't work out why they had kept it a secret. When she voiced this to the girls, Emma frowned.

'Perhaps you'll never know,' said Emma. 'Especially if Dad can't or won't tell us. Sometimes things are better left alone.'

'So many things have started to slot into place since I discovered this, you know and I'm sorry I couldn't tell you. It's just like it's all been falling into place very slowly. When I was pregnant with the twins, Mum urged me to take it easy and phoned me in London most days to remind me I was growing not just one but two babies,' said Kirsty. 'Later, when we moved back with the babies, Mum told me that she had miscarried twins before I came along.' And Kirsty could remember her dad being anxious and worried when Mum was pregnant with Emma and then Amy. She had vague memories of her mum being in bed a lot and suffering from terrible morning sickness.

Emma's gaze drifted over to Kirsty. 'That would make sense, wouldn't it? Especially with my fertility *situation*. If Mum had problems conceiving then perhaps she passed that gene to me. It at least sheds a bit of light on things,' she said, sounding a bit more reassured.

Kirsty nodded gratefully at how understanding and kind her sisters were being.

'You did the right thing by telling us this, Kirsty, and I'm glad you did,' said Emma.

Amy nodded. 'The main thing you need to know is that this doesn't change a thing between us. Not a thing.'

CHAPTER FORTY-EIGHT

It was the quietest that Meadowbank Cottage had been for a long time. All the wedding guests had left the island and Max had returned to scoop up his new wife and take her away for a couple of days. Tom and Becky were busy trying to cram in as many shifts at the hotel pool as they could. However, they had promised Amy that they would help out with the guesthouse as much as they could when she took charge.

Amy had encouraged Steve to take Kirsty to Glasgow for a couple of days. He had booked her into a spa hotel and intended on making sure she rested and relaxed. They agreed that she was shattered and had done an amazing job of holding everything together especially given the secret she'd harboured for so long. Kirsty was nervous about leaving Amy in charge. But she had also managed to enlist the help of James which reassured Kirsty a little.

Amy had told Emma about her plans to stay on and she was thrilled at her decision. 'You just have to do what is right for you. If you know, you know,' Emma teased.

Amy had tried her best to ignore her as the last thing she wanted was for her sisters to think she was planning her future around a man with whom she was *not* in a relationship. She hadn't even told him about her plans, other than to casually say that she would be extending her stay to help Kirsty out.

'Now promise me you won't set the place on fire,' said Kirsty for the umpteenth time, as they were getting ready to leave. Steve had been waiting patiently in the car but started to honk the horn.

'You'll miss the ferry if you don't hurry up,' said Amy crossly. She grabbed a tea towel and flicked it at Kirsty in a bid to shoo her out the door. 'Don't worry. I have your spreadsheet and various bits of paper with instructions. How hard can it be?' she said innocently.

Kirsty's face drained of colour. 'I will pretend that I didn't hear that. I'm out of here before I change my mind.'

'Don't worry, sis. And I'll look in on Dad a little later.'

The girls had agreed to get him checked out at the doctor's surgery as soon as possible and an appointment had been booked for next week.

'And absolutely no hanky-panky in front of the guests,' yelled Kirsty as she ran out the door and straight into James who had just arrived. Flustered and flushed, she jumped into the car. 'Go, go, go, Steve. I can't believe I just said that. Let's get going.'

James looked around puzzled. 'Was it something that I said?' he quipped. His eyes twinkled in amusement.

Amy hoped that he hadn't heard Kirsty's comment but, given his reaction, had a feeling that he had.

'Okay, so what needs to be done?'

'Good question,' she said, consulting her list. 'The guests are out at the moment and due back in a couple of hours. None of them are having dinner, so we don't need to worry about that.' She paused and chuckled. 'Thank goodness. Cooking isn't really my forte, but don't tell my sister . . . The bedrooms are all clean and tidy. I just need to check the coffee van and then pop down and see Dad.'

'It sounds like you don't need me. You have it all under control?'

She turned to look at him and cocked her head to the side. 'That's okay, you can stick around if you want to. I'm sure I can find you *something* to do.' How she wanted to lean over and kiss him. But she had to resist. There was plenty of time. Just then her phone pinged. It was a message from Josh. She beamed. 'Give me one sec,' she said, nodding at her phone.

'Of course,' he said, raising an eyebrow quizzically. 'Kirsty checking on you already?'

'Nope. It's Josh.'

'Josh? That's your friend from Vancouver?'

She nodded. '*How are you? Missing you and want to know when and if you are coming back,*' she said, reading his message aloud.

'What are you going to say?'

'Mmm . . . I will keep you posted,' she said, winking. 'Now, come on, I have things to do and people to see. Are you helping or not?'

James laughed and grabbed her hand, pulling her to him for a hug. 'You are very demanding, Amy.'

'I know. But you wouldn't have me any other way, would you?' she said, loving the feeling of being close to him. 'Now, come on.' She pulled herself away which was extremely challenging especially when he smelt so good. 'Let's go.'

James smiled fondly at her and she thanked her lucky stars they had both ended up back on the island together at the same time. She had a good feeling about this and there was no rush. They had all the time in the world . . . she hoped. Her mind was made up. This was where she wanted to be.. They had all the time in the world . . . he hoped. Unless she decided to go back to Canada. He would need to try his best to persuade her to stay.

CHAPTER FORTY-NINE

A few weeks later, Kirsty and Amy were in the doctor's waiting room with their dad when the local busybody, Anna, made a beeline for them. Groaning inwardly, Kirsty forced a smile. 'Hello Anna, how are you?'

'Fine thanks, dear, and you?' She ploughed on before Kirsty had a chance to reply. 'Are you not well? Or is it your dad? Hello, Alex,' she said as an afterthought.

Dad gave her a small smile.

'We are just fine, thanks, Anna. How about you? What are you here for?'

'My indigestion has been *awful*.'

Kirsty wanted to suggest that she cut back on the amount of wine she drank and tried to exercise more but of course, didn't.

'It's just causing me havoc. You have no idea.' She narrowed her beady eyes and lowered her voice. 'I have been a bit worried about him if I'm honest,' she said, tipping her head towards Dad. 'I already said this to your sister.' She spoke as though Amy was invisible. 'I mean, he's getting a bit forgetful, isn't he?'

Kirsty shook her head. 'My dad isn't deaf, Anna. He can hear everything that you're saying.'

Dad stared straight ahead, ignoring the conversation.

'I mean we all forget things don't we, even me, but you must be worried. Especially with all those tee-off times he's been forgetting. He'll soon talk himself out the golf circle.'

Kirsty bristled, a huge part of her wanted to tell Anna to shut up and mind her own business. But for the sake of her dad, she bit her tongue extremely hard.

'I mean if I didn't know him and about the forgetting stuff I wouldn't know.'

Kirsty exhaled through her mouth. 'What do you mean?' she said, through gritted teeth.

'Well, your dad doesn't look like he has dementia, dear.' She scratched her chin which had a few hairs sprouting from it.

'What do you mean?' Kirsty frowned.

'What's that, dear?'

'What do you mean when you say that he doesn't look like he has dementia? What on earth is that supposed to mean?' She felt her voice starting to rise and Amy placed a warning hand on her arm.

But it was Dad who spoke up. 'I'm fine thanks, Anna. Thanks for your concern. And I am here. I can hear every word you are saying. I'm not quite ready for the loony bin yet thanks very much.'

'Oh, I didn't mean to cause offence,' said Anna, her cheeks dotted with red spots. 'I was just meaning you look very well and that you don't look like a dementia sufferer.'

Fortunately, just at that moment, Nicola appeared in the waiting room to de-escalate the situation. 'Hi, Anna, the doctor will see you now,' she said, putting a hand gently on her shoulder.

'Yes, don't let us keep you,' said Kirsty, her voice dripping sarcasm.

'Well, there is no need to be rude, Kirsty, is there?'

Kirsty couldn't believe the way Anna had just spoken to them. She reached over and clasped Dad's hand, feeling him tighten his hold. She knew he was scared, and Anna's outburst hadn't helped one bit.

'Well done for putting her in her place,' said Amy.

'Just to let you know, Anna,' said Nicola in her soothing voice as she led her from the waiting room. 'We don't talk about dementia sufferers anymore. It's not very nice language to use. We talk about people living with dementia . . .'

Kirsty was grateful that Nicola had appeared when she had, and that Amy was with them too. In fact, she was hugely relieved that Amy had decided to stay. She wasn't quite sure how she would have coped without her and having a few days away with Steve after the wedding had given her a chance to recharge her batteries and think about things. The girls had been so supportive when she told them the news about her adoption, and they had all decided that now wasn't the best time to broach the subject with Dad. Causing him more stress just now was the last thing they wanted to do. Kirsty had brought him in last week so the GP could take some blood and urine samples and he had asked him a series of questions as part of a memory test.

Nicola appeared a moment later. 'Come on, come through now.'

Fortunately, the waiting room had now emptied, and Kirsty and Amy followed Dad into the doctor's appointment room.

'I am sorry about that. Some people don't know when to stop talking,' she said. 'And there is a lot of ignorance around dementia, as we know. Now Alex,' she said, turning to look at him. 'The doctor will be through shortly to have a chat with you about the test results.'

'Okay.'

Kirsty saw his eyes were bright and knew he was trying to put a brave face on things.

Nicola reached and patted his arm. 'This is scary, I know, and all the information can be overwhelming, Alex. But Kirsty and Amy are here with you, and we are all here to help. I know it's easy for me to say but try not to worry too much.'

The GP arrived with his folder. 'Hi, Alex, how are you doing? It's nice to see you.'

'Hello there, doctor,' said Dad.

'Well, we have the results back from your tests,' he said still talking directly to Dad, 'and your blood and urine are all clear. Which is good as we needed to rule anything else out. But it would seem that our suspicions are correct.'

Kirsty felt her heart plummet as she watched her dad begin to cry. She hadn't seen him cry since her mum died.

'I understand it can be hard to get your head around. But the good news is that it is at its very early stages.'

'What does that mean?' interjected Amy.

'It means that your dad, Alex,' he said looking back and addressing him, 'has a mild impairment and is in the early stages. The symptoms you told me about are very common in the early stage of dementia. So the forgetfulness and the shifts in mood you've been experiencing. I know you said you'd been feeling more down than usual. You also spoke of struggling to keep track of conversations? And feeling very tired at times?'

Dad nodded, dabbing at his eyes.

'The good news is that at this stage, unless you want it to, life shouldn't change too much. Lots of people actually don't get diagnosed with dementia until much later. Now you know though, that will hopefully help you realize what is changing and what is happening. I hope you will feel less worried.'

Kirsty was stunned, letting the news sink in. It wasn't exactly a shock, the signs had been there for a while but still it felt like they'd been dealt a blow which didn't seem fair, especially after the loss of their mother.

'This is a lot to take in,' said the doctor looking at them all. 'Give yourself some time to process it but the main thing to do is to focus on the things that you *can* do. I've got these leaflets here with more information and some really useful coping strategies. From what Nicola said it sounds like you've all been doing some of these anyway with the sticky notes in the kitchen and reminding Dad to pace himself. And in the meantime, we'll refer Alex for some post-diagnostic support.'

Kirsty nodded. 'Thank you, Doctor. Amy is here and staying with Dad too which is a help at the moment until we all get our heads around this.'

'Thank you, Doctor,' said Dad standing up and shaking his hand. 'I appreciate you doing all of this.'

They walked outside, Dad flanked by Amy and Kirsty on either side. Nobody spoke and Kirsty racked her brain trying to think of something appropriate to say that would lighten the mood. However, it was their dad who spoke first.

'Well,' he said. 'At least we know what's going on and we'll just have to deal with it. I couldn't do this without your help, girls. Thank you so much.'

Kirsty put her arm around her dad, pulling him close. She glanced over his head at Amy who gave a small smile.

'Anyway,' he said, 'remember what your mum always said? It's not the end of the world . . .'

'Until it's the end of the world,' they chorused together.

EPILOGUE

Two months after the wedding

The summer was nearing an end and Kirsty could barely believe that Emma's wedding had been two months ago. Emma and Max were happily settling into married life in Edinburgh and Kirsty and Steve had promised to visit them in September once the twins were both settled and starting their new adventures . . .

Kirsty gulped as she pushed the thought away. Life had been an emotional rollercoaster of late and she could only deal with one day at a time. Fortunately, Dad was settled, and everyone felt less stressed now he had a diagnosis of dementia. There was no doubt that having Amy here was a huge help and it was definitely making a difference to all their lives.

Kirsty knew that Amy living with their dad wasn't a long-term solution. However, before her mind spiralled into a whirl of anxious thoughts, she reminded herself that they all had to take things a day at a time.

Dad seemed the most happy and calm that he'd been since Mum's death, which was such a relief.

Amy and James seemed to be taking things slowly, but Kirsty knew that she was besotted with him. She had noticed all the glances they exchanged when they thought nobody else was watching. Seeing her relaxed and happy was wonderful, especially as James seemed equally as smitten and had also been great with their dad too.

Things seemed to have changed for the better.

She reached for her glasses, keen to try and deal with a few emails before she made the most of the rest of the day. The guests who were staying wouldn't be back until later and she was keen to enjoy the sunshine while she could.

Amy and James had also been a great help at getting the coffee van up and running on a regular basis and that had brought in a lot of walking tourists and of course, income. There still wasn't enough to do what they wanted to do in terms of the renovations, but she had stopped worrying about that too. They would get there some day.

Kirsty opened her laptop and refreshed her emails. Scrolling through them quickly, she groaned when she saw an email from Trudy and Chuck, the fussy American couple from the start of the summer. Did they really want to rebook so soon? Her heart plummeted at the thought of dealing with them, *again*. But as she started to read the email, she couldn't quite believe what it said.

Jumping out of her chair, she slammed the lid down and began pacing the room. Had she imagined what they were proposing? She glanced out the window and saw the kids on the lawn with Steve. They had found the old badminton net and Dad was sitting on the bench under the sycamore tree, watching. She smiled. They were all that mattered.

'You okay, sis?' called Amy. Kirsty hadn't heard her come in. 'I've just been for a run. It's so nice out there. I'll have a quick shower and then get back to my coffee duties.'

Kirsty looked at her sister, wondering how she had managed without her. Amy was already talking about submitting plans to the planning department to convert the barns so she could have a yoga studio and therapy room at some point when she could raise the funds.

'Are you okay?' Amy asked again, glancing down at her phone as it pinged. 'Oh, it's Emma. Checking that we're around as she may pop over at the weekend.'

'Great,' said Kirsty in a flap. 'Though they may need to stay with you and Dad?'

'Of course,' said Amy.

'It's wonderful having you here, Amy. Thank you . . . and oh God, I don't know what to make of this. But come and read this email.' Her heart was racing as the words tumbled from her mouth.

'Calm down, sis, what is it that I am looking at?'

Kirsty opened up her laptop again and pointed at the email from Trudy and Chuck.

> *We loved our stay so much that we have recommended you to our film-making friends who would like to shoot some of their next film on the island and at Meadowbank. Let us know your thoughts and if you are happy with this then we will send your details on. They will of course financially reimburse you for your time. The fee for a month is always extremely worthwhile and so makes financial business sense for you to consider . . .*

'Wow,' said Amy, her eyes glistening in excitement. 'Just wow! This sounds promising, doesn't it? And makes up for that stupid competition you missed out on earlier in the summer.'

'Indeed,' said Kirsty. 'It even just about makes up for them being such pain-in-the ass guests.'

Amy hugged her and the pair jumped up and down in excitement.

'Come on, let's go tell Steve and the kids and Dad,' she yelled.

As they ran into the garden to break up the badminton game, Kirsty realized that regardless of the amazing offer, none of it mattered. She had everything and everyone who was important to her right here, right now.

They were *her* family and always had been and always would be. That was all that mattered, and this summer's island wedding had been just the occasion to remind her what was important and how much she loved them all. It was the summer that everything had changed and their bond as a family had grown even stronger.

'Guess what?' she yelled in excitement. 'You will never believe who has been in touch . . .'

'Who?' said Steve looking over.

'Trudy and Chuck!'

He burst out laughing. 'I was not expecting you to say that.'

'Don't worry,' she said, throwing her arms around his neck. 'It's all good. In fact you won't believe what they said . . .'

THE END

THANK YOU

I would like to thank you, the reader, for choosing to read *A Summer Wedding on Arran*. I hope you enjoyed the story of Kirsty, Emma and Amy as much as I enjoyed writing it. The island of Arran has a really special place in my heart and I hope I have done it justice and inspired you to visit!

If you enjoyed *A Summer Wedding on Arran* then please do leave a review on the website where you bought the book. Every review really does help a new author like me.

You can find me on Twitter, Facebook and Instagram (details on the 'About the Author' page next).

Please do get in touch for all the latest news. I look forward to chatting with you.

Huge thanks again, Ellie x

THE CHOC LIT STORY

Established in 2009, Choc Lit is an independent, award-winning publisher dedicated to creating a delicious selection of quality women's fiction.

We have won 18 awards, including Publisher of the Year and the Romantic Novel of the Year, and have been shortlisted for countless others.

All our novels are selected by genuine readers. We are proud to publish talented first-time authors, as well as established writers whose books we love introducing to a new generation of readers.

In 2023, we became a Joffe Books company. Best known for publishing a wide range of commercial fiction, Joffe Books has its roots in women's fiction. Today it is one of the largest independent publishers in the UK.

We love to hear from you, so please email us about absolutely anything bookish at choc-lit@joffebooks.com

If you want to hear about all our bargain new releases, join our mailing list: www.choc-lit.com

Printed in Great Britain
by Amazon

25324679R00142